CW01512352

To my dear friend
Mike

Best wishes for 2025
Roger

Missing In Action

Based on True Events

E. W. Butcher

Copyright © 2022 E.W. Butcher

All rights reserved. No part of this publication may be reproduced, distributed, or transmitted in any form or by any means, including photocopying, recording, or other electronic or mechanical methods, without the prior written permission of the publisher, except in the case of brief quotations embodied in critical reviews and certain other non-commercial uses permitted by copyright law. For permission requests, write to the publisher, addressed "Attention: Permissions Coordinator," at the address below:

www.ewbutcher.com

ISBN: 978-1-7396978-1-5

This book is dedicated to my wonderful family who are so supportive in everything I do, especially to my wonderful wife Svetlana, for all the outstanding investigative work upon which much of this story is based.

Contents

Prologue 1

1. The Escape 3

2. The Overture 13

3. The Bridge 35

4. The Panzers 49

5. The Battle 78

6. The Crossing 104

7. The Prison 125

8. The Angel 154

9. The Walk 165

10. The Watershed 178

11. The Partisans 193

12. The Finale 236

Epilogue 257

Acknowledgments 263

About the Author 265

Prologue

It had been coming for some time. Following its calamitous defeat in the Great War of 1914-18, the total collapse of the German economy, along with the ensuing constant chaos and turmoil in the country, provided the ideal breeding grounds for the rise of Adolf Hitler and his extreme, far-right, Nazi party. As they consolidated their grip on power throughout the 1930s, the regime became increasingly bellicose, with ambitious plans for expansion and conquest.

Between March 1936 and September 1938, Nazi troops marched, unopposed, into the demilitarised Rhineland and also annexed Austria as well as the Sudetenland.

Emboldened by the acquiescence of the major world powers to these actions, Hitler ordered his mighty forces to invade Poland on the 1st of September 1939. This was the final straw for France and Britain, who both declared war on Germany. However, this didn't stop Poland being occupied by forces from both Germany and the Soviet Union, with whom Hitler had unexpectedly made a non-aggression pact.

The following eight months saw very little military action in mainland Europe, however, on the 10th of May 1940, the phoney war ended abruptly, as the Nazi forces launched their utterly devastating blitzkrieg attacks. In a mere six weeks, they defeated the might of the allied armies ranged against them, and ejected the British from mainland Europe with their tail between their legs.

With most of western Europe, including France, Belgium, Luxembourg and the Netherlands, now occupied, Hitler was convinced it was only a matter of time before Britain would make peace. Under the leadership of Winston Churchill however, this was never going to happen and the formidable Luftwaffe, was ordered to destroy the Royal Air Force in preparation for an invasion of Britain.

Although the German Luftwaffe was unable to decisively defeat the British in the summer of 1940, the British posed no imminent threat, so Hitler's eyes turned east instead. He'd always wanted to see Germany expand eastwards to gain Lebensraum (living space) for its people, so he ordered plans to be drawn up for an invasion of the Soviet Union. Hitler only expected the war to last a few months. Little did he know the maelstrom he was about to unleash.

Chapter 1
The Escape

In contrast to recent days, it was unusually clear and sunny, with a biting wind blowing away any thoughts that the summer warmth would return any time soon. Like sardines packed tightly into a tin, it was hugely uncomfortable. They had been crammed together in the back of a truck doing all they could do to keep warm for what felt like hours. The pain was still intense, the hunger, and especially the thirst, were almost intolerable. However, the overriding sensations that they simply couldn't escape, no matter what they tried, were the abject cold, the relentless tiredness, the constant pain and the awful, disgusting and rancid smell, mainly concocted from a mixture of diesel fumes, stale urine, mixed together with vomit and blood.

Valia stared down at the thick, roughly cut, wooden boards that formed the flooring on the back of the truck. It was difficult to concentrate on anything other than the biting chill that was persistently gnawing away at every exposed piece of his emaciated body.

With his friends on one of the other trucks in the convoy, Valia had obdurately remained silent since the start of the journey, as he trusted nobody on his truck.

Just about the only thing that'd kept him going through the last few harrowing and tortuous months, was his overwhelming drive and desire to get home to see his family again. He'd promised his wonderful, loving mother that he'd come home safely, and he was determined to fulfil that vow, one way or another.

They had no real idea where they were heading. Was it to be a drive to a bullet in the back of the head, or had the men in black another macabre plan for them? Since their capture a few months earlier, life had been nothing short of unbearable, insufferable desperation. It had been simply impossible to relax, even with their tired, battered bodies screaming for some sleep, the threat of torture or even instant death, was ever present, even now.

The winter months had seen horrendously low temperatures, with a deep, thick snow blanketing the countryside. At least now, with the spring finally bursting forth, and with temperatures finally rising above freezing, it felt more bearable. It was more bearable, but only just.

Over the last few days, the snow had started to thaw, and there'd been a nasty mixture of heavy rain, snow showers, as well as depressing, damp and penetrating mists. All of which conspired together to make travel very difficult indeed. In contrast, today had actually been beautiful, with unbroken sunshine and clear blue skies. Not that they could really appreciate it, as the grimy, smelly canvas canopy covering the back of the truck obscured most of their view. The deep throbbing growl of their truck's diesel engine drowned any attempted conversation.

With the spring thaw now taking hold, the season of rasputitsa was upon them. At this time of year, any attempt to travel on an unpaved road or across country was likely to be extremely difficult owing to the atrocious muddy conditions caused by the melting snow and ice. This was certainly the case now as the dirt track they were travelling along, was starting to turn into a horrendous morass.

As hard as the small convoy tried, it wasn't travelling as fast as they'd hoped. It was now already well into the afternoon and the foreboding shadows, cast by large trees in the adjacent forest, were lengthening by the minute. Despite the best efforts of the drivers to navigate a smooth course on the treacherous track, the Nazi guards sitting alongside the prisoners were becoming quite agitated with the constant slipping and sliding of the truck. Every so often, the truck would lurch violently as its wheels lost traction in the muddy quagmire, and it would slew violently across the road. They had already had to stop several times, and each time, some of the prisoners were forced out of the truck to push it back onto a more stable part of the track.

On top of everything else, the prisoners were in an extremely sombre mood. An earlier stop had resulted in a couple of their number, having successfully helped to right their truck, being mown down in a hail of bullets after they had tried to bolt for the nearby trees.

Without warning, Valia heard loud shouting. Urgent, panicked shouting. The trucks abruptly veered off the track and came to an abrupt, grinding halt. Then, the all-too-familiar crackle of gunfire broke out. Rifles and machine guns burst into action in unison. The guards from the trucks behind them were out in the mud, firing into the air. Then they heard the unmistakable sound of rapidly approaching engines, which swiftly grew louder and louder as they quickly roared overhead. They must be ours, thought Valia, with a mixture of hope and trepidation. Suddenly, the convoy was being raked with red-hot metal. Bullets and shells and bombs. Guards fell. Holes ripped through the canopy of his truck, and blood splattered around him in all directions from those that had been hit. Valia watched in disbelief as the truck behind him jumped several feet into the air before it erupted into a ball of flames. The deafening sound and shock wave of the explosion swiftly followed. Trepidation turned to panic. They were under attack. Another bomb hit and enveloped another truck nearby. It was chaos. Everybody in Valia's truck was doing their utmost to get out, pushing and shoving and shouting and jumping.

In a short time, Valia was half-pushed and half-jumped from the back of the stranded vehicle. He immediately lost his footing as he landed on top of one of his fellow prisoners, causing him to topple over, spreadeagled in the soft, cold, filthy mud. Almost immediately, he felt other bodies falling on top of him, and he struggled with all his might just to crawl away. As soon as he was able, he used his mud-coated hands to try to wipe away the filthy sludge covering his face.

He sensed movement in all directions. The shouting was intense as orders were screamed to the guards in German, Ukrainian and Russian. Then came another aerial assault, as the convoy was strafed a second time. Bullets and shells were exploding all around him and all along the convoy. As they continued their rapid fire, the guards' concentration was still firmly focused on the attackers in the air. Valia's eyes darted around as he tried to comprehend the mayhem that now ensnared him. Screaming and shouting continued from all sides. All he could hear was the constant gunfire, with contorted bodies falling all around him.

Valia glanced up and saw two planes climbing. Both had a distinctive red star on their wings. Valia's emotions veered violently between happiness, disappointment, fear and terror. The fact that they were friendly planes that were attacking the convoy made him happy, but the fact they could just as easily kill him, terrified him at the same time. Some of his fellow prisoners roared their approval, but Valia thought to himself, "Where were these planes when we desperately needed them a few months ago?"

Then out of the corner of his eye, he caught a glimpse of several other planes coming from a different direction. He'd seen so many of these planes over recent months, he instinctively knew they weren't friendly.

As tumult ensued, Valia quickly realised that many of his fellow prisoners were dropping, some screaming in agony, others just falling lifeless to the floor. The guards were no longer firing at the planes overhead that were beating a hasty retreat, but they were now firing at the prisoners themselves.

Immediately, his mind switched to survival mode. He only had one thing on his mind: RUN.

Missing In Action

The track the convoy had been traversing along just happened to be in a forested area, with dense fir trees and remnants of brown, rotted foliage encroaching towards the track. Valia fixed his eyes onto the nearest trees and, in a split second, was on his feet and running for his life. He could hear bullets whizzing past him and smashing into the trees ahead, throwing sharp splinters everywhere. He slipped and fell several times in the thick, cloggy and extremely viscous mud, but his overriding thought was simple: run, he simply must get to the tree line. After what seemed an eternity, Valia finally breached the foliage and the cover of the trees before diving head first under a nearby bush. Miraculously, he had managed to evade the swarm of bullets that had been fired in his general direction.

He could hear whistles and shouting and screaming behind him. Some of the prisoners had nowhere to run and were mown down in a hail of bullets where they stood; others hadn't even made it out of their trucks. A few had snatched weapons from dead or injured guards and were fighting back. Bullets were flying everywhere but, within seconds, the resistance was killed off. Literally killed.

The guards then concentrated all their efforts on liquidating any remaining prisoners as quickly and efficiently as possible.

With the adrenaline still pumping furiously through his body, Valia took stock of the very precarious situation he now found himself in. He very slowly and carefully manoeuvred himself into a position where he wouldn't give himself away, but he could still observe what remained of the convoy.

The shouting and screaming seemed endless, with officers barking orders to their subordinates. Although the gunfire had subsided substantially, there was still a regular crack of a rifle or a revolver as the guards went among the remaining prisoners, making sure they were all dealt with. Any sign of life was met with a bullet to the head. There was no mercy.

There was still an occasional burst of machine gun or rifle fire aimed into the forest, as the guards tried their best to shoot any remaining runaways. Obviously, some of his comrades must have also managed to get as far as the shelter of the woodland, but these were now being hunted down and shot. It appeared to Valia that most of the activity was taking place on the other side of the track. Guards were rushing everywhere, and he could hear a crack of gunfire each time a runaway was located.

Without daring to move, Valia surveyed the scene. There were a couple of crashed motorcycles up front, with six trucks spread haphazardly behind them. Three of the trucks had been destroyed by bombs and were effectively burning hulks. Each of the other trucks was riddled with bullet holes. Dark smoke belched into the late afternoon sky.

As his senses slowly returned and his breathing steadied, Valia realised that this was the chance he had long been waiting for. The snow that had been thick just a few days previously had been turned to slush by the rainfall of the previous day. Valia looked hard, but couldn't see any obvious signs of footprints on the ground that would give away his location.

There was only a handful of guards on his side of the track. Maybe, just maybe, he might be able to get away without being seen. Valia had dreamt of such a moment ever since he'd been captured along with all his comrades-in-arms a few months earlier, but he never imagined that such an opportunity would actually come along after the trials and tribulations he had had to endure since then.

Valia had to decide what to do next. The decision he would make could literally be the difference between him living or dying. As the different options raced through his mind, he needed to think logically and carefully.

The first option was to stay hidden where he was, safely ensconced in some thick bushes. This had the advantage that the guards were very unlikely to see him, let alone find him, except by accident. Then he remembered the dogs. The guards always had extremely fierce dogs nearby. He remembered harrowing stories back at the Prison Camp in Kremenchug about how such dogs were used to hunt down any escaped prisoners. Okay, so there were no dogs in this convoy, but how certain was he that they wouldn't bring dogs along, and soon? Staying where he lay was not really an option, so he mentally crossed that one off the list.

The next option lasted no more than a second in his mind. Why not stand up slowly, hands aloft, and just surrender again? However, that was plainly the most stupid idea he'd ever dreamt up. The guards appeared to be dispatching every prisoner they found. His fate would almost certainly be sealed if he chose to give himself up.

The only other plausible option was to get away as fast and as far as possible. However, he needed to be particularly careful not to disrupt any foliage or wildlife, lest he give away his position and, with it, more than likely, his life. The only question was when.

As the shouting and shooting began to die down around the convoy, Valia noticed that the guards had kept a couple of prisoners alive, and one of them was his good friend Oleg. It appeared that they'd been tasked with dragging the dead prisoners' bodies to the side of the track. Body upon body was slowly dragged through the thick sludge and arranged, one next to another, in a single line. Valia couldn't work out who they were.

To his horror, Valia noticed that one of the officers was counting the bodies. This wasn't good, if they realised they hadn't accounted for all the prisoners, they'd be out searching the forest again, and this time with even more venom.

A few minutes later, Valia heard the drone of approaching aircraft once more. He counted four of them. This time, as the planes flew overhead, the leading plane dipped its wing slightly, as if giving a salute. There was no red star on these planes. There was just the depressing sight of the black cross and swastika.

As Valia contemplated the best route to get away from his temporary secluded lair, he guessed that almost all the bodies had been accounted for by now. Then he saw the two remaining prisoners forced to kneel next to them: a sight he had so often witnessed over the previous months. The sound of two pistol shots rang out, as the lifeless bodies slumped to the ground to join their comrades in death. Valia's eyes filled with tears. After all he'd gone through together with Oleg, Valia was distraught. Tragically, this was no time for sentiment and he needed to concentrate, and to concentrate hard.

Valia heard some more shouting, this time in Ukrainian. Then he saw some of the guards starting to search the other side of the track where most of the action had taken place earlier. They obviously knew they were missing some prisoners. Valia had to move, and he had to move now.

Covering him in all their glory, the shadows of the tall trees lengthened by the minute, as the sun started to set at the end of an otherwise beautiful spring day.

The adrenaline kicked in again. He began slowly crawling under the bush, then onto the next tree, then the next, and so on, until he no longer heard any commotion behind him. He needed to keep moving. Anywhere, so long as it was away from that terrible scene of carnage he'd just left behind.

After a couple of hours on the move, the forest had become thick with trees, with just the occasional clearing separating the giant, evergreen sentinels. Darkness was enveloping the forest in its vice-like grip, only punctuated by the faint starlight far, far in the distance. Valia was now almost totally exhausted, and desperate for sleep.

Having spent most of his young life growing up in the countryside, Valia was reasonably familiar with this type of environment, and had some basic idea of what he would need to do to survive. He had learnt at a young age to identify all the delicious mushrooms, nuts and berries that would be safe to eat, and he knew how to get enough water to quench his thirst.

Valia's main concern was the cold. All he had on him were the rags that used to pass as a uniform of the Soviet Red Army along with his boots, which somehow, he'd managed to keep hold of, but that was it. He had nothing else. Nothing to start a fire, no knife to cut anything. It was just him and the forest, and he was determined to get as much as he could out of it.

The temperature was dropping like a stone and must have been well below freezing again now. He'd already got used to eating grass at the prisoner-of-war camp in Kremenchug, so he managed to eat a little more here. To quench his thirst, he broke the ice that was slowly forming over some puddles to get some water.

In a small clearing, he found a nook in between the roots of some trees that was surprisingly dry. This would be his bed for the night. He gathered several branches of fir and these would hope-fully keep him warm enough to stay alive while he was finally able to sleep.

Valia had lost track of time, but he figured it must be late March, or early April by now, and as such, there were still likely to be a few edible plants around. He told himself that he'd search for them once he woke the next day. That is, if he woke up the next day.

Despite being over 1,000 kilometres south-west of his home village of Yakhrobol, the surrounding forest looked and felt so familiar, so much like some of the countryside not too far from his home, and despite his dire situation, he surprisingly felt a lot more relaxed than he had done for many months. He was alone. Nobody was shouting at him. Nobody was making him work. Nobody was beating him. He felt very, very weary, so he lay in his cosy little nook and covered himself with the fir branches. As he lay down, he gazed at the beauty and brilliance of the untroubled sky above. It felt like a completely different world to the one he'd managed to escape from just a few hours earlier.

As darkness enveloped him, Valia gradually fell into a fitful state of slumber. A dreadful darkness was racing around in his mind, those indelible, dreadful images. The awful sights and experiences he'd endured over the past few months continually circled in his head. It was like a never-ending nightmare: the constant, mindless beatings he had received, the sight of his friends and comrades being slaughtered on a whim. How could he ever escape this endless horror?

Although yearning for a deep sleep, it was nigh on impossible as his senses were still in overdrive. After what seemed like no time at all, he woke with a start as he heard a cracking noise nearby. He stared over to where the noise had come from, focusing his tired eyes against the dawn light. He spotted a couple of elegant looking deer feeding, no more than 20 metres away. He surveyed the horizon some more, before he felt able to relax again.

As Valia's senses started to kick in, he felt a cold shiver run through him. The air temperature had definitely plummeted through the night, and he could sense that the cold tentacles of winter were yet to fully loosen their icy grip. A grip that could easily be deadly, especially if you happened to be, all alone, outside in a forest.

After gathering some berries and a few nuts from the surrounding trees and bushes, Valia realised it was time to move on again. But to move where? He was behind enemy lines, so no matter where he went he'd have to be really careful. The only viable option would seem to be to try and get back to his own lines, but where were they likely to be now? It'd been at least a few months since he'd been captured, after desperately trying to help defend the City of Kremenchug. Had the Red Army counter-attacked and maybe even now were approaching his position, or had the Nazi juggernaut smashed its way even further into the heart of his Motherland? Had Moscow fallen? He had absolutely no way of knowing.

Overhead, from time to time, he would see and hear either single or groups of aeroplanes. None of them had a red star. The swastika was omnipresent.

Finally, he concluded that the only realistic choice he had right now would be to head off in a north-easterly direction and hope for the best. Valia started walking. It would be a long way home from here.

Chapter 2
The Overture

Valerey Alexandrovich Ermolaev was a strong, well-built and very fit young man of 24. He was of an average height when compared to his contemporaries, measuring in at five foot and seven inches. His blue eyes and warm smile radiated an inner confidence and determination that grew from his upbringing in the sometimes, very harsh Russian countryside. Although his name was Valerey, he was known to everyone, as Valia.

Late, one cold, grey, afternoon, at the tail end of autumn 1939, not long after finishing his training to become an electrician, Valia returned home after a hard day's work. He'd been busy helping his neighbours cut up logs, which would be essential for them during the fast approaching winter.

As always, whenever Valia arrived home after an arduous job, his mother would greet him with a piping hot cup of tea and a welcoming, warming, smile. This day was different though. Although the smile was still there, Valia could sense an unease in his mother. She was pensive, and visibly on edge. He didn't say anything straight away, but after taking a couple of sips of the refreshing brew and placing the cup gently onto the immaculately laid dining table, he asked, "Are you okay Mama, you don't seem to be yourself this evening?"

With a slightly trembling voice, his mother replied. "I picked up the post earlier." Then she stopped. The words just dried up, and she couldn't carry on. She simply pointed towards a large unopened brown envelope, sitting on the table, just behind the jug of water. It was addressed to Valia.

She looked on anxiously as he picked it up and carefully opened it. Valia glanced over to his mother and could tell from the look on her face that she was dreading to hear the news. He carefully unfolded the neatly typed letter before slowly reading and digesting each line of it in turn. He looked over to his mother once more, and this time could clearly see tears starting to well up in her eyes.

It was the letter his mother had long dreaded. Even though they both knew it was coming, it was still somewhat of a shock, that now, it was finally here.

Without saying a word, Valia walked across the room and gave his mother a big hug, before whispering softly, "I'm sorry Mama, it's the call-up for national service." Valia paused, just long enough to give his mother a small, neatly folded, white handkerchief to dry her eyes. "I've been selected for the Army, and I've only got a week before they pick me up. I then have to report to a camp near Moscow, to start my basic training."

His mother couldn't say anything. She just wanted to hold him tight. She didn't want him to go.

Sensing his mother's angst, Valia did his best to comfort her. "Don't worry, please don't cry. After all, it's my duty, isn't it? Please don't be sad or afraid for me, I promise you, I'll be fine."

It was, of course, a hugely important milestone for such an immensely patriotic young man, to be able to serve, and to help protect his country. It was simply the ultimate honour, and to be joining the mighty Red Army was like a dream come true for Valia.

He knew he'd soon be embarking on a truly life changing adventure, and it filled him with an almost innocent sense of excitement. He was looking forward to the many stimulating experiences that were sure to come his way, but he was also filled with an overriding sense of sadness that he'd soon have to leave his close-knit family behind.

Coming, as he did, from the tiny village of Yakhrobol, which was situated amidst the largely flat and featureless countryside to the east of the Yaroslavl Oblast, Valia hadn't had much of an opportunity to travel anywhere of real note just yet.

Even though the metropolis that is Moscow, was located less than 300 kilometres south-west of his home, as far as Valia was concerned, it could just as easily have been as far away as the moon. He'd never even had the slightest chance to visit the nation's capital and explore its many wonders. At least he hadn't just yet.

The furthest extent of his travel to date, was to the strategic, and historically important city of Yaroslavl, sitting as it did, on the banks of the mighty Volga River, just over 30 kilometres, as the crow flies, west of his home. Yaroslavl always prided itself on being a large, modern, industrial city, yet, at the core of its beating heart, lay a beautiful cultural centre dating back many centuries. Valia was intrigued by the city. It was exciting, it was fascinating, it was grimy, yet still beautiful, but for a country lad, it really was quite daunting.

One of his favourite places to visit though, was the small town of Krasny Profintern, which also nestled, very happily on the banks of the mighty Volga, just a few short kilometres away from his home. The small, bustling town had largely grown up around the very large, and well known, starch and treacle factory, which provided meaningful employment for the majority of its population in and around the town.

Valia loved to visit the town, especially during the summer, as the strong, but beautifully sweet aroma of the treacle, permeated the air.

Over the years, Valia had got to know many of the boat captains from the town, and he frequently managed to talk his way onto one of their boats for a day out. There, he'd be able to enjoy himself, relaxing and fishing, and generally letting all the worries of the world pass him by.

Before heading off to join the army, Valia managed to enjoy some time in both Yaroslavl and Krasny Profintern with some of his friends, but, as he was well aware, time waits for no man.

Within the week, and on a decidedly chilly morning, a large, lonely military truck came meandering along the single, muddy track, leading into Yakhrobol, where Valia, like his father before him, had been born and bred.

Lined up with Valia were a couple of other conscripts from the village, each accompanied by their extended family and friends. As the huge, dirty, dark green vehicle came to a halt, just outside the large, red, brick-built community centre, Valia turned to his family. Firstly, he bade farewell to his sister Vera, with whom he shared a huge bear hug, as well as the obligatory kiss on each cheek. Then he turned to his two brothers, Anatoly and Victor with whom he regularly enjoyed making plenty of the extremely strong, homemade vodka, commonly known as Samogon. As he embraced them both tightly, Valia had a little surprise for them. "Oh yes, and before I forget, you should know that I've put an extra special bottle of the Samogon we made last year onto the top shelf in my bedroom. I promise you, we'll drink the whole bottle together, but only when we're all safely home again. Don't forget, not a drop of it before then, promise me." The brothers both nodded, and then shook his hand warmly, before Valia turned to his wonderful mother.

It had been eight years since the untimely death of his father, and although Valia missed him tremendously, he knew just how much more his beloved mother must have missed him. She'd worked miracles bringing up her four children under extremely difficult circumstances, and Valia knew she would be disconsolate at the thought of any of her sons having to leave home.

Everyone's emotions were in tatters as Valia finally approached his mother. She already had tears running down her face. After all, Valia was her baby. He was, and always would be her little boy. Valia embraced her tightly "Mama, please don't worry about me, I'm a grown man now. Rest assured, I really can look after myself you know ." Tears started to form in his eyes too. "Never forget I love you," she whispered in his ear. "Promise me you'll come home. My heart will never be whole again until you do. I love you my son, never, ever forget it." Valia knew how hard it must be for his mother, but he really had to go. "I promise you Mama, no matter what happens, I'll come back to you. I love you so much." His mother held him tightly as long as she possibly could, before, as all good Russian mothers do, she stuffed, just a little extra food into his bag for the upcoming journey.

Leaving it as late as possible, Valia finally jumped aboard the truck to join the other conscripts already on board. Within a few short minutes, the huge vehicle started to accelerate, back down the track in the direction it had originally come from.

Looking back towards his family, Valia waved and shouted his goodbyes. His family slowly grew smaller and smaller until they were gone. His sadness at leaving them was tempered though, by the anticipation of the adventures to come.

To travel anywhere in the Soviet Union without an internal passport or a special permit was extremely difficult for most normal people at that time. In fact, actually getting hold of one was a virtual impossibility, especially to those who lived in the rural areas. Simply getting the opportunity to move around the country was a real eye opener for Valia. He knew that this might be his one and only chance to travel anywhere of note, so he really needed to make the most of it.

The basic training that Valia received in the small, cramped and overcrowded military camp on the outskirts of Moscow was a bit of an eye opener for Valia. He'd never witnessed quite so much extreme violence first hand before, and he learnt very quickly that he needed to be quite careful who he spoke to, and also how he should speak to certain individuals. Fights between the conscripts would frequently erupt over the smallest of things, and bullying seemed to be quite the norm. Petty theft, often the spark for even more violence, was never far away either.

Luckily for Valia, his confident and outgoing nature allowed him to make friends quite quickly, and he adroitly stayed well clear of most of the trouble.

As for the instructors, a few of them seemed to take an almost sadistic pleasure in making Valia and his comrades exercise regularly outside in the open countryside in the sub-zero temperatures. Although Valia could understand the need to get used to winter warfare conditions, he really didn't like it when they periodically hosed them down with freezing water once they'd finished. The pain he felt afterwards was almost unbearable.

With the high probability of injury during their training, it was quite common for conscripts to find themselves in the hospital block at one time or another, and there were even a few reported fatalities whilst Valia was at the camp.

Early one particularly cold morning, just a couple of days before Valia was scheduled to complete his basic training, the conscripts assembled on the large, icy parade ground as usual, ready for yet another mind-numbingly exhausting day of exercises. As they were busy lining up ready to start, Valia noticed a small group of smartly uniformed soldiers approaching. He hadn't seen them in the camp before, and immediately started to feel apprehensive and slightly on edge, especially after he noticed their blue trousers and their matching blue hats, circled with a very distinctive red band. It wasn't every day that the secret police come to visit, and to say that the NKVD had a brutal reputation was a bit of an understatement. You just knew that if they were in the area, somebody was sure to be in trouble, and very big trouble at that.

With the weak sunlight doing its utmost to try and penetrate the frigid air, one of the NKVD officers approached the head instructor, and after a couple of minutes of hushed conversation, he started to address the massed conscripts, in a deep, loud, and somewhat malevolent voice.

"May I congratulate you all. Comrade Mikhaylov has just informed me how well everyone in this training group have done over the duration of your course. Naturally, on behalf of the state, we're delighted that you'll soon be in a position to defend our glorious homeland. However, as everyone has exceeded their training targets, we'd like to invite any one of you who would prefer not to fight for the state, and return home and act as a reservist right now, to step forward and join my colleagues over there. Of course, you may be called up again in future, but you won't be required to head to an active military unit once this training course is completed."

The NKVD officer pointed to his five colleagues who were stood, stony-faced at the corner of the parade ground, before turning to the head instructor again, and resuming their deep conversation.

Valia couldn't believe it. Was it really as simple as that. Could he really go home right now and help his beloved mother again? Then the realisation of the situation hit him. As six of the conscripts marched proudly over to the NKVD officers, Valia twigged what was going on. He looked at the six men, each of them was quite shy in nature, and they really hadn't gelled that well with the rest of the men. He felt sorry for them, but it really was of their own making.

A couple of minutes later, the six men, all smiling, accompanied by the NKVD officers strode off towards one of the small decrepit wooden sheds towards the edge of the camp.

It wasn't long into the days' exercise when Valia first heard the terrifying screams emanating from the shed. The howls of pain continued for a good 30 minutes before they eventually started to subside. As Valia was busy completing yet another set of 50 push-ups, he spotted a large truck making its way, very carefully, towards the shed. Just a few minutes later, the six men staggered out with their hands tied firmly behind their backs, and a hood covering their heads. They were very roughly bundled, one by one, into the back of the waiting truck, with what looked like blood covering each of their uniforms. The smiling, chatty, NKVD officers soon following in good order. With everyone aboard, the truck started to trundle towards the camp exit, and they were soon gone.

As Valia's group moved onto star jumps, one of the conscripts exercising alongside him muttered under his breath, "They won't be going home any time soon, will they? I'll bet they're off to the Gulag. That's the NKVD for you, nice bunch, aren't they?"

After successfully completing the gruelling, three-month period of intensive basic training, Valia was posted to the newly formed 56th Air Defence Battalion, who were stationed in the strategically important industrial city of Kharkov, which was located very conveniently on the Kharkov River, on the eastern side of the Ukrainian Republic.

It wasn't too long before Valia was hard at work training to be an anti-aircraft gunner. Although his primary task would be that of loading shells into the gun, he also needed to have a practical knowledge and experience about each of the other roles needed to operate the gun, just in case he was ever called upon to use one of them.

As with most Soviet Air Defence Battalions of the time, the 56th was made up of three separate batteries, each of which would be made up of four standard 76-millimetre air-defence guns, mounted on a four-wheeled trailer with twin outriggers, and pulled by a tractor. Each gun would normally have an active crew of ten men, and they were expected to fire at least 20 shells per minute. When you added in the other ancillary personnel, such as cooks and medics, the 56th Battalion comprised approximately 150 men and women in total.

Valia was assigned to the crew manning one of the guns in the third battery, and Valia, being Valia, wasted little time getting to know some of his new comrades. Coming from all corners of the Soviet Union, they were certainly an interesting bunch.

Alexei was a bubbly character who hailed from the one of the plethora of suburbs to the south of Moscow. Slightly shorter than most of the crew, he was of a very slight build. In fact, he looked to be almost painfully thin. He was a bit of a joker though, and he always, thoroughly enjoyed playing pranks on his comrades whenever he possibly could.

When it came to work though, he was a totally different animal. He was so cool, calm, calculating and deadly serious that he commanded immediate respect from the rest of his comrades. Unsurprisingly, he was soon a very popular member of the crew.

Igor was actually a reasonably local lad who came from the nearby city of Kiev. He was a really tall, strong, burly individual who worked closely with Valia, and was also responsible for loading shells into the gun. He wasn't very talkative, but when he did speak, everyone in the crew took notice. Valia liked his company immensely, and they complemented each other really well.

Maxim was the baby of the crew. Having only recently turned 18, he hadn't even started to shave properly yet. Although he was usually the butt of most of the jokes, the whole crew soon became very protective of him. He'd grown up on the Black Sea coast not too far from Sochi, so he really didn't like the cold weather one bit.

Michail, had been appointed the leader of the third battery, and as such commanded a certain degree of respect. He was actually one of the more experienced soldiers in the Battalion, having served for a few years in the far east near Vladivostok. Like most of the crew he was strongly built, and certainly somebody you wouldn't want to pick a fight with.

Oleg on the other hand was a strange one. He didn't really appear to do too much at all, even when the gun was in operation. He always tried to skip duties if he could and his mind always seemed to be somewhere else, be it scheming on some weird or whacky plan, or just getting a good deal on something. However, he was surprisingly popular with the crew, simply because if you needed anything, anything at all, Oleg was the man to be able to get it for you.

As a totally new unit, the first couple of weeks together were quite fraught, with every member of the crew sizing each other up. Occasionally, a seemingly trivial argument would blow up into a fully fledged fist-fight, but generally, the level of violence was nowhere as bad as it had been in the training camp. As the crew started to get to know each other a little better, along with their strengths and weaknesses, the first tentative signs of working together as a cohesive team started to emerge, then slowly, as the days passed into weeks, they stated to bond together into quite a formidable outfit.

As the bitterly cold winter months of 1940 slowly morphed into the springtime of 1941, the comrades of the 3rd Battery gradually became adept in all the different tasks needed to operate their big guns, from the manual loading procedures, to the range finding, to the firing. Each job started to become second nature to all of them.

The mood within the 56th was good too. They had regular meals, regular training, and being part of the biggest and best army in the world, felt really good.

Occasionally during their downtimes, they would look back and discuss the developments of the last few years. It was hard to digest just how far the nation had come under the leadership of their revered leader, the Great, Beloved, Comrade Joseph Stalin.

As the weeks ticked by, it was becoming more and more frustrating for many in the crew, especially Maxim. They were desperate to be deployed as soon as possible so as not to miss out on any possible action.

One day, while resting up in their barracks, Maxim asked, "When do you think we're going to get to move out Valia?".

Valia scratched his head. "To be honest, I'm not really too sure, but I'm convinced it won't be too much longer. What do you think Michail?"

Michail stared out of a small window whilst pondering the question for a short time, before standing up, and slowly pacing around

22

the room. "Well, it's quite difficult to say for sure right now, as things seem to be changing pretty rapidly all the time."

"You can say that again." Valia interjected.

Michail mulled over the question a little more before continuing. "Well, I don't know about you, but I never thought for one minute, even a couple of short months ago, that we'd be at peace with both fascist Germany and also Japan. I really didn't see it happening."

"I'm sure Comrade Stalin has it all planned out." Alexei butted in, before a smirk flashed across his face.

"Yeah, yeah, I'm sure he has," said Michail, "but seriously though, just look at things. We've managed to grab a large chunk of Poland without any major problems. We've got the biggest and best army in the world, and Hitler and his mob still have a war on their hands with the British. Maybe our Glorious Leader does actually know what he's doing, just for a change."

As the words fell out of his mouth, Michail quickly looked around the room. Luckily, he was nowhere to be seen. He knew he'd have been in big trouble if Kirill had heard him making disparaging remarks about their Glorious Leader like that.

Looking somewhat bored with the conversation, Igor gave his take on the situation. "Well, you know that so-called glorious victory we had in Finland over the winter months. I've heard from a couple of men from another unit, and they swear blind it was almost a complete disaster. A massive cock up all around apparently. They'd been involved from the beginning, and apparently the losses we took were staggering."

Maxim looked perplexed. "Well, how can that be? All the papers are saying it was a great victory, and look, we've taken a large slice of Finland as our own."

Igor rolled his eyes a little. "Maxim mate, do you really believe everything they put in the papers. I know which news I prefer to believe, and that's the comrades who were actually there, not the tripe they want you to believe in the newspapers."

Michail quickly brought the conversation to an abrupt close.

23

"Igor, you'd better be careful, if Kirill hears you talk like that, you can expect a swift visit from the NKVD, and you can be sure it wouldn't be a social call, I can promise you that. Anyway, get yourselves ready, I think the fire's already lit."

Valia and his colleagues had just finished another successful training sortie with their trusty 76-millimetre guns. They'd become exceptionally adept at their job, often being able to fire in excess of the requisite 20 rounds per minute. In fact, Kirill had been so impressed with their recent training figures, that he'd finally recommended that they were ready to become fully operational, to Battalion commanders.

The summer weather during 1940 had been unseasonably dull and wet, however that Friday evening was an exception. It was fabulous, with hazy sunshine and a gentle, warming breeze. In the confines of their military barracks, the men of the 3rd Battery were going to have a celebratory meal of fresh fish, vegetables, and the obligatory vodka or two. They were determined to properly mark them becoming a fully operational part of the 56th Air Defence Battalion.

Valia and his comrades had congregated around a fire pit that was situated in the middle of a small, muddy piece of open ground nestling between a couple of large, newly built blocks of flats. He couldn't quite believe the large number of fishes being grilled. Obviously, Oleg must've been working his magic again.

Word of the party quickly spread, and in no time at all, a large crowd had arrived and were mulling around, chatting and drinking, and eating. It looked like it was shaping up to be a really good night.

As the comforting, homely aroma of grilled fish permeated the air, Kirill Popov noticed some faces he had no recollection of seeing before. Kirill, the political commissar attached to the 3rd Brigade, slowly rose to his feet and very purposefully strode out to intercept them. He wanted to know who they were, and what were they doing so close to the revelry going on behind him.

After a few, terse, and intimidating questions, Kirill relaxed.

The strangers were actually comrades from the 505th Air Defence Battalion who'd only just taken up residence in one of the adjacent blocks of flats, and were simply strolling around to get a feel for their new camp.

Compared to most of the soldiers in the 56th, Kirill was a slight figure. He was very skinny, and wasn't particularly strong. Horn-rimmed glasses perched on a slightly elongated nose, and with his jet-black hair and dark eyes he exuded a slightly sinister appearance. Despite this, as a political officer, he carried much authority, and he was unusually popular for somebody in such a position. After a few further introductory pleasantries, Kirill issued the men of the 505th a cordial invitation to come and join in with the celebrations and share a few vodkas.

As the stunning orange hues of the setting sun illuminated the skies during a long, pleasant evening, the comrades started singing the traditional folk, and patriotic songs which had become a tradition at such gatherings. Kalinka, as always was a great favourite. Even new songs, such as Katyusha, were belted out with unbridled pride. Not surprisingly, the singing gradually grew louder and more boisterous in direct proportion to the quantity of vodka being consumed, and there were copious amounts of that.

As the evening drew on and darkness started to creep across the camp, Valia spotted a strange, quiet, slightly withdrawn, and even troubled looking individual standing all alone, just a little back from the massed chorus. Although he was dressed in the uniform of the 505th, there was something about his demeanour that put Valia on edge. As the minutes ticked by, the man made no attempt to move. He just stood there, motionless, staring high into the sky, as if he was looking for something that simply wasn't there. Eventually, a slightly unnerved Valia had had enough, and decided to find out what was going on. He strolled over in a determined manner. "Hey, who are you, and what are you doing here?"

The man slowly lowered his gaze, and looked Valia up and down. "Hello, my name's Dmitry and I'm from a small fishing village not too far away from Leningrad. Sorry, I'm just thinking about some old friends of mine. Friends who are no longer with us, and I won't be seeing again."

The man sounded more lost than threatening. Valia decided to introduce himself. "Hi, I'm Valerey, but you can call me Valia if you like. Everyone else does. I'm originally from a tiny village called Yakhrobol in the Yaroslavl Oblast. Is everything okay? You look as if your mind is somewhere else."

Dmitry was silent, and staring into space again. Then Valia noticed a nasty looking bunch of scars to the left side of Dmitry's face. They looked absolutely horrendous, and must have been causing him great pain.

A few seconds later, and sensing Valia's gaze focussing on his unsightly scars, Dmitry tried to put him at ease. "Oh, please don't worry about them, they don't hurt any more. They did for a time, but not anymore."

"Valia, it was Valia wasn't it?"

"Yes, you can call me Valia. How the hell did you get those scars, they look really nasty, especially the one running down past your nose."

Dmitry looked aimlessly away, and stared into space once more. Valia felt quite uncomfortable. Then Dmitry's whole body suddenly appeared to shudder, before appearing to return to normality again. "I'm sorry. It's my memories. Sometimes I just can't control them."

Rather than feeling threatened, Valia now simply felt sorry for Dmitry. "Would you like to talk about it, I hear sometimes that can help?"

Dmitry slowly nodded. "Okay. Wait here and I'll get you a drink." A couple of minutes ticked by before Valia returned with two small glasses, filled to the brim with vodka, as well as a full bottle tucked safely under his right arm.

A smile slowly ambled across Dmitry's face as Valia offered him one of the glasses, only to spill a little before Dmitry could take it.

Then, unusually, before Valia could say a word, Dmitry made a toast. "To old friends and heroes, let their memories never fade." Immediately, Dmitry's face seemed to go vacant again, as he looked lost in his memories.

Valia was perplexed, he wasn't sure what to do. However, after studying Dmitry's tormented face for a little while, he did the only logical thing he could think of. He raised his glass before replying, "To old Friends."

Something seemed to click inside Dmitry, and with that, the smile returned to his face. With both men finally making proper eye contact for the first time, the two new comrades clinked their glasses together, before proclaiming Na Zdorovie in unison. Without further ado, they each downed their vodka in a single gulp.

It wasn't easy to age Dmitry, but it looked to Valia like he was in his early thirties, and he'd obviously taken quite a beating at some point in the recent past with those terrible looking scars.

Valia crouched down and recharged their glasses with some more, clear, neat, vodka. Looking up at his new friend, Valia said softly. "Okay, in your own time, would you like to tell me your story?"

Dmitry's eyes started watering and blinking rapidly, almost as if he was about to shed a tear. He was obviously not comfortable, and seemed to be struggling to get a grip on reality. It took a few moments, before slowly, very slowly, and very purposefully, he composed himself, and began to tell his tale.

"Let me see, where should I begin. Well, I guess a good place would be at the start of the Winter War. Coming from Leningrad, I found myself in the 42nd Rifle Division that moved into Finland on November the 30th. I remember it well. We were all in such high spirits, and we were really expecting a quick and easy victory over our northern neighbours. That's what our officers told us to expect, so we were really confident."

Valia and Dmitry sank another vodka. Dmitry continued whilst Valia filled the glasses once again. "We very quickly made ground at first. It was all so easy, it almost seemed like a walk in the park. Unfortunately, that didn't last long though. Frankly, we were expecting the Finns to give up quite quickly, but they never did. They put up extremely stiff resistance and often attacked us with swift hit and run strikes. They really were masters on skis. It started to seem to us that they could get in, execute a devastating attack, cause absolute mayhem, and then leave, almost as if they'd never been there. We hardly ever heard or saw them until it was too late."

"Our officers kept pushing us forwards, saying that we had a huge numerical advantage, and that our artillery would be able to pulverise them into submission. They kept promising that it'd only be a short time before it was all over. Just one more concerted push and the Finns would surely collapse. They were so, so confident."

"I vividly remember one attack we made in particular. Our artillery had pounded them for several hours before we moved in on foot. We found dozens of dead bodies without a scratch on them. They'd apparently been killed just by the shock waves from the massive concussive blasts of our shells that had exploded in the nearby vicinity. It must have been truly awful to be on the receiving end."

For a short time, Dmitry seemed to disappear into his own world again, before snapping out of it and continuing. "No matter what we tried though, the Finns just kept going, they just wouldn't stop fighting." Dmitry paused for a minute, while sharing another vodka with Valia.

As he was finishing off his final pieces of delectable fish and cucumber, Alexei strolled over to join them. "You two look like a barrel of laughs, what's going on here Valia?"

Valia introduced Alexei to Dmitry, who slowly continued his tale. "It's almost impossible to describe how awful it was, we lost so many men in those first couple of months. If it wasn't the Finns, it was the bitter, biting, deadly, cold."

The winter of 1940/41 had been one of the coldest on record in that part of the world. Raging blizzards and gale force winds regularly hampered the Soviet military manoeuvres.

"Do you know what? So many our comrades simply froze to death that we lost count. It was unbelievable. They were literally frozen solid, just like a wooden board. I tell you something, fighting a war in temperatures below minus ten degrees centigrade is almost impossible, but trying to fight a war where temperatures regularly get below -30°C is plainly stupid."

Dmitry paused for another minute as the horrific images played out in his mind once more.

"We even came across the frozen bodies of dead comrades, cynically propped up by the Finns for us to see. I think they were meant to be a macabre warning to us. It really was horrifying."

It was patently obvious to Valia that it was becoming extremely difficult, and even painful, for Dmitry to continue to recall those horrendous events.

"I remember that I was in a small platoon that had just started digging into the snow to get some shelter for the night, when out of the blue I saw a blinding flash somewhere to my left. I vaguely remember hearing a hail of gunfire before almost immediately being knocked off my feet. I think I must have lost consciousness for a short time, as I don't remember anything immediately after that. It was only a little later that I slowly became aware of shouts and screaming around me. Shots were still being fired, and I could dimly hear the sound of the occasional explosion nearby."

Valia noticed the blood starting to drain from Dmitry's face, as he recalled exactly how he had earned those fearful looking scars, that had torn mercilessly down his upper body and face.

"I started feeling an intense pain to the left side of my body. I remember a distinct sensation of warmth too. That certainly took me by surprise. When I opened my eyes, I couldn't focus on anything properly. Everything looked hideously distorted. It took a good few minutes rubbing them, before they eventually started to focus properly. I looked down and could see that I was covered in blood, but the worst thing was, I was also covered in what looked like body parts too. I distinctly remember screaming an unholy scream. I also vividly remember feeling each part of my body in turn to make sure everything was still in one piece, and they weren't my own body parts."

By now, Igor, Maxim and Michail had also popped across to see what was going on. Even Kirill had joined them. They too were spellbound by Dmitry's story. "Luckily, a few of my comrades appeared above me and started patching me up as best they could. It was only then that I became aware that I'd had been hit by a few pieces of shrapnel from a mortar shell. My unfortunate comrade who'd been a just couple of meters to my left hadn't been so lucky. An almost direct hit had literally blown him to pieces."

Dmitry was now totally lost as the horrific scenes replayed themselves over and over again in his mind. A tear or two welled up in his eyes as he finished the tale.

"They did a truly fantastic job managing to get me out of that hellhole still alive. I don't remember much about anything after that, I think the shock must've knocked me out. Anyway, I do remember waking up one afternoon in a hospital bed. It was in Leningrad. I stayed there for a couple of months, while the worst of the wounds healed."

"Here, you might as well take a look at the rest of them." With that, Dmitry unbuttoned his shirt and slowly removed it. The disfigured flesh had seared all down the left side of his torso and bore the marks of the horrendous lacerations he'd received. There was no doubting that he was lucky to still be alive.

They were all lost for words. Even Alexei, who would normally make a quip about any situation, was left dumbfounded.

To try and raise their spirits, Kirill charged everyone's glasses once again, and made a toast. "To all our valiant soldiers, wherever they may be. You are heroes all." With that, they all downed their vodkas, and as it was getting late, started to head off to get some sleep.

Maxim, wasn't feeling well at all though, he was decidedly queasy. He'd had far too much vodka, and far too much food too. As he approached the doorway to his barracks, he felt his stomach churning, and then, without warning, he felt very light headed. The next thing he knew, he was bent double, and vomiting all over the floor. Igor roared with laughter, and Alexei piped up "Well look at all those delicious looking bits of fish, they look really tasty Maxim, should I put them back on the fire so you can eat them again later?"

Maxim had never felt so bad, and he found he had almost no control of his legs whatsoever. He felt like lying down and dying just where he was, right by the front door. He could only muster a few slurred, and totally incomprehensible words in reply when his comrades asked how he was feeling. After a couple of minutes of jovial banter between his comrades about how youngsters just couldn't take their drink anymore, Michail finally picked Maxim up with a little help from Oleg. "Come on son, let's get you cleaned up a bit and into bed. You'll be clearing this shit up first thing in the morning, or you'll really be in trouble."

Meanwhile, Valia and Dmitry were still deep in conversation. "So how come you're here in Kharkov rather than recuperating somewhere nice, or even at home?"

"Well, you know what it's like. The doctors decided I was well enough to fight again, so they passed me fit for active service. Even now, I still get recurring nightmares about that awful place, and I just wanted to get as far away from it as I possibly could, so I requested a transfer from Leningrad to another unit somewhere else. I didn't mind where, just so long as it wasn't near Finland. To be honest with you, I was a bit surprised to get the transfer, but the 505th seem to be a good bunch of lads, so I'm pretty contented right now. Well, as contented as it's possible for me to be."

"That's good to hear," said Valia. "Anyway, we'd best get some sleep, as I'm sure they'll have us up early in the morning again.

Thanks for sharing your story, I could see just how much it affected you. Look after yourself, and maybe I'll see you around again soon."

With that they headed off in different directions, with Valia, only just managing to miss the stomach-churning pool of mushed-up, half-digested food and liquid lying in wait for him, just outside the front door of his barrack block.

Just two short days later, on Sunday, the 22nd of June 1941, Valia and his comrades were preparing to head out for more weaponry drills when he noticed an unusual amount of activity and apparent urgency emanating from the officers building block, no more than 200 metres away, down the hill.

A few minutes later, a somewhat ashen-faced Kirill came sprinting over to them. Blowing his whistle to get everyone's attention and to make sure they could all clearly hear his critically important announcement. It was obvious to all the comrades around him that something wasn't right. This was highly unusual. They'd never seen Kirill in such an agitated state as this before. He was obviously furious and hardly able to get his breath. After a few seconds trying to compose himself, the words simply fell out of his mouth in a fast, furious torrent of biting vitriol. "Those bastards. Those hideous, fascist, back-stabbing bastards. We're hearing that massive, overwhelming Nazi formations are right now attacking our brave comrades across the entire front". Valia quickly looked around him. Everyone was stunned. Nobody was expecting this. Not while Germany was still at war with Britain. It was inconceivable.

Kirill continued, but by now, in a slightly more controlled tone, "The Southwest Command have decided, that although there's no immediate cause for concern, it would be prudent at this point in time, to ensure that the River Dnieper area has some form of air defence cover. It's essential that the front-line combat units continue to receive critical supplies, and also reinforcement units, as and when needed. We've been ordered to deploy as soon as possible to the city of Kremenchug to help secure the vital railway crossing there. We'll be joined by the 505th, the 57th VNOS Battalion, who will be looking after the air warning, observation, and communications for us, and the 96th Anti-Aircraft Machine Gun Company. Everybody, get all your gear together. We'll be leaving at 13:00 sharp".

The mood of the 56th was bullish. After all, with over 300 ground Divisions, they were convinced that they were in the greatest army that the world had ever seen. Okay, so the Nazis might be a tough nut to crack, but with the huge advantage in manpower and resources at their disposal, there was no way that the Red Army could be defeated. It was just unimaginable.

While gathering his few personal possessions together, and carefully packing them into his kit bag, Valia's mind flashed back to his recent conversation with Dmitry. He was a little worried. If this was going to be anything like the Winter War with the Finns, they could be in real trouble. He quickly dismissed any thought of failure from his mind. Surely, they were to be victorious.

With that, he grabbed his gear and rushed to join his comrades along with Oleg. He wasn't happy at all. "It's bad for business he kept muttering under his breath."

"What's bad?" Valia asked.

"Don't worry about it, it's really not your problem," but just a few strides later, and after getting no further response from Valia, he went on, "Well, with us moving out of here, I'm going to lose my cut on the eggs that come into the camp. I'd arranged a really good deal with the local suppliers, and was getting a nice wedge of cash each week out of it. It's all going to be gone now."

Valia smiled ruefully, "Don't worry Oleg, I'm sure there's some great deals just waiting for you in Kremenchug."

A smile flickered over Oleg's lips, "Yeah, you're probably right. I'm sure I'll find something."

Once at the departure point, the assembled comrades loaded everything they might need for their deployment. All 12 of the

Battalions 76-millimetre guns were hooked up to their tractors, while the shells for the guns were carried in a mix of trucks and horse drawn carriages.

As the clock struck one, in high spirits, and singing songs, the 56th Air Defence Battalion headed off on their 250-kilometre trek, west, towards Kremenchug.

Chapter 3
The Bridge

The unassumingly, tranquil and unspoilt Valdai Hills are situated midway between Moscow and Saint Petersburg, in an area to the north-west of central Russia. Rich in lakes, the hills are not necessarily as spectacular, or as well-known as their bigger brothers and sisters around Europe, such as the mighty Alps, the imposing Pyrenees, or the strikingly impressive Ural Mountains. They do however, provide the source of some of the most important rivers that have, for over many centuries, helped to define the face of much of eastern Europe.

Without doubt, the most iconic of these is the gargantuan River Volga, which snakes its way south for over 2,000 miles to the Caspian Sea, making it the longest river in the continent. For good reason it is often known as the main artery, and the very lifeblood, upon which Russia was built.

The Daugava River, is a mere baby in comparison, and although it starts its life very near to the source of the Volga, it heads north instead of south, before emerging into the Baltic Sea.

The hills also provide the origin of the majestic Dnieper River, which drives its way for almost 1,400 miles through Russia, Belarus and Ukraine and finally out into the Black Sea.

From ancient times, these mighty rivers have served as trading routes, places to settle, and significantly, as impenetrable defences against invasion.

In the tumultuous summer of 1941, with war raging across Europe, the Dnieper River would once again be called upon to play its natural role as a significant defender, but this time, it would act as a giant, natural obstacle to the advancing armies of the German Third Reich.

After a long and gruelling journey from Kharkov, the 56th Battalion finally arrived in the City of Kremenchug and once there, promptly made their way to the critically important asset that they'd now need to protect at all costs.

At any other time, this rather mundane, yet mammoth structure, would scarcely warrant a second glance, let alone any sort of dedicated protection. However, with the hugely menacing threat, ominously approaching from the West, these were not normal times.

Striding magnificently over the Dnieper River, the mighty Kryukov Bridge, had long since been a vital cog in the local transportation infrastructure. Any major movement of Soviet men and materials to the front line by rail across the river, south of Kiev, would almost certainly have to cross the bridge. Without it, the ability of the Red Army to reinforce their front line would be disastrously impaired. It had now, as Kirill kept telling everybody, taken on a role of huge national importance.

So, it was, that Valia found himself dressed in the uniform of the Red Army on the eastern bank of the mighty Dnieper River looking westward. As he surveyed the hugely impressive scene in front of him, he knew he was ready to perform his duty, and should it be needed, he was determined to repel the approaching fascist horde, even if it were to cost him his life.

While Kirill and Michail were away, busy scouting out the best places to position their main guns and also somewhere to safely store their shells, the rest of the 3rd battery personnel enjoyed a stroll along a fairly narrow sandy bank, below the bridge.

Alexei looked pretty impressed. "Well, that's it, Maxim, that's the baby we're going to be looking after for the foreseeable future. It's humungous isn't it?"

Maxim was suitably awestruck. "I've never seen anything quite like it, it's massive."

While the comrades were waiting for Kirill and Michail to return, Alexei had an interesting thought. "You know what, I just hope we can get to sunbath on this beach a few times while we're here. It's great. I can just imagine it, a lovely, warm, sunny day sharing a nice cold beer together. We could even go swimming, the water looks so lovely, it'd be fabulous."

"Dream on." Igor said gruffly. "Once we're set up, I can't see us having the time for all that malarkey. We'll probably be way too busy anyway; can you imagine Kirill giving us any time off? It'll be drill, after drill after bloody drill. You know what he's like."

Valia's mind turned briefly to those glorious summer days that he'd enjoyed back in Krasny Profintern. They'd been wonderful. In fact, the Kryukov Bridge, towering tall in front of him, bore a striking resemblance to the railway bridge over the Volga River in the city of Yaroslavl. He vividly remembered having some delicious ice cream on the beautiful river banks there. It was such a happy time.

The sandy beach where they now stood was all but deserted, apart for a few hungry looking, stray dogs, scavenging the shoreline, looking for anything to eat. Valia was sure that during any normal summer afternoon, it would've been packed with families enjoying themselves. But, of course, this wasn't any normal summer, was it?

Maxim marvelled at all the boats shooting around the river. Some headed back and forwards across the river, some headed up and down. They were all shapes and sizes, and they all seemed to power ahead without a care in the world.

Alexei could see by the look on Maxim's face that he was formulating a question, so he pre-empted him with some possible answers. "Yes, and of course, everyone knows that the river at this point is almost a whole kilometre wide, don't they?" Maxim looked up at Alexei a little startled. "And we all know that the place on the other side of the bridge isn't actually Kremenchug, it's a separate city called Kryukov-on-Dnepr, and would you believe that the railway bridge, standing so proud, right in front of us, was actually opened in March 1872?"

A little smile flitted across Alexei's face as he watched Maxim's bewilderment. To be honest, he was stunned. How the hell did Alexei know so much about the bridge. He never normally knew anything of interest. Valia was starting to get a bit suspicious too. It certainly wasn't like Alexei to know any facts or figures about anything in particular.

"Maxim, here's a little bit of bonus information about the bridge, just for you. See those two sturdy stone abutments, one on either side of the river?" Maxim's eyes followed the direction Alexei's outstretched right arm pointed to. "Well, there are 11 equidistant stone piers between them, and those are connected by box shaped steel trusses that provide the strength and support for the bridge's deck. A railway line for a single track is laid on the cross beams of those metal trusses. There's also an additional flooring of wooden boards that provides a means for other traffic and pedestrians to be able to cross the bridge if needed." With that, Alexei allowed himself a gentle nod of approval.

Everyone was staring at Alexei in total disbelief. What'd happened to the rather ignorant Alexei that they all knew and loved?

Just then, Michail came jogging over. "Okay you lot, it's your lucky day. We've been given prime position for our three guns, right beside the bridge. The other brigades are covering other important sites around the surrounding railway infrastructure."

"I'm told that the 96th machine gun anti-aircraft unit will position themselves either side of us, while the 505th Battalion are currently getting their guns moved to the other side of the bridge, and they'll be responsible for covering the Kryukov area. The 57th VNOS company, will provide co-ordinated information about any attacking aircraft to all of us, and they'll be located alongside the 505th. That's about it for now, is that clear?"

After receiving an affirmative response, Michail continued. "Okay comrades, let's get to it, we've got guns that we need to get ready for action."

"Great," muttered Igor, under his breath. "Right next to the bridge. Is he serious? At least we'll have a nice view of the Nazi planes as they bomb the crap out of us."

In no great haste, the comrades strolled back to their guns, where they spent the next hour or so, carefully manoeuvring them into the best possible positions, and then getting them configured and calibrated ready for action. After adding some protective sand-bags, they were now prepared, and they would do their job as well as they possibly could.

Just as the work preparing the guns was all but finished, who should come loping along, but Oleg. "Sorry about that, did I miss anything important? I've been a little bit busy. What do you need me to do?" A chorus of expletives were hurled back at him, but Oleg just smiled.

In the meantime, Michail had managed to requisition a large, three story, brick-built warehouse that overlooked the river's edge, pretty much adjacent to their guns. When not on duty, the soldiers would have to sleep directly on the hard and dusty floor. As there were no beds, it certainly wasn't going to be comfortable, and a blanket was all they would have to try and keep the cold at bay. A makeshift field kitchen was also getting set up in one corner of the building, and it came as no surprise that Oleg was soon in a deep and serious discussions with the cooks there.

That evening, as the smell of fresh food permeated the building, most of the comrades enjoyed their first proper meal in a couple of days. They'd had some strikingly delicious fresh fish which tasted simply wonderful. As they were finishing up, Oleg sidled up to Valia with a huge smile on his face. "Hey Valia, how did you like the fish?"

"It was extremely good thanks." Valia responded, before the penny finally dropped, and it dawned on him. "Don't tell me, you've already got a deal on the fish, haven't you?"

"I couldn't possibly say," replied Oleg, but the huge smile on his face, sort of gave the game away.

As they were bedding down for the night, Valia quietly popped over to Alexei, and asked the obvious question. "How the hell did you know all that information about the bridge earlier today?"

With a smirk, Alexei replied, "Ah that, well you know what, on the way down to that beach, I bumped into one of the local boatmen. It seemed too good an opportunity to miss, so I asked him the same questions about the bridge that I knew Maxim would be interested in. He's always asking questions about that type of thing isn't he. Don't tell him though, it'll be our secret". They both shared a wry smile. Within 15 minutes, everyone who could, were trying their best to get some sleep.

Over the next couple of days, there wasn't much action to speak of, apart from a few training sessions that Kirill insisted upon, and the gun crews were getting somewhat bored. During their frequent breaks, Valia started to take an interest in all the trains that were crossing the bridge, just a stone's throw away from their gun position.

Throughout the day, heavily laden trains would take much needed materials and men west, towards the front. More unexpectedly though was the steady stream of overflowing trains heading east. Apparently, vital industrial enterprises and factories were being dismantled as fast as humanly possible and sent to safer locations well out of reach of the Nazis, far beyond Moscow, in an area considered safe from Nazi attack. The factories were to be reconstructed there, so that critical war production could continue unabated. As far as Valia could make out, everything seemed to be running like clockwork.

As the days slowly ticked by, Valia was struck by the calmness of

everyone in Kremenchug. There seemed to be no panic, no fret-
ting, just a stoic acceptance of the situation they were facing.
Everyone seemed to have the firm belief that after a few intensive
battles, and maybe one or two minor setbacks, the Nazis would
eventually be thrown back well before they arrived anywhere near
the Dnieper, and that the heroic Red Army would inevitably
prevail.

News from the front was somewhat sparse, but it wasn't too
long before it became apparent that things weren't going as well as
everyone had initially hoped. It also became worryingly obvious, to
Valia at least, that there appeared to be no proper defensive plan in
place for the Kremenchug region, and he wasn't slow in raising his
concerns. "Hey Michail, just a quick question that's starting to
bother me a little. Apart from us, are you aware of any other army
units in the City, or any that are scheduled to arrive anytime soon?"

Michail looked out across the vast river, as he took a few
seconds to formulate a considered response. "Well, a good pertinent question as always Valia. I've certainly not seen anything to
indicate there is, apart from some NKVD troops, but as far as I'm
aware, they're only here to specifically guard the railway
infrastructure. I'll have a chat with Kirill. I'm sure he'll know what
the grand plan is, he usually does, but I can't imagine they're going
to leave us to defend the city all alone. What commander in their
right mind is going to leave a vital river crossing in the hands of just
a couple of anti-aircraft Battalions, and a few other odds and sods?"

Kremenchug had actually been the home of the 102nd Infantry
Division, a unit made up of over 5,000 able bodied men and women
from in and around the city. However, following the news of the
Nazi invasion, the Division had been quickly mobilised and sent
north towards the Belarusian town of Bykhof, a town east of
Minsk. Like Kremenchug, Bykhof also stood as a major defensive
sentinel on the Dnieper. The 102nd were expected to help try and
block the advance of the German Army Group Centre, who were
advancing rapidly straight towards Moscow. Nobody in
Kremenchug had any up-to-date news about them though. They

hoped for the best but as time progressed, many started to fear the worst.

By early July, the war finally started becoming very real indeed. The first Nazi fighters and bombers were spotted in the distance heading in the direction of Kryukov. Action stations were called, and within minutes all the crews manning the air defence guns were lining up, preparing to start firing at their approaching prey.

The soviet air force, although large in number, was stretched very thinly along a huge combat front, which meant that the only fighter cover in the area, such as it was, came from a local air base just outside Kremenchug. Many of the planes were obsolete, especially when they were matched against the planes of the mighty Luftwaffe. The defenders of Kremenchug soon got used to the idea that they would have very little air support to rely on, if any at all. The guns of the anti-aircraft batteries were more or less it. They would be the only realistic defence for the bridge, and the city for the foreseeable future.

The excitement and nervousness grew as the dark, ominous, swarm of planes from Luftflotte 4, a Division of the German Luftwaffe set up specifically to support the activities of Army Group South, approached from the West. This was no exercise, these planes were the real deal, a genuine threat, and they would surely kill in the blink of an eye.

Valia noticed that Maxim was looking quite nervous. He was feeling pretty anxious himself too, but he certainly wasn't going to show it. "Well, here they come Maxim, get your helmet on. Just do your job, the same way you've done in training, and I promise you, everything will be just fine."

As the gun crew scurried around readying themselves for their first, real, live action, Michail brought them to order in his understated, yet authoritative tone. "Okay men, this is finally our time. This is our chance to show our worth, and to strike a blow against the Nazi invaders. Don't forget, let's work as a team, and concentrate on your jobs. Let's make our families and nation proud. Oh, and before I forget, I'll buy each of you a vodka if we can down at least one of their planes today."

As soon as invaders came within range, the 12, 76-millimetre guns of the 505th peppered the sky with their shells. Plumes of dark smoke from the exploding shells erupted around the planes. The 56th were ready. Each of their 12 guns spat fire as the order was called to let loose. The planes continued though, almost untroubled, on their chosen path through the now turbulent skies. As they finalised their approach towards the bridge, the machine gun bullets from the 96th intensified the field of fire even further as the bombers loomed large. Smoke started trailing from one of the lead bombers, and then soon after that, another too.

Repetitively loading heavy shells into the 76-millimetre gun was an arduous, physically demanding job, especially after several minutes of constant bending, lifting and placing the shells into the breach. Valia was soon getting fatigued. Stripped to the waist, sweat started to roll down his body. The muscles in his arms were burning, and he could feel the tension in his back.

He was concentrating intently on the job in hand when he heard Igor and Maxim starting to cheer loudly. Glancing up, Valia caught a glimpse of a lone, Soviet, Yak fighter engaging the enemy. It was an almost suicidal mission, but the men on the ground were roused by such brave, almost reckless actions.

Moments later the sound of explosions filled the air as the bombers started to empty their loads over an area near the Kryukov Bridge. The bombers then slowly wheeled around and headed back, the way they'd come.

Unfortunately for the Yak, it had got into a dogfight against overwhelming odds. Despite numerous attempts to out-manoeuvre the Nazi Me-109 fighters, there were just too many of them, and it wasn't too long before a trail of smoke was following the Yak to the ground in the far distance beyond Kryukov. There was no sign of a parachute. Another brave comrade, and a mother's treasured son, had almost certainly perished. With the Yak downed, the Nazi fighters turned and followed their bombers home.

Although several bombs had exploded in the vicinity of the bridge, none had hit their target. The Bridge had survived its first assault, and the air defence brigades had done their jobs well.

Over the next few days, Valia and his comrades were kept busy as they managed to successfully repulse further sporadic air attacks on both the Kremenchug and the Kryukov sides of the river. Despite the increasing attacks on the bridge, there was still very little fighter cover. Every now and again they'd see a friendly plane or two, but never anywhere in the quantity needed to drive off such a determined enemy.

Despite the aerial assaults, trains still ran the gauntlet. Right around the clock, they sent vital arms and equipment to the front, whilst evacuating a huge amount of factory paraphernalia and key personnel in the opposite direction.

Below the guns, the river traffic seemed busier than ever, as numerous boats and barges continued to ferry food, materials and people between Kremenchug and Kryukov.

As the days wore on, it became increasingly noticeable that more and more boats were starting to arrive from further up the river, mostly from Kiev. Many of these boats towed large, often defenceless, barges packed with people. Men, women and children, carrying whatever they could. Their entire worldly possessions in small suitcases or bags. Those happy, once secure family lives, destroyed.

Subsequent visits from the Luftwaffe resulted in fighters and dive bombers starting to get a taste for the river traffic, with the large barges being a particular favourite. The ubiquitous JU-87 (Stuka) dive bombers would often break formation and dive swiftly, strafing as they went. The pilots really seemed to enjoy the sport. As they hurtled down at a great rate of knots, small fans attached to their undercarriage would cause a high-pitched scream which would invariably terrify the people on board their intended target. Just as they started to pull up out of their dive, they'd release their deadly load. It was virtually impossible for them to miss.

The big guns of the 56th and 505th had to prioritise the protection of the bridge and rail tracks, so had little option but to concentrate their fire on the main bomber formations, which only left the machine guns of the 96th to do what they could to defend the near-defenceless boats and barges.

A small number of the boats had some weaponry, and those that did, would return what fire they could, but it was not uncommon to lose a boat or barge, either by simply sinking or sometimes totally exploding into a thunderous fireball.

Valia even heard of a one or two cases where boat crews had panicked at the sight of the approaching planes, and had detached the barges that they'd been towing, before making a run for safety themselves. Several times, local boat crews had needed to head out into the middle of the river during a raid, to rescue the petrified occupants of a totally defenceless barge drifting forlornly on the river.

As the days passed, news from the front, was starting to become quite grim. The Wehrmacht were advancing swiftly on all fronts. The first casualties had started to appear on the trains heading east several days earlier, and over the last day or two, Valia had seen a huge increase in the number of seriously injured. He was feeling somewhat pensive, and it was becoming obvious that the optimism everyone had initially felt when they'd first arrived in Kremenchug was fast dissipating.

Since February, the charismatic, and experienced General Mikhail Petrovich Kirponos had commanded the Kiev Military District. However, at the outbreak of Operation Barbarossa, this was transformed into the Southwestern Front, commanded by Marshal Semyon Budyonny. Even so, General Kirponos retained command of the defence of the entire Kiev region.

There was even a notable visit from Marshal Georgy Zhukov, who disagreed about tactics with General Kirponos, and this played a significant part in the Red Army defeat at the battle of Brody.

With Zhukov forced to return to Moscow due to the critical situation developing in the Bialystok, Minsk, Smolensk area, Divisions of the Southwestern Front were soon fighting a desperate defensive battle in the region around Uman, just 200 kilometres south of Kiev and little more than 300 kilometres west of Kremenchug.

Despite the increasingly close proximity of the Wehrmacht and it being in a highly important strategic location, Kremenchug and the surrounding area still appeared to have very little in the way of any organised or coordinated military defence. Not surprisingly, most of the Southwestern Front reserves were being directed to protect Kiev, but surely somebody, somewhere would realise that the areas either side of the city along the Dnieper River would also need some sort of organised protection too.

With no imminent signs of any significant reinforcement to the defences of Kremenchug, and almost in a state of desperation, the City leadership decided to raise their own militia. Two regiments were raised in Kremenchug, and one in Kryukov. They totalled barely 2,000, largely untrained volunteers. Many were too old or too young for the regular army, but they happily volunteered without hesitation. Some of the Militiamen owned their own pretty basic weapons, but many had nothing. There were no uniforms to speak of either, but the volunteers were mostly brave, courageous, and desperate to defend their city.

On the 9th of July, Colonel Pavel Osipovich Kuznetsov was appointed as the commanding officer of the 75th Aviation Division, but somewhat to his surprise, he was also appointed as the new military commandant of Kremenchug and the surrounding areas. He was charged with organising the defence of the city, the bridges and all river crossings. All the military units of the city, including the air defence Battalions, as well as the local militia Regiments, now came under his direct command. Colonel Kuznetsov also had the additional authority to utilise any military units retreating through Kremenchug, as he saw fit.

The same power was given to his deputy commandant, Major Vorobyov, who was appointed commander of the Kryukov Regiment of the Kremenchug people's militia.

As the days ticked by, and the volume and intensity of the aerial attacks increased, the air defence Battalions continued to stubbornly defend as best they could. So far, the Kryukov Bridge had somehow miraculously remained intact, allowing the all important military resources to continue to head to the front.

Monday, the 21st of July, awoke with another dull, drab cloudy sky. It didn't take long though for the now, ever so familiar, bombers to mass on the horizon. As usual the 505th guns took the lead, and began their barrage of fire as the planes came within their range. The 56th and 96th soon followed, and the sky was filled with a carpet of bullets and shells once more.

Bombs started exploding in and around the city, but vitally, the Kryukov Bridge remained intact and defiant. As the morning encounter played out, a couple of Luftwaffe planes were hit, and they were soon heading towards the ground with smoke belching out behind them. One crashed somewhere towards the outskirts of Kryukov, the other was heading directly into the Dnieper. The air defence batteries kept pounding away, producing a relentless hail of shells, and soon, as so often, the main formation wheeled around and started to head for home.

Just then, out of the corner of his eye, Valia noticed something moving very fast. It was almost skimming the water, and it was heading directly for the bridge. It was no longer trailing smoke. The Stuka they thought they'd destroyed only a few short minutes earlier was still very much alive. Before they could bring their guns to bear, it was directly above the bridge. It dropped its deadly cargo, and the bomb almost immediately smashed into the fourth span of the bridge, exploding with a vengeance. To Valia's horror, the taut metal truss buckled and splintered like it was a giant piece of wood, and within seconds, the tangled mass of metal crashed into the cold, uncaring, waters of the river below.

With its throttle now set to maximum, the Stuka accelerated and climbed away as quickly as it could, evading the hail of bullets and shells at its tail, it headed west to re-join its squadron in triumph.

Valia and his comrades were devastated. They'd been hoodwinked. The smoke that had been billowing from the wings of the Stuka had just been a clever, elaborate ruse to make it look like it was no longer a threat. As soon as he felt safe to do so, the Stuka pilot had driven home his ultimately successful attack.

It mattered not, the bridge had finally been breached.

Chapter 4
The Panzers

Peter Schmidt was starting to feel a little fatigued. Unsurprising given the almost constant action he'd seen over the last three months. His unit had been on the move for weeks, often with little more than a fleeting, cursory sleep. They must've covered hundreds of miles, and to top it off, they'd just successfully concluded yet another major battle.

The weather had been really bad for the last week or two, but at least the more aggressive rain had kindly relented for the day. Some of the thunderstorms they'd recently experienced were of truly biblical proportions, and conditions were pretty atrocious everywhere. Travelling anywhere was starting to become an issue. With very few paved roads in the area, they were spending most of the time driving along simple dirt tracks and these were now a slippy, filthy mass of mud and sludge. With the roads difficult to negotiate, the whole Division had almost ground to a halt in the Ukrainian countryside, somewhere east of Uman. They took the opportunity to grab a bite to eat, get the tanks refuelled and also restocked with shells. Peter checked his Halbieserne, the daily ration of food for Nazi combat troops, and picked out some hard bread and some pork. It was certainly no gastronomic delight, but when you're hungry, who really cares.

He'd also managed to get hold of some reasonably fresh water too, so he took a swig, along with the now almost obligatory pervitin pill. The pills were actually a methamphetamine drug used to combat fatigue, and also to inhibit fear, but they'd become very popular amongst the front-line soldiers, and were quite widely used.

With short blonde hair, blue eyes and standing just a tad over six-foot-tall, Peter was the epitome of the Aryan model that the Nazis espoused. Like the rest of his unit, he was strong, tough as teak and had stamina to burn. At the tender age of just 21, Peter had already seen more in his short life than many people experience in their entire lifetimes.

Along with the rest of his crew, he'd already fought his way through Poland, France, as well as Yugoslavia, and they were now in the middle of blasting their way through the heart of the Soviet Union too. They were totally convinced that within weeks, victory would be within their grasp.

By now, Peter and the crew of his Panzer IV tank were extremely proficient, having served together since the very beginning. They had a special bond, one forged together in the heat of battle, where they'd shared together so many death-defying experiences. Their bond was unbreakable, unshakable and eternal. Peter was the driver, and he had learnt to master his 25-ton beast like a duck to water. It was easy for him.

Hans, at the age of 26, was the elder statesman of the crew and he also just happened to be the tank commander. He oozed confidence, and always had a calm and level head, even under the most extreme circumstances. During combat, his clear, succinct commands were never once questioned by his men. With just a few, calming words from Hans, Peter would instinctively, and immediately know where the tank needed to go, it was almost telepathic. The crew trusted Hans like no other commander, and they trusted him with their very lives many times over.

Wolfgang had known Peter since they'd been at kindergarten

together. He was the gunner, and a pretty devastating gunner at that. His hit rate was fantastic, and it always came as something of a shock when he actually missed a target.

Peter always felt a bit sorry for the ox that was Werner. When the action got white hot, as loader, he got through so much work making sure the gun was always primed and ready to fire. He also needed to make sure there were enough shells loaded whenever they had a replenishing stop. It wasn't an easy task unloading a myriad of spent shell casings, and then stacking up to 87 new shells safely in the bowels of the tank.

At 22, Franz was a very important cog in the smooth operation of the tank. He was the radio operator, so was a key component when communicating with the other tanks in their Regiment. When called upon, he also needed to man the machine-gun whenever they encountered infantry or civilian opposition. He'd chalked up quite a few kills over the last couple of years.

They were a very close-knit team, they knew how to fight well, and more importantly, they knew how to win well, even when the odds were stacked high against them.

While the Division were waiting for orders to advance once more, Peter and the crew were loitering at the side of the road and within a few minutes, they started discussing their next likely destination.

"So where do you think we're off to next Peter?" Werner enquired.

"No idea to be honest, I just hope the roads improve a bit wherever we're going." Peter didn't like such slippery ground conditions, it made steering just that little bit more difficult than normal.

Wolfgang mused, "I bet it's Kiev. You know, I've always fancied a visit there. It was capital of the old Kingdom of Rus don't you know. Supposed to have some beautiful churches too. I'd love to see them."

Franz started chuckling to himself. "Well, if we do go there, the last thing you'll get to see is any beautiful churches. You know what the Luftwaffe are like. They'll have flattened everything by the time we get anywhere near them. They like that sort of thing don't they."

Wolfgang momentarily seemed a little downbeat. "Yeah, I guess so. It'd be such a shame if they were all wrecked though, wouldn't it?" He contemplated the likely destruction of the churches some more. "It seems such a waste, but, I guess that's just what happens in war."

As the crew continued to speculate about their next move, Peter's mind started to wander.

He'd been away from home for so long now, that he was starting to miss the beautiful City of Würzburg, where he'd been born and bred. Tucked away, as it was, in the distinct, Franconian region to the north of Bavaria, it was a wonderful place to live.

With the prominent Marienberg Fortress, majestic in its splendour, overlooking the city from its lofty position on a hill, high to the west of the River Main, and the plentiful vineyards providing such beautiful scenery, and even better tasting wines, Peter really longed to be back there. In fact, he was as certain as anyone could be, that he'd be back in just a few, short, months' time, when the war would most unequivocally have been won.

Throughout their childhood, Peter and Wolfgang had lived just a few streets apart from one another, and having attended the same schools since they were at kindergarten, they'd become almost inseparable.

Growing up during the 1930s was not easy though. Their teenage years had been such a very turbulent time. There were often violent scenes in the streets, and they weren't averse to getting involved in a bit of thuggery themselves.

Since the Nazi party had come to power in the early 1930s, it had been quite normal for boys to join the Hitler Youth movement, and Peter and Wolfgang had been no exception. They particularly enjoyed the many activities and opportunities that the organisation provided, and they especially treasured that special camaraderie that only the very entitled could understand and enjoy. Being so well organised, and run along military lines, they even started to think of the Hitler Youth movement as their own, private, mini army.

Although neither of them enjoyed school that much, they both excelled at sport, with Peter, quite a talented number nine, and Wolfgang, a pretty reliable goalkeeper in both the school and local football teams.

It was certainly a tempestuous time for many people. The Nazis recognised the Germanic and Nordic peoples as "The Master Race," and several policies were implemented across Germany, in order to improve and maintain a Germanic-Nordic Aryan supremacy. It was really drummed into the whole populace from every direction. It was during this period of time that Peter and Wolfgang, like most of their contemporaries, had really embraced the idea. All the school textbooks espoused the theory, the posters plastered around the city espoused the theory, the newspapers were full of it, and the radio reminded everybody of it on a daily basis.

Everywhere they went, they were surrounded by reminders of their genetic superiority over other peoples. Pretty much all of Peter's friends held very similar views and beliefs. They were totally convinced that they were a superior race in every way, and were just proud that they'd been born in this time, and in this place, and were a product of such superior Aryan lineage.

Looking back at his earlier years, Peter had been horrified that he'd actually played, and even been friends with some Jewish neighbours. He couldn't understand how his parents could have let him mix with such undesirables. He was so pleased when the Jews were finally banned from attending school. As time had gone by, he had first pitied them, but now, like all fair-minded patriots, he fiercely despised them.

It seemed just a natural progression for both Peter and Wolfgang to find themselves taken under the wing of a somewhat notorious gang of thugs, known as brownshirts, who'd patrol the streets most nights, and set upon anyone they suspected of being Jewish, or any other undesirable.

One distinctly clear, and warm evening, Peter and Wolfgang were making their way home from a Hitler Youth meeting, when Peter heard the telltale shouts and screams of another unfortunate victim being accosted nearby. Keen to join the fray, Peter shouted as he started running along the street towards the melee, "Come on Wolfgang, we don't want to miss this, it'll be fun." Four burly looking men were busy accosting a slightly built man. Two of the men were holding the hapless victim by the arms, while the other two were punching him repeatedly with vicious intent. A pair of glasses with one arm broken off, and both lenses severely cracked, lay on the floor near his feet, whilst blood was pouring from both his nose and mouth.

As Peter and Wolfgang approached, the man looked over to them through his badly swollen eyes, and in a voice only just audible, cried out. "Peter, is that you? Help me, please help me Peter."

The old man was barely recognisable, but Peter slowly realised that it was his old doctor, Dr. Horowitz. The doctor who'd treated him many times when he was a young boy, even when Peter's parents couldn't afford the payments for those treatments. Despite this, Peter didn't lift a finger to help. He simply stood by and watched until the flurry of punches finally stopped, and the men let the doctor fall, unconscious, in an undignified heap by the side of the road.

Wolfgang was curious. "Who was that Peter? He seemed to know who you were."

The four brownshirts, now liberally splattered with Dr. Horowitz's blood, now also looked at Peter with a great deal of interest.

Peter stared at the barely breathing body on the floor, before replying. "Nobody I know. I tell you what. Why don't we go and smash the windows at the Cohen's shop just around the corner again? I've heard that somehow, they've already been able to replace the windows we smashed there last week."

Wolfgang didn't need a second invitation. "Great, there's a pile of stones, just over the road from there, come on, there's no point hanging around here."

With that, Peter, Wolfgang and the four brownshirts jogged down the road. They were loving every minute of the mayhem.

As dedicated members of the Hitler Youth movement, Peter and Wolfgang, along with a few of their friends had been selected to represent the Würzburg youth at the tenth Nazi Party Congress. It was to be called the "Rally of Greater Germany". The boys were extremely excited, and their parents were immensely proud that they'd been selected from so many, to represent their beautiful City.

The Rally was to take place from the 5th-12th of September 1938, and it was decided that the boys would stay in a tented camp near the Nazi Rally Ground for its entire duration. As it was to be their first extended stay in Nürnberg, they were allowed to travel there a couple of days earlier, just to have a look around the city and get a good feel for the atmosphere of the place.

Early in the morning on Saturday, the 3rd of September, Peter and Wolfgang met outside Peter's home and embarked on the three kilometre walk to the Hauptbahnhof together, where they met up with their colleagues. Everyone's rucksacks were full to overflowing.

While they were patiently waiting on the platform for their train to arrive, Wolfgang turned to Peter and whispered. "I hope you've got a good stock of food with you; my mother only packed a couple of cheese rolls and a few pretzels. I think it's only enough for the train journey."

Peter smiled. He'd been in this same situation a few times before. "Yeah, no need to worry, you know what my mother's like. I'm sure I've got a little to spare if you need it. Just don't go publicising it to everyone."

A few minutes later, the train that'd be transporting them to Nürnberg, slowly pulled up alongside the platform, until it finally came to a halt. Almost immediately, the doors burst open, and the passengers on board, got off and busily made their way along the platform towards the main concourse.

As soon as the last of the passengers had vacated the train, the excited group rushed aboard to grab the best seats available. Peter and his friends were in a party mood, and just ten minutes later, the train was accelerating out of Würzburg on the short 50-minute ride to Nürnberg, the largest city, and unofficial capital of Franconia.

The atmosphere on board was almost electric, and it didn't take long before Peter and his friends were singing popular songs, as well as delving into their rucksacks for some delicious food.

The 100-kilometre journey went by in what seemed like the blink of an eye, and they were soon pulling into the Hauptbahnhof in Nürnberg.

The group were met outside the station by members of the local Hitler Youth, who accompanied them, along with members of other Hitler Youth groups from Frankfurt, Berlin and Munich on the short tram journey to their camp site, not too far away from the Rally Ground, to the south-east of the city.

After quickly and expertly erecting their tents in nice orderly lines, the various groups assembled near the entrance to the campsite.

So many tents had been put up, it was difficult to see where they ended. Peter was having the time of his life. "Isn't this great Wolfgang? Look at it. I just love it here."

"I know, it's amazing isn't it. Everyone I've met so far has been just so incredibly friendly and helpful."

Peter looked around, and there was quite a crowd milling around. "Any idea what's on the itinerary for the rest of the day?"

Wolfgang looked a little sheepish, and started biting his fingernails a little nervously. "Well, I do remember seeing an itinerary for the week at the last meeting we had in Würzburg, but, to be honest, I hadn't really taken in too many of the details. I was only really interested in the events that were to take place in the main Rally Ground."

Peter looked around some more. To be fair, he'd done exactly the same thing, and it looked like everybody else there had too.

It's only when a group of Hitler Youth leaders from Nürnberg arrived 15 minutes later that they were reminded that the first place they were scheduled to visit was the Tiergarten. It wasn't too far away, and when the boys got there, they had a fantastic time wondering around the park and visiting the plethora of strange looking, colourful and exotic animals that were on display. They spent the whole afternoon there. It was great fun. As an added bonus, as they were visiting members of the Hitler Youth, and it was Rally time, they were even given a free Ice Cream, which was absolutely delicious. As the evening started to take hold, Peter and his friends returned to the campsite, where they sang songs, and drank tea late into the night. Eventually, extremely tired, but happy, they retired to the sleeping bags in their tents, for a restful sleep.

It was another fabulously hot, sunny day when they awoke, and this time, Peter and Wolfgang were much better prepared. They actually knew that they were scheduled to visit the famous castle, around which the city was built.

This time though, the Würzburg group would be travelling by themselves, with just a couple of local Hitler Youth to help guide them around the city.

Promptly at 9:00am they left the campsite, and after a short wait, clambered aboard the tram. After a relatively short ride, they all alighted at the Hauptbahnhof again. From there they started to stroll through the bustling streets. They could almost cut the excitement in the city with a knife. Just like in Würzburg, almost all the main buildings were bedecked with huge, red national flags, each of which had a menacing black swastika on a pure white circle embossed in the centre.

Nürnberg was heaving with visitors who were there for the Rally. Lots of different uniforms were on display, with many of them strutting around like peacocks. The many street venders were busy making a good profit selling their wares, with Nürnberger

Bratwurst, Pretzel and Lebkuchen, a honey sweetened flavoured cake, being huge favourites as always.

As they started to cross the Pegnitz River using the Fleischbrücke bridge, the group paused. Peter and Wolfgang were very impressed. "Wow, look at the beautiful views along the river, Peter."

Peter was impressed with the bridge as well as the surrounding views. "What a wonderful place, it's such a beautiful city."

There was a lot of drinking going on throughout the city and it looked like the whole place was having a huge, big party. They strolled past many shops and bars before entering the impressive main market square in Nürnberg, the Hauptmarkt, flanked by some hugely imposing and very august looking churches. In the corner of the square closest to the castle stood the famous, 14th-Century, Schöner Brunnen, which, in the shape of a gothic spire, standing 19 metres tall, and adorned with 40 vividly colourful figures, looked very spectacular indeed. Each of the boys made sure they spun one of the two brass rings on the fence surrounding it, to give themselves, just that extra, little bit of good luck.

Then, further ahead, they could see the mighty fortress on its spectacular hilltop perch. Walking past the City Hall on their right, they marched their way up the steep hill to the castle, and took plenty of time to have a good look around the mighty structure.

Wolfgang was suitably impressed. "Peter, just look at the views over the city, it's simply breath-taking isn't it."

"You can say that again, I could spend all day exploring this place. It'll be such a shame to have to leave."

Ten minutes later though, one of the local Hitler Youth guides rounded them up. "I'm really sorry to interrupt you, but we need to head down again now. Don't worry, there are plenty of market stalls throughout the city you can look through, and we'll sort out a meal for you in one of the restaurants."

Eventually the group decided to get some delicious food from one of the market stalls, before heading back to their camp after another exhilarating day.

The only negative part of it from Peter's perspective was seeing so many Jewish people walking around. "Why can't they clear them off the streets?" Peter thought to himself, especially during Rally time. They'd actually only come across five Jews throughout the day, but that was still five Jews too many as far as Peter was concerned.

Over the next few days, the boys were awestruck as they attended the various sessions of the Rally. It was so impressive, and everything was on a truly massive scale. The huge Zeppelins flying overhead were even more colossal than they'd expected. The military prowess on display was mighty to behold, and the speeches were without doubt awe-inspiring. The excitement increased by the day until climaxing in a frenzy when Hitler himself arrived in all his magnificence. The way he controlled his audience with such aggressive charm and character was something Peter would never forget. These were truly wonderful times, they were etched into his heart forever. As far as Peter was concerned, Hitler was almost as good as a god.

The boys were so disappointed when the camp finally ended and it was time for them to return home again, but they promised each other, as soon as they could, they'd join the army to serve their undisputed master. They knew it was expected, it was their civil duty, and it was their destiny.

After returning home to Würzburg, it took several days to get back to normality, but the daily routine of attending school, and the Hitler Youth soon became the boring norm again. As far as Peter was concerned, the World would soon be under the sway of the Nazis, and he was part of the vanguard that would make this a reality. He was living in the right place, and at just the right time.

In November, just a couple of months later, between Wednesday the 9th and Thursday the 10th, Peter and Wolfgang witnessed, first hand, Kristallnacht in all its bloody brutality. Jewish homes and hospitals were ransacked as both paramilitary and civilian attackers demolished buildings with sledgehammers and other instruments of destruction. The rioters more or less totally destroyed both of the synagogues in the city, and most Jewish businesses were damaged or destroyed beyond repair. In fact, Peter and Wolfgang helped to smash up a few of the building as well. They'd really enjoyed it, and in a strange sort of way, it just felt totally natural to them.

A couple of days later, at their next Hitler Youth meeting, Peter and Wolfgang found themselves in front of an excitable and awestruck group of younger members who were desperate to hear some first-hand accounts of the infamous night that had just unfolded. Egged on by the group leaders, Peter and Wolfgang were more than happy to recall their nefarious deeds.

Peter began, almost apologetically, as he was quite nervous. "Well, to be honest, we really were quite fortunate. To begin with, we didn't fully appreciate the scale of the planned operations, but some of our friends from the brownshirts saw us, and called us over to join them. They said if everything went well, it'd be an awesome night, so of course we tagged along."

Peter, who wasn't a great one for public speaking, glanced over towards Wolfgang, who was pretty happy to take over the narrative. "You know what? In fact, the whole event unfolded better than we could ever have imagined. It was quite easy really. We joined along with a few hundred brownshirts as they marauded through the city. Any building with a Star of David painted onto it was fair game."

"We started off with a few shops, and smashed the windows entirely. Some of the brownshirts then shattered down the doors, and several of us went flying in. Anything that looked like it was of any value, we took, and anything that didn't we utterly trashed. We did a few shops before some stupid Jews came to try and protect their property. They got well and truly beaten to a pulp."

Peter interjected with a quick question. "Do you know the funniest bit of the whole night?"

The adolescent audience looked somewhat quizzical, yet spellbound, in the same measure.

"The idiots even called the police to come and help and protect them, and to be fair, they did come. However, they just stood back and watched the mayhem unfold in front of them, before arresting the badly beaten up scum for inciting the trouble in the first place. It was hilarious."

Everyone in the hall was in stitches of laughter, especially the adult leaders.

With more to tell, Wolfgang continued. "It didn't take too long before our group of brownshirts merged with another larger group who were already pelting the nearby synagogue with rocks and anything else they could get their hands on. I even overheard somebody saying they were going to burn the place to the ground. I was surprised that they didn't in the end, but found out the next day, that the only reason they didn't was because a lot of property was too close and many normal people's homes might also have ended up engulfed in flames if they did."

"Anyway, I digress, we smashed the doors down, and ransacked everything inside. Nothing escaped our ire."

Wolfgang looked like he'd finished speaking, so Peter, being a lot more relaxed by now, took over. "As we were leaving the ruined synagogue, one of the senior brownshirts came over to me and gave me a couple of old looking scrolls of paper. He mentioned something about Torah, but I didn't really understand what he was talking about. Anyway, I put them in my backpack, and forgot about them, as we moved onto the next target."

"It was a truly exhilarating night, which I simply loved. We didn't get home until the sun had already risen, but we didn't care a jot. I don't know about Wolfgang, but I've been on a high ever since."

Wolfgang smiled and nodded. "I couldn't agree more. It was such a fun night."

Just as the meeting was coming to an end, a tall, aristocratic looking man in a smart black uniform entered the room. He marched smartly across the hall and talked very briefly to the meeting leaders before turning and addressing everyone present. "Good evening gentlemen, my name is Hauptmann Müller. As I'm sure you all know by now, following on from the Anschluss that took place on the 12th of March, the 2nd Panzer Division that used to be based here, in our wonderful city, has been relocated, and is now stationed full-time in Austria. We'd initially hoped that this'd be a temporary deployment, and that the Division would be returning home at some point, but it now seems that they'll be permanently stationed in Vienna, and will start to be manned by our Austrian brothers."

"You may have heard rumours that the city is to raise a new Division to replace them, and I'm here to confirm that that is indeed the case, and we will soon be raising the new 4th Panzer Division in the city."

"I'm actually here in a recruiting role, and I'm looking for enthusiastic volunteers to sign up and join this new elite fighting force. Some of you might even be selected for tank crew training if you're lucky. If any of you are interested, which I'm sure some of you will be, please come and see me before you leave."

Peter looked at Wolfgang with a huge grin on his face. "That's just what I've been looking for. I'm in, are you thinking of joining too?"

"Just try and stop me." Wolfgang was hooked as well.

Within a couple of weeks, Peter and Wolfgang had started their basic training, and were looking forward to the adventures that were sure to come their way.

Only a few, short, months later, the new Division was taking shape and they were nearing full strength. It hadn't taken long, and both Peter and Wolfgang were really pleased, as they'd been assigned to the same tank crew. Not any old tank mind you, a spanking, brand new Panzer IV.

Peter and Wolfgang's parents were so immensely proud of their sons, and in fact, just a few months later, when the 4th Panzer Division were finally ready for active service, it looked like the entire population had turned out to celebrate as the tanks rolled slowly through the city, heading off to the North, in the direction of Poland.

Before dawn, on the 1st of September 1939, Hans gave the order to roll. "Okay, this is it. Peter, let's get going." Peter engaged the tracks of his beast, and along with the other 350 tanks of the 4th Panzer Division, they soon smashed their way across the border into Poland.

Peter was so honoured that his crew had been selected to be part of the vanguard of the German Army Group South's attack, and that first day, they made very rapid progress, all the way to a village called Mokra, where they finally engaged with the Polish forces for the first time.

Peter smiled as he recalled having to face an actual, real life, Polish cavalry charge. Just imagine the absurdity of it, men on actual, real, horses charging towards tanks. How ridiculous was that?

Peter called out. "Sir, I think I'm going mad. Is that a real cavalry charge up ahead? I thought those things had long since been consigned to history?"

Hans looked on in total disbelief too. "Well, we're either both going mad, or the horsemen I see charging at us are. Franz, get on the machine gun, and start taking them out."

Polish horses and men were soon crashing to the ground, as the tanks got their range. Despite this, the Nazi attack foundered, and the tanks were forced to withdraw after suffering heavy casualties themselves. This however, was more to do with the conventional Polish forces in the field than anything to do with the cavalry.

With other Nazi forces racing across Poland, the 4th Panzer Division took up a role supporting the 1st Panzer Division as they finally broke through the Polish defensive lines near Kłobuck. Just three days later, they were swiftly approaching the capital, Warsaw.

As they manoeuvred their way into the City suburbs, Hans warned, "Keep your eyes open for anything suspicious. Any news on the radio Franz?" Hans was getting worried. It was way too quiet. "Nothing new to report at the moment, sir." Franz replied.

Again, the whole crew took great pride at being selected as part of the vanguard in the menacing, mechanised beasts leading the Division into the City. They were expecting an easy ride, after all, they'd broken the back of the Polish Army just a few days earlier.

The clanking monsters continued to slowly pull themselves further and further towards the city centre. It was eerily quiet. Hans could feel the hairs on the back of his neck starting to stand on end. He could smell trouble.

Without warning, a huge blast rocked them, followed immediately by the unmistakable rat-a-tat-tat sound as bullets ricocheted off the hull of their trusty beast. Then another explosion erupted, this time to the right. "Shit, I knew it." Hans snarled, as he surveyed the horizon through his periscope. The tanks immediately in front and to the right of them were in flames, with their crews scuttling out as fast as they could.

Hans screamed, "Peter, get moving. Get moving now. Wolfgang, target and fire at anything hostile that you can see." Peter didn't need to be told, he was already manoeuvring the tank around the burning hulks ahead. Wolfgang was targeting flashes from the buildings up ahead. As they moved forward, Hans was cursing under his breath "those bastards." He could see the crews of the stricken tanks either being engulfed in flames or cut down as they tried to get away to safety, by withering Polish fire from the surrounding buildings.

Wolfgang pulled the trigger and seconds later the wall of a building ahead collapsed in a heap. Peter drove hard as the number of explosions around him intensified.

They'd driven straight into a trap. This wasn't how it was meant to be. As more and more tanks became victims, the advance slowly ground to a halt. They were now almost sitting ducks. Peter didn't like it at all. There was virtually nowhere to go. Franz was busy on the radio, getting updates, and relaying information on their status.

After several minutes, that seemed like an eternity, he shouted "It's the order to retreat, and regroup, sir."

"Okay, get us out of here as fast as you can Peter." Peter took great delight, getting the tank up to top speed, as he immediately complied with the order.

Within minutes, the whole column of tanks had turned tail, and were headed out of the City as fast as they could, followed by a hail of bullets and anti-tank missiles.

General Reinhardt, commander of the 4th Panzer Division, wasn't somebody who took retreat kindly, and another attack the following morning was swiftly ordered.

The Nazi artillery and Luftwaffe started softening up the Polish defensive positions early the following morning and just before 8:00am, with dense smoke billowing over Warsaw, the tanks started to roll again.

After their exploits the previous day, Peter and his crew were positioned near the rear, as the column advanced. Up ahead a multitude of dispossessed civilians were running around with nowhere in particular to go. It was mayhem. Many people were trying to escape the capital, while others were retreating there from areas already overrun by the Nazi advance. It was pandemonium. There were people in carts, people in cars, there were people on foot. The roads were almost totally congested with people and as the lead tanks approached them, they were effectively blocking the way.

The radio crackled into life once more. "The order is to plough right through them." Franz announced matter-of-factly. The tanks continued their inexorable march forward and it didn't take long for the lead tanks to start driving over cars, horses, and even people. Anything that was in their way was run over. Some tanks even started firing on the utterly defenceless civilians. It was absolute carnage.

It really didn't matter to Peter, they were in the way, there was no other route to take and they really didn't have time to stop to let them get out of the way. Defenceless men, women and children were brutally crushed or mown down in a hail of bullets. It was a massacre, nothing less.

As the blood-splattered tanks rumbled further into the City along the road, hemmed in by tall buildings on either side, they encountered a very hastily erected barricade blocking the road. The tanks at the front of the column engaged the apparently lightly defended obstruction and continued their unrelenting advance to remove it. Within seconds, the leading tanks were being peppered with bullets and shells were flying everywhere. A few tanks were quickly in flames. From the rear of the column, Peter could witness it all. The first thought that went through his mind was, "Shit, not again," as Hans debated whether to continue advancing or halt where they were. Wolfgang was already trying to target any enemy positions he could spot.

Then, ahead of them, they quickly became aware of flames on the road. Not just individual tanks on fire, but the whole road ahead was in flames. The road was burning, how could this be?

Hans screamed. "Reverse, reverse now, as fast as you can Peter. Go, go, go." With a huge roar of the engine, Peter fought with the controls as his tank hurtled backwards at great speed. The road ahead of them was soon just a massive sheet of flames, with thick, black, dense, choking, smoke, billowing high into the air. There was no escape for the tanks up front, or for those up to 100 metres, or so, behind them. The road was a raging inferno, with the tanks, trapped where they were, being cooked in the intense head. As the shells inside exploded in the heat, tank after tank was split open, like a tin can, from the inside. The frantic, wretched, desperate crews were simply incinerated, as they attempted to escape.

Unbeknownst to the attackers, the Polish defenders had covered the road in highly inflammable turpentine from a chemical factory that was situated right next to the barricade. It was a very simple, yet very deadly trap.

The polish defenders then charged with fixed bayonets. It was an astonishing sight. The few infantrymen that had been accompanying the tanks and had somehow managed to evade the flames, were either cut down, or were so terrified, that they surrendered there and then.

The few tanks that'd managed to escape the raging inferno retreated, like scolded animals, for a second day in succession. By the time they'd re-assembled, the Division had lost over 40 tanks. It was a heavy toll, and General Reinhardt had had enough. The Division retreated, and instead, ended up taking part in the battle of Bzura, the biggest of the Polish Invasion. The eventual breakthrough here signalled the end of major Polish resistance, and soon after Warsaw was captured by other Nazi forces. Peter and his crew had won their stripes though, and were now ready for more.

Soon after, the Division found themselves near the village of Śladów on the banks of the River Vistula, at over 1,000 kilometres, the longest river in Poland. Most of the tanks had already pulled up and their crews had managed to start getting some well-deserved food and rest.

While they were grabbing a bite to eat, Peter vividly recalled a disturbance, near the banks of the river, just a few hundred metres away. Turning towards the source of the noise, Werner asked, "What's that dreadful hullabaloo all about?"

Hans wasn't sure, "No idea Werner, let's go, take a look." Horrendous howling, screaming and shouting filled the air, then gunshot after gunshot, it never seemed to end. The curious crew came into an open area on the banks of the river, and the scene that met their eyes was one of abject slaughter. A SS paramilitary death squad, the Einsatzgruppen, were busy going about their normal, daily, business. This time, executing prisoners of war with bullets to the back of the head. The normal Wehrmacht infantry soldiers from the Division were surrounding the prisoners to make sure nobody was able to escape and any prisoner attempting to do so was shot out of hand.

About 50 metres further along the bank was a large group of local civilians, and these were literally being thrown into the river, and the soldiers were taking pot shots at them.

Peter chirped, "Hey, that looks like fun, how about we go and join in?" and with that all the crew members apart from Hans jogged over to the river bank. They too started taking pot shots with their pistols at the defenceless, drowning men, women and children as they floated past. The bank was soon full of soldiers taking pot shots, while the Einsatzgruppen continued their ruthless dispatch of the Polish prisoners of war.

Hans was disgusted. This was no way to fight a war. But what could he do or say against so many of his own countrymen who'd obviously been so indoctrinated into believing that all prisoners were little more than vermin and needed to be destroyed. It was also likely that many of the soldiers were probably still high on the effects of their pervitin. It didn't matter either way, as their commanding officers were actively encouraging murder.

A couple of hours later 252 prisoners of war and 106 civilians were dead. Unceremoniously killed, in cold blood.

The crew were in jovial mood as they returned to their tank. Werner boasted, "I'm sure I got at least five, how many did you get Wolfgang?", "I'm not sure but I definitely bagged a couple."

Hans had a very uncomfortable night's sleep, as his conscience pained him, but in the end, he needed to keep his "unpatriotic" thoughts to himself. He certainly didn't want to end up in front of the Einsatzgruppen himself.

After the surrender of Poland, the 4th Panzer Division found themselves in the Lower Rhine region, close to the Dutch border, to get some well-deserved downtime, rest and recuperation.

As most of the men in the Division came from Franconia, its men had a reputation for enjoying a beer or two, and they certainly enjoyed the local brew here. They'd been very pleasantly surprised with the quality and especially its taste. Why, it was almost as good as some of the beers back home. Peter and his crew mates just loved to have a few beers in a nice bar, especially when there were some good-looking girls around, of which there were a great many.

Although they had a great time imbibing in the various local bars, Peter had been a little surprised to see quite so many Jewish people still around the town. It was a little unnerving for him. What were they doing out and about? Most of the crews ignored them totally, but a few would indiscriminately punch or kick them as they tried to hurry past.

When a very pretty, dark haired, young Jewish girl was accosted by a small group of very drunk infantrymen, nobody said anything at all. Peter saw them drag the girl down a quiet looking side street, and soon after, just a few minutes later, he could hear her screams. The cries of help went unanswered, and didn't last long. They were swiftly ended as the single crack of a gunshot reverberated around the streets. Peter and the rest of the crew strolled on without a care in the world. Such was the wonderful life in the Master race.

After such a relaxing break, a deep sense of foreboding came over the whole crew when finally, the orders to move into France came through. Peter recalled the whole crew being very apprehensive and distinctly on edge.

Werner was obviously getting quite nervous as the hours ticked down to zero hour. "Peter, how do you think it's going to go?"

Peter pondered the question for a little while. "Well, this time we won't be facing the Poles, but the French as well as the British. I'd imagine we'll have a real fight on our hands. I'm sure it'll be intensive, and it's certain to be tough. Nevertheless, I've got full confidence in every one in this crew, and I'm sure that the senior commanding officers know what they're doing. We'll be just fine. I just hope we don't get dragged into the same trench type warfare that destroyed so many of our countrymen just over 20 years ago."

Under the dashing leadership of General Paul Ewald von Kleist, the tank formations quickly smashed through the piecemeal defences of Liège and Charleroi as they sped through Belgium and northern France. They kept battering their way through the poorly organised defenders, who were clearly in disarray, at full speed until they reached an area near the town of Bethune, not too far from the French coast. Here, they were joined by several other Panzer Divisions before their first proper engagement with the British. Heavy fighting ensued as the British and French rear-guard tried to cover what was rapidly becoming a hugely desperate evacuation from the hostile beaches around Dunkirk.

With the Panzer Divisions in a prime position to totally crush the stranded, and virtually helpless British forces on the beaches, a totally unexpected turn of events unfolded. "Sir, you're not going to believe this," Franz said, "we've got an order to hold our ground." The crew were dumbfounded. "Can you double check that Franz." Hans asked, "Surely that can't be correct." After a few further calls to verify the veracity of the order, Franz was soon able to update Hans. "Sorry sir, it's confirmed. We need to hold our ground here, and not make any further advances until ordered to do so."

Peter couldn't believe it, nor could the rest of the crew. Here they were, just a few short kilometres away from taking the British out of the war altogether, and they had to stop. It made absolutely no sense at all. As they waited, refuelled and replenished, the infantry Regiments finally caught up with the tanks.

Werner wasn't happy at all. "What the hell are they playing at?" Peter and Wolfgang both concurred. "I know, I know. It seems like a strange decision to me too, but you know very well not to question an order. There must be a good reason for us to halt. We wait here." Hans was firm. The line of authority could never be questioned.

As the hours dragged on, and with no sign of further movement, all the crews were aghast at the decision. "Why, why, why?" was a common thought. The general consensus was that it was absolute nonsense.

Above them, the Luftwaffe continued with their aerial assaults. The tank crews could hear the constant explosions in and around the Dunkirk area, not too far off, in the distance.

Some of the tank crews were frustrated, some were even furious. They'd seen a total, stunning, victory, easily within their grasp, but just because of some ridiculous decision, they were now watching that opportunity slip through their fingers. Peter and the whole crew were getting more and more disheartened as each wasted hour ticked by, and ship after ship, fully laden with totally defenceless enemy soldiers, who'd been there for the taking, headed back to Britain.

It was three whole days before the order to resume the assault arrived, and by that time, a large proportion of the British and French had left the beaches at Dunkirk and were already safely ensconced back in Britain. So, whether by design, or by accident, this was not going to be the week that the war would end after all.

Encountering hardly any resistance of note, the 4th Panzer Division then sped south, at speed, through France, until they reached the foothills of the Alps at Grenoble. It was while they were here, that the French, meekly agreed an armistice with Germany.

When Franz received the new on the radio, a big smile extended right the way across his face. He was so excited. "Sir, I've just received some great news from command. The French have given up. Apparently, they've signed an armistice. As far as head-quarters are concerned, the war is over. We're to remain stationed here, until further notice."

An unexpected, yet almost instant burst of triumphal euphoria broke out amongst the crew. They were all quick to hug each other, and pat each other on the back. They had met, head on, many huge threats and challenges over the last few weeks, and as a team, a very close-knit team, they had successfully overcome each one.

"Is that it? Have we really won? What about the British?" Werner just couldn't take it in. He'd been expecting a long, drawn out war, as had the rest of the crew, and he was simply stunned.

Hans, didn't usually get too involved with informal crew discussions, but this time, he was happy to join in. "Well, I think you can safely say that we have won. With the French out of the equation, the British won't have a chance to take the war to us again. In my

71

opinion, their only logical course of action is to sue for peace. I've heard several rumours that that's what the Führer is hoping for and expecting anyway. Let's wait and see what transpires over the next few weeks, but I would expect us to finally get some proper rest now."

The rest of the crew just couldn't stop smiling for the rest of the day.

The following day, the whole Division was formally ordered to remain in the Grenoble region until further notice to quell any potential uprisings, but mainly to rest, relax and generally enjoy themselves in the area.

It was very picturesque, with the mountains rising from the River Isère. The tank crews loved visiting the cafes and bars, and quite a few of the local ladies seemed to take quite a liking to the tank crews too. What could be better?

Within a couple of weeks, members of the Gestapo, the official secret police of the Nazis, started to arrive in the City, and it wasn't too long after that, that a great many of the Jews in the area were being rounded up and loaded into open cattle trucks at the railway station. Some of the Divisions' infantry had been roped in to help with the movement of these undesirables, and their commanding officers were only too pleased to oblige. Some of the soldiers took great pleasure beating Jews at random, and a few Jews were even shot, whether or not they were trying to escape.

After a couple of months enjoying the delights of France, the Division were finally allowed to return to their home city to rest, recuperate and re-organise themselves. As the tanks rolled back into Würzburg, they were hailed as conquering heroes. The streets were thronging, bands were playing, the beer and the wine were flowing like water. It was a huge party. Both Peter and Wolfgang managed to visit their parents who were so happy to welcome them home. They must have been the proudest parents in the world. It was evidently clear now that Germany was the master of all Europe. The master race had prevailed, just as the Führer had promised.

After a few days relaxing with their family and friends, the crew reported back for duty where Hans had some unexpected news. "Welcome back men. I hope you've enjoyed your fun over the last week. Anyway, it seems like we'll be moving. There's a new Panzer Division forming, and our Regiment has been earmarked to provide it with some experience and backbone."

"Great, I bet that just means a lot more work." Muttered Wolfgang under his breath.

"We'll be heading off to join the 14th Panzer Division in a couple of days from now. Any questions?"

There was silence. The crew was a little stunned, and somewhat disappointed to be leaving the 4th Panzer Division, but they were bound to feature prominently in this new Division, so they were looking forward to plenty more good times ahead.

Over the winter months, the new Division trained intensively until they were ready for active service, and in early April 1941, they joined in with the invasion of Yugoslavia. Led again, by the charismatic General von Kleist and his 1st Panzer Group.

Peter and his crew were a little disappointed though. Only a couple of weeks after crossing into Yugoslavia they'd already reached Sarajevo without any real opposition to speak of, only for the Yugoslavian forces to totally capitulate. Within days Peter and his crew were heading back west again. The whole thing seemed to have been a huge waste of time and effort.

By mid-June, Peter and his crew were posted to an area, not too far from the Soviet border, where it soon became apparent that something major was at hand. It was becoming obvious that there was a huge build-up of Nazi forces in the vicinity. He'd even seen some small units from friendly countries such as Finland and Romania passing by.

Peter was anxious, yet excited at the same time. It was a similar feeling to the one he'd experienced just before the invasion of France. All their invasions up to that point had been successfully completed in double quick time, and they were hoping and praying for a similar outcome here. They were supremely confident that they'd defeat anything the Soviets could throw at them, and the eventual outcome would be total, unmitigated victory.

Early in the morning of the 22nd of June 1941, the Nazis initiated the invasion of the Soviet Union. Operation Barbarossa had begun. A torrent of 3,000,000 men from the Wehrmacht poured forward toward a largely unprepared, and disorganised Red Army.

Army Group North's task was to advance to, and take Leningrad, along with the entire Baltic Sea coast, Army Group Centre was tasked with advancing through Belarus and then driving straight on to take Moscow.

Peter and his crew now found themselves as part of the German, 17th Army, and they came under the auspices of the formidable, Army Group South, who were tasked with advancing towards, and conquering the Ukraine, and then driving on to secure the oilfields of the Caucasus, a region between the Black Sea and the Caspian Sea.

Directly opposing Army Group South was the Red Army's Southwestern Front, which contained the largest concentration of the Soviet forces anywhere. With a geography lending itself to good defence, the Soviet commanders were highly confident of eventual victory too.

For several days, Peter and his crew enjoyed an easy ride. With the Panzers concentrated in tight packs, they quite simply punched and blasted their way through any opposition that they came up against. They'd often encounter the occasional brave, even reckless Red Army attempts to attack them, but these usually consisted of small, uncoordinated groups. This was easy meat and drink for the hunters. It seemed to Peter and his crew that the Red Army didn't have a clue how to fight a war.

This wasn't totally surprising, considering the huge number of officers that had been purged in the years prior to the war by Stalin. There were in fact, very few experienced officers left in the Red Army that could actually mount any sort of co-ordinated and concerted defence.

Wolfgang didn't care. He was happy, he was racking up kill after kill. It was sometimes intense work, but he was enjoying it. It was all too easy. They were advancing at pace, and gobbling up huge swathes of land.

The Panzer Divisions had refined a tactic that was very well practiced by now. It involved avoiding direct engagement with any large enemy mechanised units at all. They simply by-passed and then encircled them in a pincer movement. The enemy would then be destroyed by the infantry units that were following behind as well as being bombed into oblivion by the Luftwaffe.

By the end of June, with huge casualties inexorably mounting up, the Southwestern Front command ordered a retreat of the Soviet forces to the Stalin line to set up a new defensive front to protect the major city of Kiev. They were confident that they'd finally be able to halt the Nazi advance there. They were certain. They simply had to hold.

Unfortunately, these fortified positions, had not been maintained for quite some time, and by 1941, most of them were in disrepair, and virtually undefendable.

Just a couple of weeks later, Peter and his crew had reached an area near Uman. A big battle was obviously brewing as intelligence had reported that both the 6th and the 12th Soviet Armies were in the vicinity. As usual, the 1st Panzer Group with General von Kleist at the head, was thrusting ahead and leading the main attack. The Russians had counter-attacked as they'd done so often in the past, and as usual, they'd been easily crushed.

The battle raged for several days with counter attacks being parried, and thrusts being halted dead. There were destroyed tanks, weapons and people everywhere.

It wasn't too long after that, that the Soviet armies tried to retreat to a more defendable position once again, but this time there was nowhere to go. As so often in the past, they'd been out-flanked by the Panzers. There was just no way through them and it became blindingly obvious that there was going to be no escape. As August dawned, the remnants of the once proud 6th and the 12th Soviet Armies were in complete tatters, and the surviving pockets of men soon started to surrender in droves.

With wrap-up activities being undertaken behind him, General von Kleist was already heading south-east towards the Dnieper with his trusty 1st Panzer Army. Peter and the other units of the 17th Army were heading east towards the Dnieper River and some city called Kremenchug.

Peter's gentle reminiscing was rudely interrupted as Hans came strolling over and called a quick meeting with the whole crew. He'd been at a tank commander's briefing.

"I know this place is the arse end of beyond, but this is where we are right now. We should be moving again very shortly, and this time we'll be heading towards the city of Kryukov, which is located this side of the Dnieper River. Directly across the river from there is the city of Kremenchug, and the plan is to take that as soon as we can."

The crew looked around at each other with quizzical looks. Peter, smiled wryly, as nobody had a clue where Kryukov or Kremenchug actually were. "What about Kiev?" Wolfgang had so wanted to go to Kiev. "Typical, some crap sideshow," muttered Werner, "I bet we won't get much action there."

Hans carried on, "Some excellent news from our intelligence though, they've estimated that over 200,000 enemy have been accounted for in that last battle. It seems at least half of them were killed or wounded." Franz piped up "That means there must be at least 100,000 prisoners." Peter and his crew were jubilant, they really were becoming invincible.

Peter thought for a few seconds, "Hans, any idea what the hell they're going to do with that number of prisoners?" Hans quickly replied. "To be honest, I haven't got a clue. I don't think anybody has even thought too much about prisoners, certainly not in those sorts of numbers. Maybe the Einsatzgruppen will deal with them for us?"

Wolfgang joked, "Well if they treat them like they did the Polish prisoners at the River Vistula, I'm sure we won't have to worry about them for long." Everybody started laughing.

"Oh, and one final thing, apparently the 40th reinforced reconnaissance Battalion have just reported back. They're already close to the Dnieper River. They were last reported approaching a small village called Pavlysh, just a short distance from Kryukov. The 13th Panzer Division were supposed to be leading a surprise attack in that area tonight but they've been held up by the treacherous conditions, and won't be there for at least another day."

"The original plan, was for the 13th Panzer Division to cross the river and hold the railway bridge for us to cross when we get there. It now seems likely that the 40th Battalion will push on themselves anyway and try to take the railway bridge tonight."

It was time to get moving again, as they'd be needed to reinforce the assault, and get across the river as soon as possible. The tanks had been refuelled and restocked and the pervitin was starting to kick in. On the commander's order, the tanks started to roll as fast as the conditions would allow. They were finally heading east towards Kremenchug and the Dnieper River.

Chapter 5
The Battle

Since being appointed as the overall commandant of Kremenchug, he had become increasingly concerned about the precarious state of the city, and even more so about the surrounding region. Colonel Pavel Kuznetsov was a worried man. Exactly how was he supposed to defend such an important sector with so few men, and with such insufficient firepower or equipment?

There was some limited aerial cover in the form of the 75th Air Division, whose pilots he knew would fight bravely, but as their commanding officer, Pavel knew full well, they would have a huge task on their hands against the vastly more experienced Luftwaffe.

In Kremenchug itself, the 56th Air Defence Battalion, along with the attached 96th machine gun company were already hard at work, doing whatever they could to fend off aerial assaults on the railway bridge as well as some other important sites around the city.

On the ground, a Division of the NKVD was specifically tasked with the protection of the bridge, as well as the other railway infrastructure in and around the city.

Apart from that, there were the two recently formed Regiments of the Kremenchug Militia made up of local volunteers, plus a few other small detachments of soldiers tasked with protecting key industrial buildings and warehouses.

Across the river in Kryukov, the 505th Air Defence Battalion, along with the 57th VNOS Battalion were also busy dealing with the Aerial threats.

The 4th bridge-building Battalion, the 2nd company of the 540th mine-sapper Battalion and a third Regiment of the Kremenchug Militia, made up of volunteers from Kryukov, completed the line-up.

Totalling just a few thousand men in total, it was hardly a force to make the advancing Nazi Panzer Divisions quake with fear. What most worried Pavel though, was his total lack of any form of mechanised units or heavy artillery that he'd be able to tactically deploy. Tanks, that's what he badly needed at his disposal, and he had none.

To add to his worries, the report he'd just received about the critical damage to the Kryukov bridge felt like a punch in the stomach. Although he'd expected it at some point, Pavel had hoped it wouldn't have been quite so soon.

The profound implications the loss of the bridge would have to the sector as a whole, and to the support for the 12th and 6th armies in Uman in particular, didn't bear thinking about. The news really was a huge blow.

Pavel knew he needed to act quickly, and hastily convened a meeting to discuss the options available to him. Within a couple of hours, 15 prominent members of the city leadership committee sheepishly entered into his bustling office.

"Gentlemen, take a seat. Thank you for all for attending this, critically important, meeting at such short notice. As, I'm sure you'll all be fully aware by now, our railway bridge has been hit and put out of service. It's imperative that we find an alternative way of getting our men and equipment moving across the river again as soon as possible. Obviously, the number one priority has to be to get the bridge operational again, and as fast as possible. However, in the meantime, we also need to identify some practical short term, temporary solutions which we can put in place. Chief engineer, do you have an update for us?"

The eyes of everyone, now sitting down around the large, rectangular, wooden table, fell onto the short, stocky man, sat just a couple of places to the left of Pavel.

With dense, thick clouds of cigarette smoke permeating the entire room, the city's chief engineer nervously shuffled the array of papers lying in front of him, and cleared this throat with a short, stunted cough. "Thank you, Colonel Kuznetsov. With your permission, I'd like to run through our initial investigations into the damage sustained by the Kryukov Bridge with you."

Pavel nodded his agreement. "Do continue, but please try to limit your findings to just the most pertinent points, if you will."

"Of course, sir. My team have undertaken a very quick survey of the damage to the bridge. The affected piers look to have some very superficial damage, which I would estimate should be fixed within a few days. As for the damaged truss, unfortunately it's beyond repair, so we'll need to procure a replacement. We've already looked into this, and believe that we've got a couple of factories in the city that should be able to manufacture it in a week or two. So, I'd estimate that, provided we have the relevant personnel, and work around the clock, it'll take between 14 and 16 days to get the bridge fully operational again, with a replacement truss fully installed, and a new set of rail tracks put in place. Can you authorise this work to commence immediately, sir?"

"Thank you, chief engineer, I hereby order that all possible resources be made available to you for this task. However, if you feel you need anything else, anything at all, just let me know."

Pavel continued. "In the meantime, until the bridge is operational once more, we've got a significant logistical headache on our hands. There's still a huge amount of men and equipment that need to cross the river. To help try and mitigate this, I'm immediately ordering all available boats and ferries in the area to work around the clock, and that any boats not already being used for transportation, be requisitioned and put onto this task. This small flotilla will have to be the lifeline between Kremenchug and Kryukov for now."

Pavel knew full well that it'd be impossible to carry everything needed across the river using just the boats, and some form of road bridge was now desperately needed. It was crucial, and it was needed fast, no-matter what.

"Finally, gentlemen, we are desperately in need of a road bridge across the river. I don't care where it's located, but I urgently need it to be up and running in the next few days. I'll leave it to you to find a suitable site, and get all the necessary work completed. I'm sure I don't need to remind you; just how critically important this is."

With that, the meeting concluded, and the somewhat worried committee members left Pavel's office deep in discussion.

As it lay directly between the two banks of the river, and only just downstream of the stricken Kryukov Bridge, it didn't take too long to identify the "Bolshoi Island" as the most promising, and in fact, only realistic site, for the crossing to be built.

The river workers were soon hard at work constructing a temporary pontoon bridge with a capacity of up to 100 tons, and this was rapidly completed and moved to its position between the left bank and the Island itself. Another small pontoon bridge was also swiftly constructed and put in place connecting the island to the right bank. By the 4th of August, the new crossing was finally completed and ready for use.

The morale of everyone defending the city was lifted, if only a little, with this news, and it was a great fillip to the 56th and 505th to see the traffic once again flow across the river.

In parallel, work on providing the temporary replacement truss for the railway bridge was progressing well. Within just a few days of the bombing, a new metal truss had almost miraculously been manufactured, and was being floated out to the bridge, on two very large barges. Despite the now continuous air attacks, work to repair the Kryukov Bridge continued at a pace.

The 56th and 505th were now defending both the restoration

work on the crippled Kryukov Bridge, as well as the Bolshoi Island crossing. There was no respite for Valia and his comrades at arms. The Luftwaffe continued their attacks unabated, with the intensity increasing by the day. It was getting to the stage where the gun crews were totally exhausted. They often found themselves in-between raids, nodding off, right beside their guns.

Despite their tribulations, the massed guns from the air defence Divisions continued to defy the Luftwaffe's best attempts to destroy many of the important centres within Kremenchug and Kryukov. They were certainly giving as good as they got.

On a few occasions, their own positions had even been targeted, and a couple of those attacks had been very close calls indeed. Getting showered with dust and debris from an exploding bomb certainly wasn't very high on Valia's list of enjoyable experiences. He could think of very few things worse than a Stuka bomber diving straight at you with that dreadful, terrifying scream, all guns blazing, spitting hot metal everywhere. It was a thing of nightmares.

By the 6th of August, work on the installation of the new truss was progressing well, in fact, so well that there were high hopes that the bridge would be open for business again in just a few short days' time.

Contrary to official intelligence reports indicating that the Nazi advances were being repulsed far away from Kremenchug, Pavel was becoming increasingly worried about the dearth of military forces at his disposal. He needed to prevent an enemy crossing at all costs, be that at Kremenchug itself, or over the large stretches of the river either side of the city.

If he was to have any chance of defending such a large tract of land in the face of a full-scale Nazi assault, he desperately needed more men and equipment. He really needed additional soldiers, artillery, and tanks, especially tanks.

He sent an urgent message to the Southwestern Front command, more or less pleading with them to send any available forces his way.

However, at the headquarters of the Southwestern Front command, General Kirponos and his staff had been digesting the situation at Uman. The outcome there had been quite unexpected, to say the least. In fact, it really was quite catastrophic. There'd been high hopes that they'd have halted or even pushed back the Nazis there, but those hopes had sadly been left in tatters on the unforgiving, heavily saturated, Ukrainian plains.

Having realised that there was nothing more that could be done to save either the 6th or the 12th army, they now turned their full focus onto the defence of Kiev. This was now, without doubt, their top priority, bar none, and any other areas were regarded as largely superfluous. Despite this, General Kirponos obviously noted the situation in Kremenchug, and an order was sent to Colonel Afanasyev, the commander of the 297th Rifle Division.

Over 120 kilometres to the north of Kremenchug, in the town of Lubny, Colonel Afanasyev immediately began preparations for his Division to deploy to the Kremenchug area. It might take a couple of days to get the full Division ready to move, be he anticipated that they'd arrive in Kremenchug in three or four days' time.

Although the senior commanders regarded the 297th as fully operational, they were in fact only recently formed and were a very inexperienced Division, lacking even some of the most basic equipment that they'd need to deploy. Moreover, they lacked the one thing that Pavel had really wanted. They had no tanks.

By now, Pavel was under no illusion about the difficulties the defenders of Kryukov and Kremenchug would face if they had to attempt to halt any potential Nazi offensive that might be coming their way. To this end, he needed to be sure that they'd prepared some sort of organised defensive lines in place just outside Kryukov, even if they were only used to buy some precious time. The most critical thing though was to ensure that the Nazis weren't able to cross the river immediately.

Earlier that morning he'd called Colonel Platukhin, and Major Vorobyov, commanders of the Kremenchug Militia to a meeting. "As I'm sure you're aware, the current front is pretty much in a state of flux, with nobody 100% sure where the Nazis actually are. The latest information we've received from intelligence is that they're still at least a few days away from here, and that the main thrust of their attack appears to be towards Kiev, and not in this direction." He paused pensively. "However, to be honest with you, I don't trust what intelligence say, they've been wrong so many times before. As we've got a major bridge across the river here, I'm pretty convinced the Nazis will be targeting us, sooner rather than later, so we need to get some organised defences in place as best we can. I'm sure you don't need me to spell out the dearth of men and materials we've got available to defend this entire area, but we've simply got to make the best use of the limited resources that we do have."

Colonel Platukhin responded, "What's your priority, Sir, we can set up some defensive positions near the bridge, or would you prefer them outside Kryukov?"

"Well, you know the terrain around here far more than I do, so you'll have a much better idea of the key places we can use to put pressure on any attackers, but I suggest you take a team out and reconnoitre the area south-west of Kryukov, as I think that's the most likely direction of any imminent attack. See where we can set up the best defendable positions, and report back to me as soon as possible. Ideally, when they do come, which I'm sure they will, we can hold them outside the town."

"Oh, and the good news is the Southwestern Front have finally decided to send us some reinforcements, of sorts. With any luck, they should arrive in a just few days' time."

Major Vorobyov perked up with the news. "At last. How many tanks are they sending us?" Pavel's response wasn't what they'd hoped to hear, "No tanks I'm afraid. We're only going to get a single, inexperienced Rifle Division. Not great I know, but at least it's something."

There was a deafening silence for a few seconds as the Militia commanders digested the news. The enormity of their task they now faced, almost seemed to overwhelm them. "Are you telling us we're really going to have to try and defend against a heavily armed marauding enemy, with no heavy guns to speak of?"

"Well, there are the Anti-Aircraft guns I suppose, but yes, that appears to be it for now. I'm still trying to impress on General Kirponos the need for some tanks down here, so you never know, we might get some later, but for now, that's it. Unfortunately, these are the cards we've been dealt, and I'll admit, they're not a strong set, but let's fight like demons, and pray for a miracle. Report back to me as soon as you've identified the best places to deploy our limited forces, and we'll do our best to set up a formidable defence."

Colonel Platukhin and Major Vorobyov headed straight out with a small team of the local militia and reconnoitred the area south-west of Kryukov. After a few hours, they'd identified some suitable defendable positions along the heights, north of the villages of Pavlysh and Onufriivka, just 10-15 kilometres outside Kryukov.

After returning, they reported their suggested defensive positions to Pavel, and having perused the large map on the wall, he quickly agreed. It was also agreed not to immediately deploy the Kremenchug Militia into the area, but wait until suitable engineering work had been completed in those positions to make them more defendable, which would probably take a couple of days at most.

Later that afternoon, just after 16:00, the phone rang in Pavel's office. Alexander, one of Pavel's staff took it. It was the railway station master in the village of Pavlysh. Pavel overheard Alexander admonishing the poor unfortunate woman. "How dare you make up such a fabricated story like this. You know you can be shot for spreading false information and rumours." Pavel caught the general gist of the conversation and came over. "What's all this about then?"

Alexander was a little surprised that Pavel had taken such a keen interest in the call. "Sir, it's the Station Master at Pavlysh. She's claiming that a convoy of Nazi tanks, motorcycles, trucks and soldiers have just arrived there, and that they're moving through the village, house by house."

"That's nonsense," exclaimed Pavel. "That can't be possible. Platukhin and Vorobyov were in Pavlysh just a couple of hours ago and didn't mention encountering any enemy units in that vicinity at all. They can't be in Pavlysh. Tell the station master to mind her jokes or I'll go there and shoot her myself."

Alexander went back to the phone. It was dead. He tried calling back a few times, but nothing.

Not far away, in the small village of Pavlysh, the 40th German Reconnaissance Battalion had arrived. The troops were busy cutting communication lines, and checking all the buildings for any potential sources of resistance. The Station Master had been beaten and forced outside with the rest of the population. The troops were searching for food and weapons, especially for food. They were really hungry. Outside one house, three young children, all under the age of ten, had been happily playing just a few minutes earlier. As the Nazis approached, they were swiftly lined up as if to be executed. The children screamed and screwed their eyes tight in anticipation and terror. A volley of shots rang out. The soldiers started laughing. They thought it was hysterically funny. They'd actually fired into the air. The children on the other hand were in floods of tears. They were absolutely terrified, but at least they were still alive.

Despite Pavel thinking the call from the Station Master was questionable to say the least, he thought it prudent to double check, especially as the line to Pavlysh was now dead. If the Nazis really were there, he needed to know, and he needed to know fast.

He called for a couple of aircraft to urgently take stock of the situation. Within minutes the planes were approaching the Pavlysh area, and through the thick cloud, quickly spotted numerous military vehicles, including a few tanks.

As they couldn't positively identify the forces as being the enemy, the lead pilot decided to descend to get a better look. It was a fatal mistake. Bullets were soon flying all around him from the machine guns below. Within seconds, the plane burst into a ball of flames and fell to the ground on the outskirts of the village. Immediately the other plane staffed the column below, and after dropping its bombs, made a hasty retreat, heading back to safety as fast as it possibly could.

"I understand. Thank you." Pavel put the phone down. The blood had drained from his face. He was stunned. It was the confirmation he'd been dreading. The Nazis were already in Pavlysh, and from there, they could easily be at the River itself in less than an hour.

"Sasha, please get Major Vorobyov on the line immediately." It took several minutes, but eventually Alexander got through.

Pavel was staring intently at the large map on his wall. There were lines scribbled all over it, and the latest were worrying him the most. "Ah, Major Vorobyov, not good news I'm afraid, it looks like the Nazis are alrcady in Pavlysh. They may have advanced further by now. We need to know exactly where they are, and at what strength. I need to understand what we're up against. Get some men out there, find out what's going on, and report back to me immediately." He slowly placed the phone down, his hand trembling a little.

Pavel was racking his brains for an impossible answer. How could he defend the river crossing with so few men, and no tanks? A few minutes ticked by, then, "Sasha, order the Kryukov militiamen to be deployed immediately, and put the Kremenchug militiamen on immediate standby. Any other available Military resources we can spare should get over to Kryukov now. Then get me General Kirponos on the phone, as soon as you possibly can."

Valia and his comrades were dead tired by now, resting alongside their gun, when Kirill came running up to them. "Comrades, they need some support over in Kryukov immediately. We still need to be operational here, but we can spare a few volunteers. Who wants to go?"

All the comrades looked at each other nervously. Nobody seemed to be overly keen on the idea. "I'll go," said Michail, but Kirill quickly dismissed the suggestion. "Sorry Michail, but as leader of this gun, you'll be needed here."

A few seconds passed, then a proud and loud voice rang out. "I'll go. Maxim, you coming too?" Maxim was taken aback a little, but didn't really have an option, as Valia had more or less taken Maxim under his wing, and he couldn't let him down now. "Of course, Valia, let's go."

Kirill seemed happy. "Thank you, comrades. You'll be temporarily placed under the command of a Major Vorobyov, report to him as soon as you get over to Kryukov."

Maxim and Valia grabbed their rifles, and several belts of ammunition, and swiftly headed off to the pontoon bridge, before hurrying over to Kryukov with six other members of the 56th.

Major Vorobyov, was a busy man, but Valia and his colleagues managed to report to him as quickly as they could. He was just heading out towards Pavlysh with a few of his trusted militiamen. "Nice to have you aboard men, stay close to me for now". With that they started heading down the road.

Pavel was staring intently at the map on the wall. Surely there was something more that could be done, but he just couldn't see anything obvious that would drastically change the situation. Their position was extremely perilous to say the least. Without warning, his deep concentration was abruptly interrupted. "It's General Kirponos on the phone for you, Sir."

"Very good, thanks Sasha." Pavel detailed the latest situation, as far as he knew it, and outlined the defensive options available to him. None of which sounded remotely viable. General Kirponos was shocked. Nobody was expecting the Nazis to reach Kryukov quite so quickly.

The General immediately ordered Bomber squadrons to be scrambled, and continuous air attacks on the Nazi positions to commence. They had to somehow slow down, or even halt the attacking enemy forces before they could get to the river.

Back on the ground, a small group of the Kryukov militiamen who'd been tasked with scouting out the Nazi positions were heading along the main road towards Pavlysh, just south of the small village of Malamivka, when out of the blue, three Nazi tanks burst through the tree line and headed straight towards them. Within seconds, they could see fire belching from the machine guns on the tanks, as the clanking monsters continued to ominously grind their way forwards. The tanks fired again. The inexperienced militiamen were terrified, and in blind panic, were soon sprinting as fast as could back towards Kryukov with bullets flying all around them as they fled. The petrified militiamen kept going as fast as they could until they were met by Major Vorobyov with his body of other militiamen.

Without any hesitation whatsoever, Major Vorobyov turned his machine gun directly towards the fleeing group and shouted as loudly as he could, "Stop there you miserable cowards. Stop right now." The men hesitated, not sure what to do next. Just to ram home his point, Major Vorobyov swiftly fired a short volley of shots into the air just above them.

"Get back up there, and fight like the heroes you were always meant to be." The very real threat of them being shot as cowards had the desired effect, and stiffened their resolve somewhat. Turning around again, they headed straight back down the road to confront the approaching demons. Maybe they would be heroes after all?

Maxim whispered, "Are you thinking what I'm thinking Valia?" Valia had a wry smile on his face, and whispered back "I think so. They really have no idea just how lucky they are, do they? I'm sure if they'd run into a NKVD unit, they would've been shot on the spot as deserters and traitors."

Major Vorobyov badly needed to get a view of the evolving situation on the ground. "Come on, follow me." They quickly headed up a hill with a good vantage point over the road. With a standard pair of binoculars, he scanned the countryside ahead, and spotted several positions held by the Nazis, but it didn't look like the huge numbers that he'd half been expecting to see.

They did have tanks though, and they were heading quite swiftly down the road.

Major Vorobyov whispered to his radio operator. "Put me through to Lieutenant Aleksandrovich of the 505th." After a couple of minutes, the radio operator, who never ventured too far away from the Major, handed him the radio.

"Aleksandrovich, it's Vorobyov here. We've got a major problem. There're a bunch of enemy tanks, heading directly towards Kryukov, and we've got nothing available here to stop them. Can you spare some of your guns to try and halt them for us? We've got a couple of comrades from the 56th here who should be able to assist with directing your fire."

"Yes, Major, of course, put one of them on the line and as soon as we have some coordinates, we'll commence firing straight away."

Valia, took the radio, and studied a field map that the Major had just handed to him. After a few seconds determining the position of the tanks on the map, he passed on the approximate coordinates. Within a minute the first salvo of shells erupted. They were a little way short of the tanks, so Valery relayed that information back to the 505th. Their next salvo of shells was on point. The tanks ground to a halt as if they'd been taken by surprise, and were assessing the situation. Another salvo hit the area around the tanks, and with that, the tanks started to retreat.

After a little while longer, Major Vorobyov took the radio and called a halt to the shelling, and thanked Lieutenant Aleksandrovich for his invaluable help. In the meantime, Valia could hear planes in the sky. They didn't have the usual sound he'd been accustomed to. They made a deep, growling sound, which started to vibrate everything the closer they got. They weren't Luftwaffe planes, they were Soviet bombers. Before long, they were overhead and emptying their loads onto the Nazi positions. There must have been at least 20 of them. The explosions shook the ground as each bomb exploded in a great ball of fire.

As the sound of the planes faded into the distance, and the plumes of smoke drifted higher into the sky, Major Vorobyov scanned the countryside for movement once more. There was no large-scale movement of any note.

Major Vorobyov got through to Pavel on the Radio. "Sir, the enemy doesn't look to be a substantial force right now, I'd say it's likely to be a scouting group. It looks like we've managed to halt their advance for now, but the worrying thing is that they're likely to be followed, sooner or later, by some additional major armour."

"Thanks Major, keep me abreast of any further developments."

"Will do Sir. Can I also suggest you deploy the Kremenchug Militia Regiments over here as well now, and maybe we can hit them hard with a surprise attack and maybe even push them back?"

"Okay, we'll put a plan of attack together, and I'll order the men over later tonight."

With that, the call ended and Pavel wrote an entry into the logbook: "19:00. Major Vorobyov and the Kryukov Militia, assisted by the guns of the 505th halt initial incursion by Nazi tanks, and support forces."

The bombing on the Nazi positions intensified, and for the first time in weeks, the unrelenting progress of their advance was checked. The swift drive to take the Kryukov bridge had, for now, been thwarted.

Pavel asked Alexander to contact the Southwestern Front Headquarters again. He was now starting to feel beyond desperate. He still only had a fraction of the defenders he needed to fight a swiftly strengthening enemy, and that enemy was already in a dangerously close proximity to Kryukov.

As General Kirponos was too busy to talk with Pavel, he was instead put through to the political commissar, one Nikita

Khrushchev. Pavel apprised Khrushchev of the precarious situation he was facing, and once again pleaded the case for some tanks to be sent to Kremenchug.

The almost dismissive response from the man who would one day become First Secretary of the Communist Party, and leader of the Soviet Union, was almost soul destroying to Pavel. "Thank you Kuznetsov. I understand your situation, and as much as I sympathise, you really do need to understand that we're under far greater pressure here in Kiev, and as such, we need all the tanks we can lay our hands on in this area. You are instructed to do everything humanly possible to hold Kremenchug, and I'm sure you'll engender your men with the patriotic zeal and fervour needed to fight off the enemy. Whatever happens, the Nazis must not be allowed to cross that river."

With that, the call abruptly ended. Pavel was quite irate. He was no better off, and if anything, he'd been left in an almost totally impossible position.

Meanwhile, General Kirponos and Khrushchev were just as worried as Pavel about the fast-moving situation on the ground. They were massively concerned about the possibility of Kiev becoming encircled by the Nazis, and had started to lobby Stalin into allowing them to strategically withdraw the Red Army forces in a controlled manner to avoid such a possibility.

Despite their frequent and increasingly desperate pleas, the simple response from Stalin was always the same. The order remained, "Stand and Fight, not one step back."

At 22:00 that evening, Colonel Afanasyev, received updated orders from the Southwestern Front headquarters, which he instantly acted upon. The 1055th Rifle Regiment were immediately deployed onto trains and sent with all haste towards Kremenchug. They took a few pieces of artillery with them, but they had no tanks. Their primary task was to prevent the Nazis crossing the Dnieper, but

also to provide support in whatever way they could in the upcoming defence of Kryukov.

Back in Kremenchug, as the rapidly collated scouting reports were being scrutinised by Pavel and his staff, the picture on the ground was slowly becoming clearer. There was now, clearly no doubt that Major Vorobyov and his brave rag-tag militiamen, along with the critical heavy gun support from the 505th had thwarted a surprise Nazi attack, which easily could have rolled straight through to Kryukov and reached the Dnieper. They may even have been able to force their way across the river that night, which would have resulted in the whole strategic defence of the Kiev region being critically compromised. Vorobyov and his militiamen were indeed heroes.

Frustrated that their initial attack through to the river had been halted, the Nazis had dug in, and their artillery started to do some talking of its own. They had plenty of it, and they knew how to make good use of it. The citizens of Kryukov and Kremenchug soon felt the full ire of the enemy.

Yet another damp and miserable day dawned, with constant rain showers soaking everybody through to the skin. Valia and his comrades hadn't had any sleep to speak of, and were by now starting to get exceptionally tired. They'd got used to the almost rhythmic, constant pounding of heavy guns, but this was somehow different. It was a little unnerving not to be firing them, but to have shells whizzing over their heads. The Nazi shells were wreaking havoc somewhere in the distance, somewhere in Kryukov and somewhere in Kremenchug. Like all the defenders, Valia was somewhat apprehensive, but stoic. They were all focused on one single task, and that was stopping the Nazi advance for as long as they possibly could.

Major Vorobyov called over to Valia and Maxim. "You two, come with me." Valia was simply pleased to be moving, as he'd felt far too exposed on the hill. As they were carefully making their way down the hill, the sound of sporadic gunfire echoed all around. "I'll need you to help out as best you can. You probably don't know yet, but the rest of the Kremenchug Militia crossed over to Kryukov overnight and are being equipped at a holding site just down the road. Most of them are already adept in the use of their weapons, but some of the youngsters will need a crash course, especially those getting guns for the first time. Just try and make sure that they have the basics, and know how to fire the bloody things properly."

After a 20-minute hike, they arrived at a clearing where those fighters who were still weaponless were being issued with a rifle and a couple of belts of ammunition each.

In one area of the clearing, Valia and Maxim quickly initiated some very basic shooting drills for anybody who needed them, whilst another area had been turned into a temporary munition's factory. Crates of empty bottles were piled high, and barrels of petrol had been assembled together. Several men were scurrying around, busy filling the empty bottles with petrol, and then stuffing a rag in the top of each bottle. If they could get close enough, these very simply produced Molotov Cocktails would be the weapon of choice for attacking the tanks. Large numbers of militiamen were given the improvised bombs as they left the clearing for the hills.

As the morning wore on, there was no significant movement from either side, although there were intermittent cases of fire-fights breaking out as the opposing forces probed each other's positions for any weaknesses. In the meantime, the Nazi artillery and Luftwaffe kept peppering large areas in both Kremenchug and Kryukov in a ceaseless bombardment.

The 1055th Rifle Regiment had hoped to arrive in Kremenchug very early in the morning to help reinforce the defenders, however, because of the constant shelling in and around Kremenchug, their train was forced to stop 20 kilometres north of the city. The soldiers weren't happy at all. With virtually no sleep to speak of, they were already tired, and now they found that they needed to yomp the remaining distance to Kremenchug on foot. The roads were deep in thick, dirty, slippery mud, and it really was immensely energy sapping having to drag themselves and their equipment through it. It was onerous and miserable, especially in the rain. Eventually though, during the early afternoon, and after several hours of slogging their way across country, they finally slipped and slid their way into Kremenchug.

A small group of militiamen hesitantly approached Major Vorobyov as he was busy directing some of his men into specific positions on the nearby hillside. "Sorry to interrupt Sir, but do we have permission to leave." The commander looked at the disparate group quizzically. He was stumped for a few seconds. "Sir, we've just received news from the Carriage Factory, they're hard at work dismantling the equipment right now, but they need us to help, as they don't know how some of the machinery can be safely disassembled. We've waited here as long as we possibly can, but we really need to go now."

The penny dropped. Major Vorobyov was aware that some critical factories were being dismantled, and some of his men would need to be released at some point, but he'd been promised that they'd be replaced by men from the Car Factory in the city. "Also, Sir, most of us will need to accompany the machinery, as we'll be needed to reassemble it at the new factory somewhere east of Moscow. I'm very sorry to let you down, Sir."

Major Vorobyov needed every spare body he could in the upcoming fight, but knew he couldn't stand in their way. "That's okay soldier, you've done all you can while you've been here with us, and the needs of the state must come first. Permission granted, good luck men."

The group turned and headed off in the direction of Kremenchug. "Any sign of the men from the car factory yet?" Major Vorobyov shouted after them. "Sorry Sir, they should've been here earlier this morning, but we haven't seen them yet, maybe they can't make it after all?", and with that, the men carried on as fast as they were able to go. Major Vorobyov was dismayed, the Kryukov militia now only totalled around 300 fighters. How was he meant to stop the expected, overwhelming, Nazi attack with so few men?

By mid-afternoon, Colonel Georgy Afanasyev finally arrived at the drab, concrete building that passed as the headquarters of the Kremenchug Defence Forces. Ascending the noisy concrete stairs to the second floor, he entered Pavel's office. It was a few seconds before anyone noticed he was there. However, a large smile broke out across Pavel's face when he finally spotted him.

Pavel was so relieved to see some help finally arrive, even if it was only a single Rifle Regiment. He strode purposefully over and warmly greeted the new arrival with a firm handshake. "Colonel Afanasyev, it's so good to see you. I'm just sorry it's not under more convivial circumstances."

Colonel Afanasyev was tired and just a little irritated after the tiresome journey there. "Good afternoon Colonel Kuznetsov, it's a pleasure to meet you too. However, unfortunately to tell you, I have orders from the Southwestern Front to relieve you of your command. As soon as you've apprised me of the current situation here, you can head back to the 75th Air Division, and carry on as their commanding officer once more."

Pavel was highly delighted. He could finally get back to the job that he loved once more, as well as finally being able to get rid of the huge amount of stress that had fallen onto his shoulders over the last few weeks.

Over a few small glasses of the finest vodka available, Pavel provided Georgy with a fully detailed rundown of all the defensive positions, as well as the currently known positions of the enemy. After an hour, Georgy was happy that he fully grasped the situation, and with that Pavel bid adieu, and made his way to the staff car waiting outside.

The latest aerial reconnaissance had located at least 20 Nazi tanks that looked threatening to the west of Kryukov, so Georgy immediately deployed the newly arrived 1055th to dig-in near the village of Checheleve, which he hoped would be enough to halt an expected attack from that direction.

The incessant Nazi shelling continued ad nauseam, and was striking all areas of the city, but especially in the areas near the river crossings. Despite this, reports coming in had confirmed that the Kryukov Bridge was now only a couple of days away from re-opening, as the heroic workers continued to toil away, right around the clock.

Even though the temporary wooden pontoon bridge had, by now, received several direct hits, it was still, quite remarkably, functioning as well as could be hoped for, as any damage was quickly patched up by specialist teams of boat workers.

Unfortunately, for the men of the 1055th who'd just started crossing it, a shell smashed directly into the middle of a company of their troops, sending blood and body parts in all directions. "Welcome to Kremenchug." muttered one of the boat workers who'd seen it all before, as he surveyed the latest carnage in the middle of the bridge. After a short pause, while the debris was cleared and the bridge made safe again, the remainder of the 1055th continued their advance.

As soon as they took up their defensive positions near Checheleve the Nazis spotted them and the men of the 1055th came under immediate mortar and shell fire. It was not a very pleasant place to be, that was for sure, in fact it was decidedly dangerous.

Major Vorobyov had requested that some of the guns from the 505th be deployed further forward, and as they moved to cover the western approaches, Valia, along with the handful of volunteers from the 56th joined up to help them.

The weather was truly awful again. Yet another thunderstorm was drenching everyone. It was unpleasant and very uncomfortable. No matter what they tried, they just couldn't get themselves dry, or warm. All the defenders were on edge, with any sudden sound or movement met with an instinctive and overriding sense of fear. Adrenaline levels were constantly high. They needed to remain alert, and ready for combat at the drop of a hat.

Valia sought out Dmitry who had been with one of the guns

that was moved forward. It was good to see him again, and they managed to have a quick and relatively quiet chat. Like most of the defenders, Valia's eyes were red raw and aching after so little sleep over the last few days. It was an awful time.

Each minute seemed to last an eternity as they waited, and waited, and waited. Minutes turned to hours. Nothing except the sound of mortar and artillery shells flying overhead. The Luftwaffe would show up at regular intervals, just to keep them on their toes too. Peering into the distance for any hint of movement was so stressful. There was no respite for any of them.

Unbeknownst to Georgy and the defenders near Kryukov, the positions held by the relatively lightly equipped, and nimble 40th Reconnaissance Battalion were now being gradually replaced by the extremely well equipped, and hugely experienced 13th Panzer Division, who had finally arrived in the vicinity following their tortuous journey, mainly owing to the terrible state of the muddy roads.

During the remainder of a dull and dreary day on the 8th of August, the Nazi command prepared their forces for what they were sure was going to be a crushing assault on Kryukov. They would use their tried and tested tactic of encirclement, where two separate pincer thrusts would encircle all the defenders on the West bank of the river. One arm of the pincer was planned to drive around the north of the defenders, whilst the other arm of the pincer would force its way around the South. The planned meeting point, and target for both thrusts was the railway Bridge itself. The attack was scheduled to commence at 6:00am the following morning.

An unusually bright, moonlit sky ushered in the 9th of August, as there was finally a break in the rain. Just after midnight, as the Nazi units were preparing for their own attack, the combined forces of the local militia, along with support from men of the 4th Bridge-Building Battalion, attacked towards the Nazi positions down a hill to the south of Kryukov, near Onufriivka. The rag-tag militiamen, adorned as they were in a wide variety of assorted clothing, drove back the startled Nazis. Fearing an organised counter-attack by regular Red Army soldiers, the Nazis started to withdraw their forces. The tanks, hidden piecemeal in cornfields were ordered to retreat to a position where they would have a much better field of fire.

Despite the heavy Nazi machine gun fire raking the ground around them, the militiamen, patriotically roused by their political commissars, captured an observation post on the Ostraya Mogila mound. The men in the militia cheered. They smelt blood. They felt like heroes. They celebrated their first taste of victory. It was good.

It didn't last long though. After retreating for two kilometres, the tanks found a suitable place to deploy properly. Turning to face their attackers, withering fire was soon cascading down onto the militia positions. The tanks slowly started to move forward again in unison, firing as they went. Heavy mortar, artillery and machine gun fire soon joined in, and the militiamen were now under extremely ferocious fire. Colonel Platukhin, the overall commander of the militia, was hit in the thigh of his left leg by a fragment from a Nazi shell, and swiftly evacuated back to Kremenchug, leaving Major Vorobyov in overall command of all three Militia Regiments.

By 4:30am, the momentum of the Soviet assault had all but petered out, and the number of militia casualties started rising steadily as the Nazis found their range. It was carnage, militiamen were falling right, left and centre. The desperate situation only worsened as the sun's rays started to dance around the countryside, and visibility improved. It really was a dire situation. The Nazi tanks and artillery were safely out of range of the militiamen's rifles, but they themselves were well within the range of the Nazi guns. To say the odds were stacked against the militiamen was an understatement.

The main problem with a Molotov Cocktail is its propensity to ignite when hit with a bullet or a piece of shrapnel. Unfortunately, many of the militiamen had been issued with Molotov cocktails, and several of them were quickly turned into writhing, contorting infernos as they were hit, and their blood-curdling screams were horrific. The militiamen that were able to, made every effort to retreat to a new defensive line higher up the hill, but they were pursued all the way by the unrelenting Nazi fire.

By 6:00am, the Nazi units had retaken the entire area they'd very briefly lost in the preceding hours. They had also taken around 100 militiamen prisoner. Dressed as they were, in their normal, drab, every day, civilian clothing, they looked a motley crew indeed. Some were injured, others were not. It made no difference. The order came down from the Nazi brigade commander for all civilian insurgents to be shot on the spot. The captured militiamen were all rounded up together and taken to the side of a nearby field. There was nowhere to run, they were penned in tightly by Nazi soldiers surrounding them to the front and sides with a fence behind them. A truck pulled up and the tailgate dropped. From inside, a heavy machine gun vented its fury and the militiamen dropped one after another. After a few minutes of butchery, the deadly fire ceased. Infantrymen wandered amongst the bodies, ensuring there was no survivors, with a bullet to the head of anyone that so much as twitched.

The battle raged on. A detachment of the NKVD came to the aid of the remaining defenders, who were now holding a defensive line further up the hill, but the military might, stacked against them, was simply overwhelming. At least five tanks moved to within 150-200 metres and started firing at point blank range. Other artillery, mortars and machine guns joined the fray. Casualties were colossal. The defenders had no chance.

Despite the minor inconvenience of the night-time assault by the Soviet defenders, on the dot of 6:00, with typical German punctuality, the Nazi offence commenced, as originally planned.

The right pincer of the attack, moving around the south of the defenders, made very swift progress. The defenders, ostensibly assigned to hold this area had been involved in the overnight raid, and as such were in no position to now oppose any attack. As the Nazis continued to drive their assault forward, they finally entered the centre of Kryukov itself, and it was here that they finally met up with some defensive force of note. There was bitter fighting and the defenders used every nook and cranny, every cellar, every building they could to hold back the Nazi advance. It was bloody, bitter and fierce. There was intensive hand-to-hand fighting, as well as numerous Molotov Cocktail attacks, with the resulting fireballs of terrified human flesh.

As the attack started to falter in the face of desperate and heroic defence, the Nazis simply upped the ante, and increased their firepower by deploying additional heavy artillery and tanks to smash their way through with simple brute force.

The progress on the left pincer of the attack, moving around the north of the bridgehead, was altogether more difficult. Here the defenders were supported by the guns of the 505th. Valia and Dmitry were with them, helping ensure the guns were always ready to fire, and making sure there was no shortage of shells for the guns. It was onerous work, but it was critical work. Nazi attacks on the guns failed to silence them, and they continued to roar out their defiance.

The battle around Checheleve was ferocious. SS troops had tried to take the village a couple of times, but each time they had been repulsed. As attack after attack rained upon the defenders, casualties mounted. Almost all the political commissars, company and platoon commanders and over 100 men were killed as the struggle throughout the morning wore on.

Now at breaking point, and no longer in any position to resist, most of the remaining defenders withdrew from Checheleve, and quickly made their way to the pontoon bridge crossing, and headed back to the left bank, and the relative safety of Kremenchug. Around 100 personnel remained to cover the retreat, and in the end, a few of these were taken prisoner as the Nazis finally steam-rolled their way through the village.

After the 1055th had retreated across the bridge, it didn't take long for the central barges to be separated, and with that, the pontoon bridge disintegrated into flotsam, drifting aimlessly along the Dnieper.

Bolshoi Island itself was now a death trap. The Nazis started shelling it at will. Many tried to swim to the left bank, some managed to scramble ashore, but many met a watery end as they were washed away in the fast-flowing waters of the river.

Eventually, several river-men from the port of Kremenchug bravely brought their boats to temporarily plug the gap in the bridge, allowing most of the people still stuck on the island to cross safely back to Kremenchug.

On the right bank, the noose of the encirclement was tightening, however, the remaining defenders continuously performed heroic deeds as they systematically retreated in good order, until they held just a single last line of defence, a small area of land, just in front of the Kryukov Bridge itself.

Major Vorobyov, along with a handful of fighters and militias, with the support of what remained of the 505th, held this last line of defence for a further two hours. The area was made up of military warehouses and a sawmill, and from hastily improvised positions, they inflicted significant losses on the Nazis as they tried to drive home their attack. It was during this battle, that the 21-year-old commander of the 505th, Lieutenant Aleksandrovich, was killed. After almost constant action, the 505th were down to its last few remaining shells.

The Nazi tanks concentrated their firepower on the anti-aircraft positions, and eventually, a lucky shot from one of their shells detonated among the few remaining boxes of the 505th shells causing a huge explosion that was easily visible across the river in Kremenchug. With that the guns of the 505th finally fell silent. The gun crews made sure that their guns were totally inoperable before they headed swiftly to the Dnieper. Under extremely heavy enemy fire, they, along with Valia, Maxim and Dmitry, managed to get to the left bank on improvised rafts.

The final act of defence on the West bank consisted of a hastily dug trench right in front of the Kryukov Bridge, along with a single armoured machine gun position.

With the massed ranks of the 13th Tank Division fast

approaching it was plainly evident that the Kryukov bridge could no longer be held. The defenders had done their utmost. All efforts now switched to preventing the Nazis actually being able to cross the bridge to Kremenchug.

Colonel Afanasyev immediately ordered the destruction of the now almost completed 4th span of the bridge. A large barge holding the span in place was removed on the Kryukov side, and blown up. The barge, together with the truss of the bridge, massively distorted by the explosion, went to the bottom of the river.

The very last few defenders on the right bank came from a variety of units, but they continually repulsed Nazi attempts to get onto the bridge. They had supporting fire from guns on the left bank, but once the armoured machine gun position had finally been taken out, there was virtually no hope.

The final defiance came from a couple of machine gunners located adjacent to the bridge. They continued to fire until their ammunition was spent. Throwing away the guns into the river, they crossed the river as fast as they could.

By that evening, the battle of Kryukov had ended. About 2,000 lightly armoured defenders had attempted to hold back the might of the Third Reich. Almost half of them had been killed, captured or were missing. They had gloriously failed, but as the Nazi commanders noted of their attack, it hadn't been easy.

The job of properly destroying the bridge to prevent its use by the Nazis now fell to a small group of Red Army engineers, and a couple of days later, the 5th span of the Kryukov Bridge was also destroyed along with the piers of the 4th and 5th spans. On the remaining spans, sleepers and beams of the railway superstructure were removed. The Kryukov Bridge was effectively dead.

Valia was still alive. He'd been hardened in the merciless furnace of battle, and, along with his comrades still stood defiant on the left bank of the Dnieper River, in Kremenchug.

Chapter 6
The Crossing

Since capturing Kryukov, the Nazis had been relentlessly reinforcing their positions on the right bank of the river. It was simply soul destroying for Valia and his comrades to see the vast scale and rage of weaponry now gradually being lined up against them. They were just grateful for the imposing Dnieper River that flowed swiftly between them, as it alone, formed the impenetrable barrier that the Nazis were simply not able to cross.

Almost immediately, they found themselves facing an intolerable around-the-clock bombardment from the Nazi heavy artillery, whilst in the air, the Luftwaffe continued with their habitual, brutal raids, raining down destruction and devastation throughout the city. The pressure was growing incrementally on the defenders by the day.

The constant stream of murderous munitions cascading into the assorted districts of Kremenchug was simply terrifying, and really difficult to deal with emotionally. After several days on the receiving end, many in the 56th were at their wits end, with their nerves almost completely shredded. Valia could see it in their eyes. They would stare blankly into the distance for a few seconds, before reconnecting with reality again. He'd seen that same, almost ghostly, stare somewhere before, and it was starting to worry him. It was becoming crystal clear to everybody still in the city, that the situation was now desperate, and their end could come at literally any moment. It was a frightening prospect.

With most of their guns now redeployed away from the river to defend other important sites across the city, Valia and his comrades continued do what they could to defend the skies across the city, and it was almost like a small, personal victory, whenever they actually managed to down an enemy plane.

Of course, Dmitry had, by now, been officially seconded into the 56th, and was diligently working alongside Valia in the third battery. They made a great team.

In amongst all the devastation on the ground, Kirill, as the political commissar, knew that he needed to keep his men's morale as high as possible, after all, it was his job to keep them fighting. Often, he'd try to raise the men's spirits, by getting them to sing songs. It wasn't easy though. The men were, by now, physically exhausted, as well as being mentally fatigued. Whenever they did manage to muster a muted, half-hearted, sing-a-long, it generally didn't last long because they were simply, too tired.

Despite feeling like he'd been totally abandoned, Colonel Afanasyev was still trying as hard as he possibly could to get more troops and equipment to help defend Kremenchug and its surrounding areas. His ever increasingly desperate pleas to the Southwest Command for more men and equipment were almost invariably ignored, as General Kirponos and his staff were so pre-occupied with defending Kiev and dealing with the Nazi bridgehead to the north of the city.

Like Pavel before him, he'd only managed to obtain a handful of additional Regiments, which meant he still had insufficient manpower, and even fewer heavy guns at his disposal. Most critically though, he still had no tanks of any note that he could deploy at all.

It had come as a massive shock to everyone when news broke that the Nazis had actually managed to cross the Dnieper, to the north of Kiev, on the 22nd of August. It immediately set alarm bells ringing in the Southwest Command Headquarters. It really was a crushing blow to the defensive plans that General Kirponos and his staff had been working on so hard. They'd been hoping to prevent any Nazi crossing of the Dnieper, at least, until the winter set in and froze the river solid.

With close to a million men deployed defending Kiev and the surrounding areas, General Kirponos was now getting very anxious about another possible Nazi encirclement. He'd already lost many tens of thousands of men in the defeats at the battles of Brody and Uman, and the thought of losing a million more was utterly unthinkable. It would be absolutely catastrophic.

Despite the many previous requests to allow the controlled withdrawal of his men from the Kiev region, each one had been flatly rejected by Stalin. This new, and very troubling development, only exacerbated General Kirponos' desire for a strategic retreat. He dispatched yet another, desperate, request to move his forces to a more defendable position, further to the East, near Kharkov.

Stalin was already in a state of deep depression and despair with news of the constant stream of defeats and retreats across all fronts. He was absolutely furious when he received the latest request from General Kirponos. He was aghast at the idea of conceding yet more land, especially as he firmly believed that the General Kirponos had more than sufficient forces to halt the Nazis where they stood. It came as no surprise to anybody, when the request to withdraw was once again, flatly denied.

Peter and the rest of his Panzer Regiment were desperately trying to catch up with the 13th Panzer Division who were up ahead, but the roads and surrounding ground were by now so treacherous, with thick, sticky mud, it was virtually impassable. What limited progress there was, was very, very slow, leaving most of the crew feeling incredibly agitated and irritated. They certainly weren't going anywhere in a hurry, and had that sinking feeling that they were going to miss out on all the action.

As they slid their way closer to the Dnieper, the radio cracked into life, and Fritz immediately relayed the message. "Sir, some good news, the town of Kryukov has been captured." It was news the crew had been anticipating, but then he unexpectedly added, "Apparently, they found the going really tough, the Soviets put up some really stubborn resistance."

Wolfgang couldn't quite believe what he'd just heard. "What, they can't be serious, surely. We've been rolling over them with no real problem for a good couple of months now, since when did the Soviets learn to start fighting?" It was a reasonable point of view considering their experiences to date, however, Hans was having none of it, "Well, mark my words, the closer we get to the heart of this vipers' nest, the harder they'll fight, believe me." Werner wasn't so sure, "What makes you think that Skip?"

"Well, I know if the boot was on the other foot, and we were defending our homeland and our families, I'd fight like a devil right to the end." There was silence for a few seconds while they took in the enormity of the prophetic words.

It mattered not, the Nazis had taken Kryukov, and were even now scouting out potential places to cross the river.

A few hours later, the radio sizzled into action again. This time it was a message directed to all tank commanders in the Regiment, so Fritz handed the handset over to Hans. It took a few minutes for Hans to fully digest the message. "It looks like they've found a possible river crossing site about 30 kilometres to the south of Kryukov. Peter, I've written down the new coordinates they've given me. Get to work on calculating the best route there, and this time we'll lead the other tanks."

Peter started to study the map that Hans had passed to him, and after a few seconds replied. "Yes, that should be no problem at all. Ready to go on your order, Sir."

Hans then appraised the whole crew with the latest situation. "As they've been pretty successful so far, it looks like the high command are aiming for another major strategic encirclement. Even now, the Dnieper has already been crossed to the north of Kiev, and they've managed to form a sizeable bridgehead on the eastern bank of the river. Additional units from Army Group Centre are being diverted south to join in with the operation too. We've just got to force our way over the river down here as soon as we can, and meet up with them a little further east."

He then got back onto the radio to the other tank commanders, to confirm their planned movements. As soon as the call ended, Hans gave the order. "Okay Peter, let's go." With that, the Panzer sprang into life once more. It was on the hunt for its next prey.

As Peter continued driving eastwards towards their new destination, it was impossible to miss the signs of the rampaging advance that had already preceded them. At each village they passed, the sky was filled with smoke, houses were either burning, or had already been destroyed. It was almost impossible to miss all the lifeless bodies, both military and civilian, lined up along the streets or slumped against walls. Old men, women and even children, some of whom were still clutching a favourite toy in their lifeless arms.

In the insane world in which they lived, this all made perfect sense to Peter. After all, for many years now, he'd been brainwashed into believing that the Slavic people, just like the Jews, were simply inferior beings, and should be purged whenever and wherever possible. It looked like most of the units advancing in front of them had taken this to heart, and any sign of resistance had been met very firmly indeed. Sometimes entire villages had been destroyed and all the inhabitants eradicated. There was no mercy. Why should there be?

Wolfgang had noticed something strange though. Something they hadn't really expected. In some of the villages a few locals had actually been out welcoming them as heroes. They were joyfully waving swastika embossed flags and cheering them on, as the life-less corpses of their former friends and neighbours littered the ground around them.

It was now the end of August, and the summer was fast receding whilst the dawn of autumn was starting to introduce itself with a wonderful display of assorted reds, yellows, and browns amongst the trees.

After a rather uneventful, but irritatingly slow journey, Peter and his crew were now safely embedded with the rest of their Panzer Regiment, not too far from a village called Dereevka that sat on the right bank of the Dnieper River. They were waiting patiently along with a huge array of military might. The thick trees of the forest that dressed right up to the banks of the river were a great place to hide. They would often see Soviet planes fly overhead before being quickly chased away by the Luftwaffe. There was no way they'd be seen from the air through that thick canopy of the forest though, it really was quite dense.

They were billeted within a kilometre of the river itself, and they were very content. They'd been re-supplied and fully stocked with everything they'd need for the coming days, and most impor-tantly, they'd received their new supply of pervitin. The whole crew were happy again.

Up against the banks of the river, there was a hive of activity. Engineers and specialists worked around the clock preparing every-thing for the upcoming crossing. Concealed and heavily camou-flaged, close to the river's edge were a large number of assault boats, most of which were able to hold between four and six men, but there were also a few larger boats that could hold up to 16 men. Just behind them was a large number of pontoons and platforms, piled up in several stacks, that would hopefully be used to build a bridge that Peter and his crew would be able to use to traverse the river.

Hans gathered the crew around for a quick chat. "Okay, as I'm sure you've worked out by now, this is going to be our crossing point over the river. The assault is planned to commence a couple of days from now, at dawn on the 31st of August. Until then, we need to make sure that we keep this area as secret as possible, so no lighting fires, or doing anything else that's likely to attract any attention from the air. To try and confuse the enemy, a few dummy sites have been set up further along the river bank and made to look like potential crossing sites, and hopefully any Soviet air reconnaissance will concentrate on those locations, rather than paying attention around this area."

"How long before we're likely to cross Skip?" asked Peter. He was keen to get into some action again as soon as possible. He didn't like all the waiting around. "As I understand it, the specialist river engineers will lead the crossings, followed by the infantry. The engineers will then quickly install a pontoon bridge to allow for the swift crossing of lighter artillery, and we'll be heading over as soon as the engineers have strengthened the bridge enough to handle our tanks. I'm not sure how long that'll be, but hopefully no more than a day or two after the first troops cross."

The crew were happy, and they were even happier when somebody dropped a crate of beer off for them. It was nice to have a short break from action, but they were desperate to get going again, and as soon as possible.

Just as planned, as dawn rose on the 31st of August, a huge Nazi artillery barrage smashed into the sparse Red Army positions on the eastern bank of the river, directly opposite them. Simultaneously, a huge number of assault boats were quickly moved to the banks of the river. The boats were specifically designed for river crossing operations, and were fast, with outboard motors that could propel them in excess of 35 kilometres an hour.

Within minutes, men from specialist river-crossing assault units were scampering and jumping into the boats, and they were immediately racing across what had just a few minutes earlier been beautifully calm waters. Spray was everywhere as the wake of the boats ahead were met by the boats following on. Within minutes, the assault troops were jumping off the boats onto the shore on the left bank. The boats never stopped, the assault troops simply jumped from the boats as they were turning to head back to the right bank to pick up the next load of assault troops. As minutes turned into hours, each boat headed back and forwards across the river virtually non-stop, delivering more and more men.

The defending troops had been taken completely by surprise, but it wasn't long before they were unleashing everything they could at the attackers. A stream of bullets and shells flew over and into the water. The steersmen, fell one after another. They had to stand up to operate the boats, and it wasn't long before many were being riddled with bullets, but despite this hostile welcome, the boats just kept coming.

Although not great in number, through the ferocity of their fire, the defenders managed to butcher many of the attacking troops. However, as more and more crack assault troops crossed the river, and with the constant hail of artillery shells pouring down on their positions, it was only a matter of time before the defending 300th Infantry Division were overwhelmed. Slowly, but ever so surely, they were destroyed.

Following hard on the heels of the specialist river-crossing assault troops came other specialist assault troops, and these were in turn followed over by two whole infantry Divisions from the 17th Army. By noon, a small bridgehead of a few kilometres had been established on the left bank of the river, and throughout the rest of the afternoon, more and more infantry poured over the river to bolster it.

As evening took hold, that initial spell of intensive fighting gradually subsided, and one of the Nazi Divisions took the opportunity to set up defensive machine gun nests on the top of a hill at the northern part of the bridgehead, whilst the remainder of the bridgehead perimeter was defended by the other Division.

As soon as the Nazi commanders were sure that the bridgehead was secure, larger, rubber rafts loaded with heavy infantry weapons, especially anti-tank guns, also started crossing the river, and soon after that, heavy guns were towed across on pontoons. After a long, exhausting day for everyone concerned, the crossing seemed to be a great success. The German 17th Army were now dug in on the left bank of the Dnieper River, and as far as they were concerned, they were there to stay.

Back in Kremenchug, there was utter confusion. Reports had been arriving through the day about a possible crossing of the river several kilometres to the south of the city, but there were also messages coming through to say that an attempted crossing had been successfully beaten back. Colonel Afanasyev was struggling to get a clear picture of the situation, and the scarcity of defenders in that area made getting hold of any concrete information, very difficult.

"What does the latest Aerial reconnaissance show?" Colonel Afanasyev was trying to get a better idea of the situation from the Southwestern Front Headquarters. "Really, so it's looking like they've already got a bridgehead in place. Any news from the 300th Infantry Division, we haven't heard anything from them for a few hours now?" There was no positive news at all. "Can you at least send me some tanks now?" The Colonel was getting exasperated.

He knew the defences in the vicinity of the reported crossing were few and far between to say the least, and there were very few roads in the area either. He was doing his best to try and organise reinforcements for the area, but getting them there quickly would be nigh on impossible. He also deeply lamented the lack of any tanks of note that he could deploy. He'd been crying out for them for days on end, and still none had come. It was looking ominously like a very predictable disaster was starting to unfold, right in front of his eyes.

Valia and his comrades were now stationed near the city's railway station, with their gun, almost hidden amongst the remains of a bombed and burnt out shell of a building. No matter how hard they tried, it was an almost impossible task to defend the station as the Luftwaffe bombers just kept coming, day and night. With the continuous artillery bombardment thrown in too, the Nazis were systematically destroying section after section of the city, almost at will.

During a rare lull in the action, Kirill quickly called a meeting of the Gun crew. "Comrades, this is the situation. It looks like we've done everything we can here, the Nazis have crossed the river south of the city, and we can expect a land-based attack on the city any time now. We've got no real means to defend the city any further, so we've been ordered to withdraw. Let's get all the gear together as soon as possible, and let's go moving. Any questions?"

Oleg was downbeat, he was going to lose another good money earner, "Where are we heading to now Kirill?"

"We've been assigned to help defend the field headquarters of the newly formed 38th Army and that's located in the small town of Semenivka, to the north of here, so we'll be heading up there."

"Come on Maxim, let's get the trucks loaded, we've got another rather urgent appointment, apparently. Let's not leave any mess behind, we need to be tidy, don't we?" Alexei was joking as always, but they were all keen to get moving as soon as possible. If they stayed where they were for much longer, they'd be sitting ducks when the Nazis attacked the city. Within the hour, the entire 56th Air Defence Battalion was heading north towards Semenivka.

As the hours slowly ticked by, Colonel Afanasyev was more and more desperate as it was becoming increasingly clear that the Nazis had managed to cross the river in great strength. He had little option but to send everything he had available to try to counter them, and somehow, try to push them back across the river.

At the river crossing, Peter and his crew were getting restless, they were crying out to get in on some of the action. They'd been moved closer to the river, but there was still no bridge in place yet. Boats and barges can carry a lot of things, but monstrous tanks were simply not on the agenda right now. The specialist engineers were working as hard as they possibly could getting pontoons set up and transported into position.

Hans loped back from another briefing of the other tank commanders, and immediately called the crew together for yet another meeting. "Things are still going to schedule, the enemy aren't causing the bridgehead too much grief, and the engineers estimate that the bridge will need to be around 400 metres long, so they hope it'll be completed by first thing in the morning."

Wolfgang started rubbing his hands, "Great, so we should be crossing in the morning then?" Hans smiled a little, "Unfortunately not. The bridge will only hold 8 tons first thing tomorrow. It'll need to be strengthened before I want to go over it, I don't know about you?" Everyone smiled. "Okay, how about we have another day relaxing here." Werner muttered.

Early the following morning, Nazi troops and equipment were soon crossing the bridge in growing numbers to reinforce the existing, and now, slowly expanding bridgehead.

In the Southwest Command Headquarters, General Kirponos was all too aware that they had a major problem on their hands. It didn't need a brain surgeon to look at the map and spot the danger. With the Nazis now across the Dnieper River both north and south of Kiev, there was a distinct possibility of an encirclement, even if the southern crossing looked like it might be a Nazi drive directly towards Kharkov.

As soon as daylight burst through the clouds they scrambled all available planes, with explicit orders to destroy the Nazi pontoon bridge and cause as much disruption to the bridgehead as possible. As the Soviet bombers approached, the Luftwaffe were already there and waiting. They were roaming, and controlling the skies. Fighters swooped and streaked through the sky which was ablaze with deadly shells and bullets. Intensive dogfights made pretty patterns in the sky. From the ground they looked so effortless, yet in the air, it was a simple, desperate, battle of survival. It was a titanic struggle. Planes were being downed with an ominous regularity. Some bombers managed to force their way through, but the pontoon bridge continued to remain unscathed.

On the ground, the panzers were still waiting for the bridge to be strengthened before they could cross. Peter and the rest of the crew marvelled at the planes performing heroics above them. It was actually quite exhilarating to watch.

With the bridgehead now firmly established, and still expanding south of Kremenchug, General Kirponos was getting extremely concerned about the possibility of a swift Nazi strike directly towards Kharkov. Such a strike would effectively bypass Kremenchug and Kiev. All available reserves were hastily deployed towards the bridgehead area, including a few obsolete tanks that they'd somehow managed to get their hands on. They needed to snuff out this bridgehead, and fast. Colonel Afanasyev had already come to the same conclusion, and had already sent most of his 297th Rifle Division in that direction the previous day.

Somehow, Valia and the 56th found themselves heading in the opposite direction, at almost a snail's pace. The roads were simply clogged up with terrified civilians, not knowing where to go, or what to do. Families, individuals, some on foot, some in cars, some in horse-drawn carts piled high with belongings. They were going in all directions, and going nowhere. Certainly, nowhere fast. Haphazard units of the Red Army were heading south towards the area of the bridgehead. Valia couldn't help but notice that the men in these units looked particularly pensive. Was this their day to die? The roads were constantly being strafed and bombed by the Luftwaffe, who seemed to bask in the joy of dominating the skies. Everyone on the road would scatter when they heard that dreadful scream as the Stuka dived onto its prey. They seemed to be following Valia around everywhere.

The bridgehead was looking to be more and more secure, despite starting to come under heavy and sustained counter-attacks from the Red Army reserves. At one point, some Soviet tanks had even managed to make some good headway near the village of Salivka, but they'd soon been annihilated by rapid and accurate Nazi 88-millimetre anti-tank gunfire.

In the meantime, the specialist engineers were continuously working on the pontoon bridge to increase its load capacity to be able to accommodate the waiting tanks, and it wasn't too long before Hans rounded up the crew again. "Gentlemen, some good news. We've been given the green light, let's get moving Peter." The tanks slowly lumbered their way the relatively short distance to the river. They had to be careful not to overload the bridge, so they staggered their crossings. With great care and attention, each tank in turn began to cross the river. Peter slowly navigated down a shallow incline onto the narrow sandy beach, before manoeuvring his tank onto the bridge. As he inched forward, he could feel the pontoons beneath him sag and lurch slightly as they struggled to take the weighty vehicle. Very slowly, moving at almost a walking pace, with its metal steel plates clanking loudly, the caterpillar tracks gradually pulled the tank further and further across the bridge. The crew could now feel the force of the river, as the bridge gently swayed beneath them.

Just as they were half way across, the crew could hear the ominous sound of approaching planes. There was no hiding place, and no turning back now. The crew felt and heard the staccato noise of bullets bouncing off their armour. Peter raised the speed a little as he determinedly carried on. The sounds of explosions around them did little to quell their fear, and one bomb must have fallen quite close to them, as it rocked the pontoon bridge a little. Almost as quickly as it had begun, the attack petered out. Peter, with a steely glare kept going the left bank, and the relative safety of terra firma was getting closer all the time. After what seemed an eternity, Peter manoeuvred his panzer off the bridge and was back on solid ground. The crew took a collective sigh of relief. None of them had enjoyed that experience.

The panzers quickly advanced to position themselves strategically along the perimeter of the bridgehead, and despite continual, concerted, counter-attacks by Red Army units, the bridgehead was now finally secure.

Over the next couple of days, more and more Nazi forces reinforced the slowly expanding bridgehead. The fighting continued to rage around its perimeter, as counter-attack after determined counter-attack was repulsed by the Nazis. Both sides sustained heavy casualties, but no matter how hard they tried, the Red Army just couldn't push the Nazis back.

In the meantime, Valia and his comrades had finally managed to get to the 38th Army Field Headquarters on the outskirts of Semenivka, and were busy setting up their 76-millimetre guns ready for any aerial assault that might be coming their way. The activity around the Headquarters was pretty hectic, with cars arriving and departing by the minute. Messages were also being relayed by horseback as well as radio. It was a very busy place. Kirill was liaising directly with the army commanders, and would visit hourly to get the latest updates.

On Thursday, the 4th of September, Valia woke up quite early, and to his relief, it was another really damp and foggy day. The 56th could relax a little, as even the Luftwaffe weren't mad enough to fly in the fog. As Valia was eating a boiled egg and an apple for breakfast, Kirill came sprinting over. Taking a few seconds to regain his composure, he relayed the latest news. "Sorry comrades, more bad news I'm afraid." The men looked at each other stoically. Surely things couldn't get even worse, could they? "The latest report is that the Nazis have forced another bridgehead across the river. This time just 15 kilometres away from Kremenchug." Maxim looked a little frightened with the new development. Valia tried to calm him. He put his hand gently on his shoulder and whispered, "Don't worry Max, I'll make sure no harm comes to you. I promise." Kirill continued, "Apparently, the 125th German Infantry Division crossed the river virtually unopposed near a place called Vorovskogo and despite our heavy artillery and aerial attacks, they've somehow managed to build a 700-metre pontoon bridge across the river within a single day. It really is unbelievable. Nazi forces are even now pouring over this new bridge, and heading north towards Kremenchug. The only obstacle now preventing them attacking Kremenchug from the South is the narrow Pesl River, and some units of the 1057th Regiment of the 297th Rifle Division. As we speak, they're doing their utmost to hold the Nazis back."

With the latest developments, everyone was in an extremely sombre mood. Even Alexei couldn't find a humorous quip. Oleg articulated what everyone was thinking. "There's not a whole lot of defenders between Kremenchug and here, is there? We could be in a spot of bother pretty soon." All they could do now was ponder the future, and pray for a miracle.

The 1057th Regiment valiantly held their positions defending the area in front of the Pesl River for three whole days, repulsing every Nazi attack, until finally, totally outnumbered and overwhelmed, they were forced to retreat behind the Pesl River, destroying all the bridges behind them as they went.

They were finally undone after Nazi engineers managed to repair a railway bridge that hadn't been completely demolished, and the Nazi attackers poured across in number.

Alongside their trusty 76-millimetre guns, Valia and his comrades were on high alert as they awoke to find the weather was still as dreary as it had been for the previous few weeks, but ominously, the recent fog had relented. This could only mean one thing. A visit from the Luftwaffe was on the cards, and like clockwork, just a few minutes after 11:00am, a swarm of planes emerged from over the horizon. It only took a few minutes before Valia and his comrades were in action again, firing for all they were worth. The swarm was relentless, ejecting bombs, and strafing everything they could. Some parts of the Headquarters were hit. Like annoying gnats, the planes just kept coming. All Valia could do was keep loading the gun, and hope they could get a few kills themselves.

The raid hadn't taken long, maybe no more than 30 minutes in total, but it had taken out the communications centre in the head-quarters. The 38th Army was, for now at least, rudderless. Without the defensive coordination that had been provided by the commu-nications centre, and having no real, meaningful, defences left, the Nazi forces finally fell upon Kremenchug itself.

After another early morning artillery bombardment, on the 8th of September, the 257th German Infantry Division crossed the Dnieper River, just north of the city near Samusivka.

Kremenchug was now in a helpless position. With Nazi forces bearing down on them from just about every direction, the few remaining Soviet troops in the city did what they could to leave the city by any means possible. By that evening, Nazi troops finally marched into an almost deserted city.

After having held up the Nazi advance for almost an entire month, Kremenchug had finally fallen.

The civilian population that remained in the city now had nowhere to go. They were trapped. Despite the majority being disconsolate, there was a sizeable minority of locals who welcomed the invaders with open arms. As the Nazi soldiers made their way through the city, they were even greeted with flowers by some.

The news that Kremenchug had fallen a couple of days earlier had been a hammer blow to Valia and his comrades. They were now even more exposed and vulnerable than they'd been in Kremenchug. The only positive thing was that no Nazi advance in their direction had yet been reported, and most of the action appeared to be taking place to the south of Kremenchug near the main Nazi Bridgehead.

The 38th Army command seemed convinced that the Nazis were going to drive directly eastwards towards Kharkov and, in what Valia thought was a somewhat reckless decision, they committed what pitiful reserves they had left to defend the area between the bridgehead and Kharkov, leaving themselves particularly vulnerable, and virtually defenceless. Valia had a sinking feeling in his stomach. He just hoped the commanders were right.

Peter and the rest of the 36th Panzer Regiment were still providing heavy weapon support for the gradually expanding bridgehead south of Kremenchug. They had been somewhat disappointed not to be involved in the charge to take Kremenchug, however, the news that Hans brought with him soon changed the crew's mood.

"As we are speaking, General von Kleist and his 1st Panzer Group, are approaching Kremenchug from further south along the western bank of the river. Once they arrive, the plan is to launch a huge pincer strike to encircle the whole Soviet Army defending Kiev. The 1st Panzer Group will lead the drive northwards towards the town of Lubny, while the Northern pincer arm heading south, will comprise the Second Panzer Army under General Heinz Guderian and the Second Army of General Maximilian von Weichs. The operation is scheduled to kick off on the 12th of September".

Hans had some even more exciting news. "Oh, and I almost forgot the best bit. The 16th Panzer Division, which are part of the 1st Army Group, apparently need some additional tanks to bolster their number for the upcoming offensive, and they want us to join them."

The whole crew were really jubilant with this fantastic news. At last, they were to come under the command of the almost legendary General von Kleist, if only for a short time. They were guaranteed to get plenty of action now.

Within a couple of hours, ten tanks had safely re-negotiated the pontoon bridge, but this time back to the West bank. It didn't take long for them to team up with the 16th Panzer Division as it lumbered along the river bank. As they passed, Peter and the other waiting tanks tagged on the back of the group. They were finally heading to Kremenchug.

In the meantime, the pontoon bridge that had been built 15 kilometres downstream of Kremenchug had now been dismantled and floated upstream to Kremenchug where specialist engineers reconstructed it just a little upriver from the destroyed Kryukov Railway Bridge. By the 11th of September, the bridge was securely in position, and that very afternoon, General von Kleist led his 1st Panzer Group across the bridge and into Kremenchug.

The following morning was yet another dull day, frequent rain showers and low clouds were the order of the day. Meanwhile, the tanks of the 16th Panzer Division were lined up on the high ground of Kremenchug, straining at the leash to head north to join up with the tanks of General Guderian. This was going to be fun.

At 9:00am sharp, they headed north at pace and ploughed straight into a couple of Regiments from the Red Army's 297th Rifle Division. Peter had taken his daily pervitin pill, and was loving the action. He was being allowed to manoeuvre more or less at will, and at speed. It was exhilarating. Hans was soon acquiring targets, and Wolfgang, was destroying them in quick time. The defenders put up the expected heroic, fierce, yet totally uncoordinated and doomed defence, which ended with the usual result. The odd Nazi tank had been taken out, but the defenders were eventually swatted away with ease.

In less than an hour, the 16th Panzer Division was past the frontline defenders, and were rampaging towards the ancillary personnel of the Division. Totally unprepared as they were, large numbers were slaughtered or taken prisoner. Peter was quite familiar now with the tactic of driving straight and true, and if there was anybody in the way, hard luck, it was more efficient to run straight over and crush them than spend time trying to avoid them. He distinctly remembered driving straight through a field hospital, and it didn't bother him one iota. Before long they ended up with clear empty countryside ahead of them, and they powered ahead at full speed.

It was around 5:00pm when the lead tanks arrived in the vicinity of Semenivka. Valia and his comrades in the 56th had a terrible surprise when totally unexpectedly, around 70 huge monsters came out of nowhere at speed, and started to attack them. Their trusted 76-millimetre anti-aircraft guns were quickly lowered to become anti-tank guns, and all of the brigades started hitting back at the tanks as hard, fast and as accurately as they possibly could. The whole Battalion were absolutely petrified, yet in a strange, surreal way, very calm at the same time. They functioned like the well-oiled machines they had become, and the fighting was ferocious.

Peter was doing his utmost to avoid the burning hulks that had come to a halt in front of him, while Werner and Wolfgang were loading and then firing at the gun emplacements as frantically as they could. Peter was pleased these guns weren't as mobile as tanks, as they seemed to be very accurate and very deadly.

Valia watched on helplessly, and tears filled his eyes, as the second battery of the 56th was pummelled to extinction. Then his battery, the third, were being targeted. They kept firing as if their lives depended on it. And their lives really did depend on it. In just a few minutes, three of the guns in his battery were totally destroyed, yet Valia and Dmitry were still loading the remaining gun as fast as they could. With terror etched on their faces, the shells continued to erupt from the 76-millimetre gun, finding their intended target more often than not. Valia wasn't counting how many tanks they'd hit, he was just concentrating on loading new shells into the gun, that was his one and only thought. Then there was nothing. He couldn't sense a thing. A shell had exploded just metres away, and a huge concussive blast had smashed both Valia and Dmitry to the ground, unconscious.

Peter, had enjoyed the little joust, and pitting his wits against the big guns that had been raging against them. As usual, Peter and his crew had emerged unscathed, despite several of his sister tanks being destroyed. He felt invincible. He was convinced he was in a lucky crew, and they could never be destroyed. As they lumbered past the mangled remains of the once obstinate and defiant guns, Peter just couldn't help himself running over the bodies that were strewn across the ground in front of him. In truth, he actually enjoyed it.

Valia, very slowly regained his senses and could just make out a loud clanking sound rapidly getting louder and louder. It was soon almost deafening. The unimaginable horror of a fast approaching tank heading directly for him met his eyes when he compelled them to open. With all his remaining energy, Valia forced his body to violently contort out of its path, and he could feel the ground around him tremble as the tank slid past just centimetres away from him.

Then he heard Maxim screaming, "Help me, I can't move." There was nothing Valia could do, he was totally helpless as Maxim screamed, and then disappeared under the tank tracks. Valia broke down in tears. He'd promised to look after Maxim, and he'd failed.

As the tanks continued on their way past the shattered guns, Valia witnessed a lone, badly wounded comrade rise to his feet with a machine gun. He opened fire at the machine gunners perched on the passing tanks. A hail of bullets immediately headed back in his direction, and defiantly, he fell dead.

After the skirmish, Peter and the 16th Panzer Division continued on their swift thrust towards Lubny, and the much-anticipated rendezvous with the tanks of Guderian and von Weichs. Eventually, the two prongs of the pincer finally met, on the 16th of September, almost 200 kilometres east of Kiev at the town of Lokhvytsia.

It took a few minutes for Valia to register the enormity of his situation. On the bright side, he was uninjured apart from a few minor cuts and bruises, but that was it. There were no weapons nearby he could use, and he could see lots of soldiers heading in his direction. They were dressed in the uniform of the German Wehrmacht. He slowly, and a little shakily rose to his feet with his arms in the air. He just preyed they wouldn't shoot him on the spot. With their rifles aimed directly at his head, a couple of soldiers approached. They quickly searched him for weapons, and shouted at him, and then indicated for him to kneel with his hands behind his head. Valia surveyed the battle scene. Most of his comrades lay dead. There were a few other survivors though, and he was pleased to see that Kirill, Oleg and Dmitry were among them. For them the fighting was at an end. They could do no more.

Chapter 7
The Prison

The situation Valia was now being forced to face would have been unthinkable just a few short months earlier. Here he was, totally defenceless, with an overriding sensation of abject loss and hopelessness. It was almost as if his entire world had collapsed all around him. Everything he had known and held dear was gone in just a few minutes, shredded, just like the tortured and twisted guns lying just metres away. They had been strong and defiant for so long, yet now they were nothing, just a pile of useless scrap metal. That's exactly how Valia felt, completely useless, devoid of meaning, and more than anything, he had a feeling of deep embarrassment. He felt that somehow, he had failed.

As the tanks were swiftly driving off into the distance, more and more Nazi infantry dutifully followed. The first group he'd encountered seemed very thorough, yet scrupulously fair. They'd ordered all the surviving members of the 56th to congregate close to one of the now hideously deformed guns. It took a little while for Valia to register the full scale of the devastation all around him. What'd been an intense and fierce battlefield just an hour earlier, had now become a scene of surprising serenity. Off in the distance, he could see hundreds of uniformed men scuttling around, like busy ants, trying in vain to keep up with their tanks.

The most poignant and desperate scenes though were of the score of lifeless bodies surrounding him. The many friends and comrades with whom he would no longer be able to share a joke, sing a song or share a vodka with. It was simply overwhelming. He could see the badly disfigured bodies of Alexei, Igor and Michail. "At least their end would have been quick, and they wouldn't have known anything about it." Valia thought to himself. He was racked with guilt and pain as he saw Maxim's young lifeless body, crushed into the ground, not too far away, in the distance. There was nobody to look after him now, and nobody to bury him. Maxim was all alone and Valia felt terrible. Nobody should die like that, certainly not somebody who was really only a child.

All 17 survivors, looked forlorn. Nobody said a word, they couldn't even look at each other in the eye. Valia soon starting thinking the worst, what was going to happen to them now? Many scenarios played out in his mind for what seemed like an eternity.

After some time, an elongated, open top Mercedes car approached them. Inside were three men dressed in black, and a civilian sporting a red armband with swastika embossed onto it. The car pulled up, and all the men got out and slowly ambled across towards them. The five soldiers that had been standing guard all saluted. They must have been important men thought Valia, but he had no notion of just how important.

These soldiers were dressed in black with what looked like lightning flashes on their collars. One of them calmly talked to the civilian for a couple of minutes, then the civilian approached the prisoners. He spoke perfect Russian, with just a hint of a Ukrainian accent.

"You are now prisoners of the Third Reich. You will be treated as prisoners of war, and as long as you comply with the orders you are given, you will be safe. Let me remind you that if you do attempt any sort of resistance or try to escape you will be shot on the spot. This will be your only warning. Do I make myself clear?"

The somewhat stunned prisoners slowly nodded. They were powerless to do anything else. The civilian continued, "I will require your name, rank and serial number." With that, he dutifully went to each prisoner in turn, and matter-of-factly wrote down their responses. Once he had the information he needed, he returned to the men in black.

After a short discussion, the civilian pointed an accusing arm directly at Kirill. The men in black calmly strode over towards where Kirill was still kneeling. All eyes followed them. Kirill was now looking quite worried. One of the Nazi officers spoke in a friendly manner in perfect Russian. "Hello Kirill. I understand you are the political commissar in this Brigade. Is that correct?" Kirill didn't know how to respond. He blinked as he stared at the smiling officer in front of him. A few seconds passed before he slowly nodded. "Thank you, Kirill." The officer was silent for a few second before continuing in a menacing tone. "I have to tell you that under *The Commissar Order* issued by the German High Command on the 6th of June, all political commissars are to be executed with immediate effect."

Then without any warning, and before Kirill could do anything, one of the other officers who was now standing directly behind him, drew his pistol, and shot Kirill in the back of the head. Blood and brains flew through the air as Kirill's lifeless body slumped to the ground. The prisoners looked on in utter disbelief. They were now understandably terrified. The officer placed the pistol back in its holster, then took out a white hanky out of his pocket and wiped a few pieces of brain matter off his smartly pressed uniform, as if they were just pieces of dirt.

The civilian, now speaking in an almost jovial tone, informed the prisoners, "I'm sorry, about that, but we are under orders that all political officers and anybody who is obviously a Bolshevik is to be executed immediately. The rest of you will be fine as long as you show no sign of resistance and follow orders. You will be joining other prisoners shortly." With that, the men turned and returned to their car. After a short conversation, they drove off in the direction of the tanks. They'd obviously got a lot of extremely important work waiting for them up ahead.

After around thirty minutes or so, a truck pulled up, and another group of soldiers disembarked. With that, the original guards jumped into a truck and headed off in the direction of the tanks. This new group of guards immediately made it clear that the prisoners needed to get up and start walking. This time, they would be heading back in the direction of Kremenchug, almost 70 kilometres to the South.

As they walked, and walked, and walked, they were joined by more and more prisoners and before long they were in the midst of a column that must have numbered well over 100, all dispirited, all tired, all hungry, and all extremely thirsty.

As night-time fell, they were finally allowed to rest. They were given just a mouthful of water each, but there was no food. Only the guards had food. Those of the prisoners who could, managed to grab some sleep, but most of them were so traumatised it was impossible. It was an uncomfortable night, it was cold, it was wet, and it was miserable.

As dawn rose the following morning, those that had managed some sleep were rudely woken by loud shouting from the guards, and it wasn't too long before the prisoners resumed their long trek towards Kremenchug. There was no talking, just abject despondency. The closer they got to Kremenchug, the column numbers swelled even further as more and more prisoners joined them.

Valia was near the rear of the column along with Oleg and Dmitry. At one point they heard some shouting from behind them. Valia peered around and saw a prisoner struggling to keep up with the column, he had a leg injury, and it was proving difficult for him to walk, let alone keep up with the column. It looked like he'd just given up, and was sitting down. Two guards were now berating and barking orders at him in a language that he didn't understand. He couldn't go on. The column continued to advance, and those near the back who had momentarily stood to watch, were swiftly ushered on. The shouting continued for a brief while, before a shot rang out. The two guards soon jogged back and re-joined the column. The prisoner, now motionless, had been tossed in a heap to the side of the road, just like a pile of rubbish.

Every hour or so, the column would be ushered off the road to make way for more Nazi tanks, trucks, and motorbikes heading towards the front. Then they'd be forced back onto the road to continue their depressing and monotonous slog to Kremenchug.

Three days after they started walking, they finally arrived back in Kremenchug. It looked very different. Many of the buildings were dressed with large red swastika flags and all the road signs were now written in German. As the column continued to trudge through the streets, a few locals hurled abuse at them. It was a real eye opener. It had only been just over a week since Kremenchug had fallen, but the Nazis had been busy, as they were soon about to discover.

The column was now a few hundred strong, and it slowly snaked its way through the city streets, and then on to what had once been the barracks of the 12th Army. Valia had been there a couple of times whilst they'd been defending the city, but it had changed beyond all recognition. As they approached, the first thing Valia noticed was the loud barking of dogs, then he quickly spotted several wooden towers around the perimeter, and each of them appeared to be manned by a couple of soldiers with a mounted machine gun pointing in, towards the barracks. The column very slowly shuffled their way into the camp, and then, onto what had once been an immaculate parade ground. There, they were ordered to line up and stand to attention. The prisoners formed disjointed lines, and stood and waited. The prisoners waited at attention for what must have been at least an hour. It was really uncomfortable. Valia counted at least six huge, ferocious guard dogs incessantly barking and baring their teeth, as their handlers struggled hard to hold them in place. It was somewhat unnerving to say the least.

Valia's eyes darted around the camp. It appeared that the grim, ramshackle and desolate looking buildings were already occupied. He also noticed what appeared to be large pens in the open grounds, enclosed with what from a distance looked to be several rows of barbed wire forming high walls. Some of these pens already contained prisoners.

Eventually, a small group of Nazi officers emerged from one of the building. They strode purposefully towards, and then swaggered up and down in front of the recently arrived prisoners, eyeing them up and down. Valia thought that they looked a little drunk. Eventually, a civilian with a swastika armband walked sheepishly toward the group of Nazi officers and a rather portly looking officer in a very fine uniform, with tall, shiny leather boots, and a peaked hat talked in German to the civilian for a minute or two.

The civilian, in a shouted address, translated for the assembled prisoners. "Welcome to your new home." Pointing to the slightly pudgy officer, he continued. "This is Major Orland. He's the chief medical officer of the camp. For you the war is over. It is only because of the extreme graciousness of the most revered leader, the Führer, Adolf Hitler, that you will be allowed to stay in this camp. You will be expected to work when necessary, and be warned, if you attempt to cause any sort of problem, rest assured, you will be punished. Your pathetic leader, Mr Stalin has abandoned you all, so enjoy your extended stay here as our special guests."

The officers took another disdainful look over the new arrivals before heading back to their office, and sharing another glass of schnapps together.

The guards motioned to the prisoners to move. They were slowly corralled into the pens, until there were a few hundred in each of them. As they were being distributed between the pens, Valia counted what must have been ten separate pens in total. There was a gap of at least ten metres between each pen, and a single gate into each pen. The newly erected barbed wire fences surrounding each pen must have been over three metres tall, it was imposing and oppressive, and there was no way that anybody was going to get through, or climb over it. Each pen had its own wooden watchtower, and there were numerous watchtowers all around the perimeter walls of the camp too.

Valia, Dmitry and Oleg had managed to stay close together since their capture, and had luckily ended up in the same pen with each other. It didn't take them long to realise the dire situation they found themselves in. There was no shelter whatsoever, they were stood in, to all intents and purposes, a fenced in plot of land. There were no toilet facilities anywhere to be seen, and no running water either. They did find an animal trough hidden away in a secluded corner of the pen with some disgusting, stagnant looking water inside. That was about it.

Over the next few hours, the prisoners started talking with one another, and they all had a depressingly similar tale. Almost without exception, they had fought until it was impossible to fight any longer. Either they had run out of ammunition, or they had been incapacitated in some way. More worryingly were the stories about the unpredictable behaviour of the Nazis. Some prisoners had been treated well upon their capture, others had been harshly beaten. Valia could easily spot those, as they had cuts and bruises everywhere. There were also several tales of prisoners being shot out of hand, and without exception, all the political commissars that had surrendered had been summarily executed.

After a while, Valia, Oleg and Dmitry got talking to a small group of inmates that had been inside the camp for a few days already. They'd been members of the 1055th, and they'd been captured near Checheleve during the battle of Kryukov. Valia and Dmitry must have fought alongside them just a few short weeks earlier. They were hungry, desperately hungry, as they'd been given hardly anything to eat since their capture.

A very scrawny member of the group called Boris, reflected on their time since being incarcerated. "Well, we got separated from the rest of our unit as they'd retreated, and when we'd run out of ammunition, what could we do? Throw stones at the Nazis?" Boris was very pragmatic about things. "The three of us put our hands up and very slowly, and to be honest, very nervously, we rose as one. I was half expecting to be shot there and then, but the Nazi soldiers that captured us, made it clear that we'd be okay, we just needed to accompany a couple of them to an area at the bottom of the hill which was obviously a temporary holding base for prisoners."

Valia, Oleg and Dmitry were speechless, and transfixed as Boris continued his tale. "It all seemed very orderly, they put the prisoners who were in uniform in one part of the field, and separated out the poor militia fighters who were in their own clothes. After a couple of hours, the militiamen were herded away just like sheep to the slaughter. Nobody knew what was going to happen to them, but about ten minutes later, we heard sustained bursts of machine gun fire, with a lot of shouting and screaming. It was all over in less than five minutes."

"Then they called for any political commissars to come forward from our group. Do you know what? A couple of them were stupid enough to do it too. Both of them were executed on the spot with a bullet to the head. Right in front of us."

"If you really want to know, I was really worried after that, I thought they were going to shoot us all. We didn't have a clue what the Nazis were going to do next. So, when they marched us into the mirror factory near the river the following day, I truly feared the worst. We were packed in the badly damaged building like sardines in a tin, but at least they didn't kill us. Well, not to start with anyway."

Oleg was curious, "So, what did they do next?"

Boris furtively glanced at his two mates. "Well, the factory building was in a terrible state. It had been heavily shelled during the battle, but somehow, at least a couple of the toilets still seemed to work. Well, they did for a short time. Just imagine a couple of hundred people using them. They were soon overflowing, and soon stank the whole factory out."

"For the first few of days we had no food at all, and hardly any water. Finding somewhere comfortable to sleep was a real problem too, as all that was available was a bare space on the filthy floor, and nothing else."

One of Boris' mates butted in. "Yes, that's something you're going to have to get used to. Hardly anything to eat. We've already had over a month of this crap, god knows how much longer we can keep going."

Valia didn't like the sound of that one bit, but he was still interested to hear more. "What did you do after that, Boris?"

A slight grimace crossed Boris' face before he continued. "Well, we were stuck inside the cavernous factory building for a couple of days until they started taking us out to clean up the streets, and start repairing buildings that'd been destroyed in the battle. There was a huge amount of rubble and debris everywhere. The Nazis certainly didn't want to clean up the mess themselves, so we were forced to do it. In some ways it was a blessing, because at least we got a little bit of bread and some gruel each day. Not much, but it was better than starving."

"How long did you have to do that for?" enquired Oleg, who was looking unusually spellbound by Boris' tale.

"We were taken out early each morning in small workgroups of up to eight men, and we were worked hard until dusk, and then they took us back to the factory for the night. It was sheer hell, and we did this every day for a month. Some comrades became too exhausted to carry on and you could sense they just wanted to give up. They were mentally and physically broken. It always ended the same way. The guards would beat them, and if they still wouldn't work, they'd be shot. It was awful. I lost count of the number of men they killed."

"Then about a week ago, we were kept inside the factory. We were very suspicious and quite worried. It seems that any change to the normal daily routine would usually spell trouble for us. But by mid-afternoon, we heard what must've been a massive column of tanks passing nearby. I managed to sneak a look through one of the shattered windows out towards the river, and I could see a huge convoy of tanks, for as far as I could see, crossing the river over what looked like a newly constructed pontoon bridge."

"I bet those were the bastards that we fought with." Dmitry sighed forlornly.

"With the huge number of tanks that I saw, I wouldn't be at all surprised. You know, not long after the tanks had crossed the bridge, most of us were marched out of the mirror factory, and were also crossing it. They moved us to this old, deserted, army base. When we arrived at the camp there was nothing much here, apart from the buildings you can see over there." Boris pointed to the somewhat dilapidated camp buildings. "Within the day, we were forced to start constructing these pens, and also the watch towers. We were worked virtually non-stop from dawn to dusk every day until we finished everything, just a couple of days ago."

"Who is sleeping in the buildings then?" enquired Oleg.

"The buildings are mainly occupied by the Nazi guards, but there are also a few locals who seem to be quite happy to help them as translators. The only prisoners inside the buildings are a few of our officers, and our doctors. I've no idea how they've managed to wangle that, but good luck to them. You know, we thought things were bad in the mirror factory, but this place is a real shithole. It's still only September, and it already feels bloody freezing at night."

A look of despondency struck Valia, Oleg and Dmitry as they grasped just how bad their situation was.

"What about this Major Orland, what's he like?" asked Valia.

"Major Orland arrived a couple of days after we did, so he hasn't been here that long himself. As a medical officer, we'd hoped that things would improve around here when he arrived, but if anything, things have got worse. He seems to be drunk most of the time, and the food, if you can call it that, has been very scarce indeed. All we ever get are a few morsels of hard bread and the odd bowl of extremely thin gruel now and again. You wouldn't believe how tasty rotten vegetables can be once you get ravenous. On a few occasions the guards have thrown some putrid vegetable into the pens, and at other times, the locals have been known to throw what food they can spare, nicely wrapped in handkerchiefs, over the fence. The Guards don't seem to mind. They seem to have a lot of fun watching the prisoners fighting each other, just to get a tiny morsel."

Valia, Oleg and Dmitry looked at each other in turn. One thing was for sure, this was no place to stay for very long, especially with the winter soon approaching.

Once Boris had finished his tale, Dmitry then described the escapades that he'd gone through with Valia and Oleg since the battle of Kryukov to Boris and his comrades. They seemed to be amazed at the suffering and hardships that they'd experienced too.

As the conversation started to dry up, Valia noted. "It's always difficult to know what the future will bring. It sounds like we need to pray hard for the best, but fear for the worst. Thanks for the chat, I'm sure we'll bump into you again very soon." With that the two groups lethargically went their separate ways.

Night came around swiftly and although exhausted, Valia, Oleg and Dmitry found it really difficult to get any sort of sleep. They were outside with no shelter, it was cold, it was wet, it was unbearable, and the dogs barking never seemed to stop. The only bed they had, was the ground they lay on, and with no proper toilet facilities anywhere, many parts of the pen were already covered in urine and faeces. It was disgusting. Trying to get any sleep wasn't helped by the guards in the watchtowers, who seemed to enjoy sweeping the camp on a regular basis with the full beams of their searchlights.

For the next few days, life in the camp followed the same monotonous routine. Valia, Oleg and Dmitry would wake up, and they'd watch the world go by. There was nothing to do. They'd have the occasional chat with other prisoners, they'd watch the guards, the guards would watch them back. New prisoners would arrive on an almost daily basis and go through the same welcoming ritual with Major Orland. It was tedium personified.

Dmitry spotted a few of his former comrades from the 505th in one of the other pens. They shouted a few comments to each other before a couple of guards arrived and quickly made it clear that communication between pens was forbidden. Dmitry did manage to find out that they'd been captured on the banks of the Dnieper because they couldn't swim, and they'd had no way to get across the river to Kremenchug. They'd been so terrified of trying to cross the river, they had no other option but to surrender.

As the days drifted into weeks, the trickle of prisoners arriving at the camp turned into a flood. All the pens were soon packed to the almost breaking point. With many more mouths to feed and no increase in their already meagre food supply, the prisoners were getting virtually nothing to sustain them at all.

All the time the weather was getting colder. Overnight frosts were now an almost daily occurrence. Winter was definitely advancing, and coming very fast.

From their first day in the camp, the biggest problem by far was the food, or more precisely, the lack of it. As each day painfully, and very slowly, dragged to a conclusion, the scant quantity of food they had to eat was becoming more and more of an issue. A few morsels of bread, tiny portions of gruel, the odd rotten turnip or potato. It just wasn't enough. Before long, their only thoughts seemed to revolve around food. They even started eating what grass remained in the pens they were incarcerated in. It was desperate. At least the guards would periodically top up the water in the cattle troughs but that too was disgusting.

As it was almost impossible for the prisoners to shave, most of the prisoners had grown quite impressive beards by now. There were a few doctors amongst the prisoners. Whilst many of them were housed in the camp buildings, others found themselves housed outside in the squalid pens along with the vast majority of the prisoners. Somewhat surprisingly Major Orland had provided them with rudimentary first aid equipment, so if the need arose, they could provide some fairly basic treatment. The doctors found themselves constantly busy attending to and treating the most badly injured, and malnourished, but they could only do so much to help. Each morning, the guards would order prisoners to take away the bodies of prisoners who hadn't made it through the night. The bodies were then unceremoniously dumped into a large open pit outside the camp walls. It didn't take too long for the stench to become overpowering.

The guards were a strange bunch. Most of them were Nazi soldiers, but there were quite a few local Ukrainians that seemed very keen to help them. Most were either translators or cooks.

As well as the officers, there were even a few "privileged" prisoners who were able to stay inside the buildings at night-time. Nobody was quite sure why, but Oleg wanted to know. He was pretty keen on the idea of sleeping in some proper shelter rather having to continue sleeping outside, open to the elements and whatever weather the sky decided to throw at them.

Quite unusually, early one morning, a group of guards approached the pen that Valia and his comrades were housed in. As usual, one of the local translators did the talking, or in this case shouting, for them. "Good morning prisoners, I hope you've had a good night's sleep? Major Orland sends his warmest greetings to you. He is a little concerned that you might be missing out on some exercise."

"He's got to be joking," quipped Oleg, who, like most of the prisoners had hardly managed any meaningful sleep in the cold, wet and freezing conditions.

"For your benefit, Major Orland has agreed that some of you can accompany us into the city to do some work. Form orderly lines, and stand to attention."

Once the prisoners had shuffled into roughly straight lines, the guards entered the pen. An officer started walking up and down the lines, and every so often he'd pause and examine a prisoner, looking them up and down in great detail. Sometimes he would carry on to the next prisoner, but with others he'd simply tap on the shoulder with his baton. Those he selected were escorted out of the pen, and once he had 25 prisoners lined up outside the pen he stopped abruptly. "These will do for now, we'll take some more if we need them." He motioned the guards to leave the pen, and he then followed them out.

Oleg was very apprehensive now. "Valia, why the hell did he pick us?" Valia, Oleg and Dmitry had all been selected, as had Boris. Valia was worried. "I wish I knew Oleg, I really wish I knew."

Just a few minutes later, they were marched out of the camp and rather than head towards the City centre as they had expected, they actually headed towards the north-east of the city. Eventually, they were marched to an open area at a place known locally as Peshchanaya Hill, not too far from the village of Peshchanoye. There were several trucks already there, and more worryingly there were a large number of Nazi soldiers, all dressed in black, milling about, laughing and joking with each other as if they didn't have a care in the world. Of course, there were a few ferocious looking dogs walking their handlers around too, the loud barking was incessant.

This didn't look good, and a sense of foreboding flashed through Valia's mind interrupted only when the prisoners were all handed shovels, and told to start digging a large pit. Even though it must have been late October by now, the digging was still extremely back breaking work, especially for the malnourished prisoners. The ground was hard from frost, and it took them the whole morning, and into the early afternoon before they were finally ordered to stop.

Valia, Oleg and Dmitry were silent. They didn't want to attract any unwanted attention from the guards or the men in black. The men in black were now playing with their guns, some had rifles, some had machine guns, whilst others had pistols. "This really doesn't look good," whispered Boris who was stood to the left of Valia.

One of the men in black jumped down into the deep trench, and walked along in front of the prisoners before halting abruptly when he noticed the terrible scars on Dmitry's face. "Let's see if this trench is big enough shall we." With that he drew his pistol and nonchalantly aimed it directly at Dmitry's head. Dmitry stared defiantly back with his steely eyes, straight into the eyes of the officer facing him.

A loud call came booming down into the trench. "Stop it Helmut, we'll need these prisoners later, there's no point wasting a bullet now. We'll have plenty of time for that later."

Helmut looked whimsically at Dmitry. "This is your lucky day prisoner." He returned the pistol into his holster, before being helped out of the trench by a couple of his accomplices. Valia looked at Dmitry, he was literally shaking. He whispered very quietly. "Don't show them your fear Dmitry." Dmitry tried the best he could to look unperturbed, but it was difficult.

One of the Ukrainian translators spoke loudly enough for everyone to hear, and pointed to a nearby truck. "Okay, you can get out of the pit now. Grab a piece of bread and some water from that truck over there." The prisoners slowly clambered out, with some difficulty, and made their way over to the truck. The bread was actually freshly baked. They couldn't remember the last time they'd tasted fresh bread. Although it was just one small piece, it was simply divine. To the starving prisoners it felt like a banquet.

"Okay, once you've eaten, go and wait behind that row of trucks. Just sit down and don't do anything stupid, or you will be shot." There were a couple of other locals, as well as the local police helping to guard the prisoners.

As he was curious to know what was happening, Valia risked asking one of them. "What's going on here then?" The guard seemed quite relaxed, and didn't seem to mind sharing the news. "Well, do you see those Nazis dressed in black. Well, apparently, they're an elite unit of Einsatzgruppen, and from what I understand, they are travelling around executing all sorts of people, but it seems they are mainly targeting Jews."

"So, what are they doing here then?" Dmitry butted in. "I thought most have them had left the city while we were still there."

The guard chuckled to himself. "Maybe so, but apparently there were still about 3,500 left in the city when the Nazis arrived. I know quite a few of them were killed when the city was captured last month, but most of them were rounded up and incarcerated in a Prison Camp, in barbed wire pens."

Oleg, who looked a bit puzzled. "Strange, I didn't see any civilians in our camp?"

The guard couldn't help laughing again. "There's more than one Prison Camp in the city you know. They must be being held in one of the others. Anyway, over 1,500 of them are arriving here shortly. You lot will be okay, so long as you keep quiet and don't cause any sort of incident. They just need you to cover up the bodies once the killing is finished. I think you're going to be taken to the mirror factory in the city centre after that, and will be put to work on a wooden bridge for a few weeks. I don't know how true that is, but that's what I've overheard the Nazi guards talking about earlier today."

About ten minutes later, a long convoy of heavily armed trucks started to pull up at the bottom of the hill and hundreds of civilians began to disembark from them. They were surrounded by a huge number of Nazi guards, so any attempt to escape would be impossible. Soon, family groups of around 25 people at a time were brought up the hill to where the Einsatzgruppen soldiers were waiting, while their ferocious-looking dogs barked threateningly.

Valia and the other prisoners looked on in utter disbelief as events unfolded. Children were ripped from the safety of their parents arms and were dragged, often screaming, to the edge of the large pit. A couple of the men in black opened up with machine guns, and the children dropped like stones. Some were dead when they hit the ground, others merely wounded. It didn't matter, those that hadn't already fallen into the pit were thrown in by the Ukrainian police, who were on hand to help.

The parents were forced to watch the carnage, and not surprisingly, most of them went insane with grief. Valia whispered to Dmitry "This is inhumane, its total barbarism. How can anybody behave like that?" Dmitry and Oleg were just as stunned. They were used to the brutalities of war, but the children. Why the children?

Some parents were total bereft, and meekly succumbed to their fate, whilst other tried to fight, but it was impossible. Every Jew brought up the hill that afternoon was shot, and thrown into the dark, desperate pit.

Valia saw some very young children, little more than babies being given something to smell. Minutes later, their lifeless bodies were also being tossed into the pit, just like some old piece of discarded trash.

The appetite of the Einsatzgruppen for blood seemed to be insatiable, and they very happily continued with their gruesome task, non-stop, until the last of their victims for the day filled the pit.

Once the shooting was finally at an end, the smiling Einsatz-gruppen soldiers compared their individual kill figures with relish. It was a daily routine, whereby, whoever racked up the most kills in the day, would get an extra bottle of schnapps to celebrate the evening with. The jovial banter continued for a short while, before they jumped into their cars and trucks and headed back into the city to rest and recuperate. As far as they were concerned, they were very happy to have completed yet another successful day's work.

Valia and the other prisoners were ordered to bury all the bodies in the pit with earth. It was a distinctly unpleasant task, as there were still moans and the odd cry for help from people that had only been wounded, and some bodies were still moving. There can't be many things worse than being forced to bury somebody that may still be alive, and many of the prisoners were physically sick whilst they toiled away, especially when they had to walk over still warm corpses to get the work finished.

Once their work was completed, they could still see the ground moving as those buried alive struggled to extricate themselves. It was appalling. For at least ten minutes the ground writhed around, before the movements finally ceased, and the last of the buried bodies was suffocated to death.

The exhausted prisoners were loaded onto the back of a truck and taken into the city centre, and on to the mirror factory, where they were to spend the night.

"Pray to God we don't have to go through that again." Oleg whispered to Valia and Dmitry. Pretty much everyone agreed, it had been a horrendous day. Images of that indiscriminate, gruesome, slaughter were certain to haunt them for the rest of their lives.

It was however, a nice change to have a little protection from the elements as they tried to get their tired bodies to sleep inside the relatively dry mirror factory.

Early the following morning, the same truck pulled up outside the factory building, and Valia and the rest of the prisoners that had been present at the massacre the previous day were forced to return to Peshchanaya Hill. It was the same routine to the previous day. They were forced to dig another deep pit throughout the morning and into the early afternoon, and not too long after they'd finished their arduous work, another heavily guarded convoy of trucks pulled up at the bottom of the hill. Hundreds more Jews disembarked, totally unaware of what was lying in wait for them. Again, groups of approximately 25 were brought up the hill to be slaughtered. Valia couldn't bear to watch as the children were ripped from their parents' arms. The frantic and desperate pleas to spare the children fell on deaf ears, as the men in black went about their efficient, yet deadly work.

The tormented howls and screams that echoed across the bleak hillside, seared themselves into the very fabric of the desolate countryside for time immemorial, a permanent reminder of the unspeakable horrors and atrocities committed in this awful place.

It was another long, tortuous and grossly disturbing day, not helped by the biting, cold wind blowing across the hillside.

The emotionally drained prisoners finally returned to the Mirror Factory Prison Camp late in the evening. Sleep was difficult at the best of times, but after the scenes of the last two days, most of the prisoners who'd been at Peshchanaya Hill could only muster a short and very fitful sleep.

The next morning was colder still, and just like clockwork, the truck arrived yet again. Oleg was dismayed. "No, not again, surely they can't have anybody else left to murder?" Oleg, really didn't want to go again. None of them did, but they had no option, and they were soon heading back to that murderous site.

As usual, the men in black were messing around while waiting for their next batch of victims, and the dogs were straining at their leashes. This time there was even a photographer on site to record their heinous crimes, they didn't really seem to care what they were doing, if anything, they seemed to be proud of it.

The day followed the same pattern as the previous two, with several hundred additional poor souls eliminated, simply because they were different.

Once the prisoners were back inside the mirror factory that evening, the local interpreter that they'd got to know over the last few days, finally had some good news for them, although some of it wasn't quite so welcome.

"Okay men, you'll be pleased to hear that there's no more killing tomorrow. The Einsatzgruppen officers, and the local police are now busy searching the city for any remaining hidden Jews. Rest assured, they will all be found, and they, along with those who have hidden them, will, all in good time, also find their way to Peshchanaya Hill. However, over the last couple of days, you've all shown yourselves to be good workers, and as such, it's been decided that you will remain billeted here for the next few weeks. You will have the honour of joining the team of workers who are busy constructing a new wooden bridge across the river. Only when the bridge is completed, will you return to your Prison Camp."

The Nazis were busy building a wooden road bridge over the Dnieper River to replace the temporary pontoon bridge that they'd quickly constructed when they'd initially captured Kremenchug. It was a huge project, with more than 1,000 prisoners working literally from dawn to dusk on the one-kilometre long structure.

With winter fast approaching, the weather was getting colder by the day. There had already been a fair few snow flurries, and the freezing winds went right through the prisoners who had no winter clothes to speak of. It was becoming more and more unendurable for the prisoners by the day.

Dmitry was doing his best to keep warm by stamping his feet, and rubbing his hands constantly. "What I'd give for a nice warm fufaika jacket right now."

"Oh yes, I'd love one of those too, and how about a comfortable pair of valenki to keep your feet warm as well?" Valia replied.

The fufaika, also known as a telogreika or a vatnik, was a warm, cotton wool-padded jacket, that soon became part of the standard Red Army winter uniform during the war, whilst valenki were traditional Russian winter boots, made largely from felt that kept the feet nice and warm.

Unfortunately, as it was, they just had the uniforms that they'd been captured in. If any prisoner had possessed any winter clothing at all, it had almost certainly already have been appropriated by some very grateful Nazi, who'd be trying to supplement his standard issue Wehrmacht uniform, which was totally unsuited, and utterly inadequate for the severe winter weather in eastern Europe.

As well as constructing the wooden road bridge, the Nazis had been hard at work, repairing the railway bridge. With new spans in place, they were now busy laying new railway track over it.

Unfortunately for the Nazis, their rolling stock couldn't be used on the standard Russian railway tracks at all, as the Russian and German railway gauges were totally different. This meant that they either needed to use Russian rolling stock, or they needed to replace all the railway lines with fresh track. As it turned out, the Russians were very good at destroying their railway stock as they retreated, so the Nazis had the huge logistical problem of having to lay new railway track across huge swathes of captured land.

Valia, Oleg and Dmitry were all assigned to help work on the wooden bridge, and their main task was to unload the trucks as they arrived with the requisite timber for the bridge. Nazi engineers would then check the timber before the prisoners manhandled it into the appropriate position to be fixed into place.

At least the almost constant physical exercise offered them a little warmth, and they even received a little more food than normal because of the arduous work they were doing. It was more, but it was never enough.

Work progressed for several days, and by now the river was starting to freeze over in many places. The guards and the engineers kept themselves warm by making themselves large fires, and using stoves which they would often huddle around.

One day, while they were waiting for the next truck to unload, Boris started chatting with one of the local translators and they ended up strolling towards one of the stoves to warm up a bit. Boris thought this was great. For the first time in ages, he was just starting to feel almost comfortable, when without warning, Nazi guards started yelling at them very aggressively. Before Boris knew what was happening, a couple of them sprinted over and bundled him to the floor before kicking him uncontrollably.

A Nazi officer sauntered over, and berated the interpreter for several minutes, before slapping him across the face. It was obvious he wasn't happy. The kerfuffle had attracted the attention of everybody in the vicinity, and they were all staring at poor Boris as he was taking a real hiding. A few short seconds later, the translator announced to everyone, "The stoves and fires are not to be used by any prisoners, is that clear. If you do, this is what will happen to you."

With that, the guards stopped kicking Boris and grabbed a couple of shovels. They then proceeded to smash his head with them so hard Boris must have died instantly, but their fury continued until his head was totally unrecognisable. It was just a ball of red mush, with his warm blood flowing like a torrent over what had been, pristine, white, frosty ground.

A couple of prisoners were called over, and they were ordered to toss what was left of Boris onto one of the open fires.

Valia felt sick. How could anybody kill somebody, just because

145

they wanted a little warmth? Surely these people were not normal? How could any sane person behave in such an utterly barbaric manner? Surely it was not possible, surely? It was totally inhuman. If only it was some gruesome nightmare from which he'd soon awake.

By the time the new road bridge had finally been completed, hundreds of prisoners had died. Some fell into the river and drowned. Some simply froze to death. Some starved, whilst others were shot on the flimsiest pretext. The Nazis treated the prisoners with the utmost contempt, and they didn't care how, or even how many of them died.

Although the majority of the Jews that had remained in the Kremenchug area had by now been exterminated, Valia, Oleg and Dmitry still made the occasional day trip to Peshchanaya Hill to dig yet more dark, chilling pits for the Einsatzgruppen on their frequent return trips. As well as the few remaining Jews who'd been discovered hiding around the city, the executions now started to include some of the local population, as well as many prisoners of war.

By the end of November though, there was not enough work left to keep all the prisoners in the city, so most of them were transferred back to the Prison Camp that was now officially known as Stalag 346A. As the column of prisoners started shuffling in the direction of the Prison Camp, the guards became extremely trigger happy, and seemed to enjoy shooting prisoners for almost any reason.

Any prisoner so physically exhausted that they couldn't keep up with the column were soon shot, right by the side of the main road. Others were shot if they were seen to be accepting any food being offered to them by some of the city inhabitants.

Major Orland was of course delighted to welcome them all back again, and after a very short speech in the freezing cold, they were swiftly re-housed in one of the outdoor pens.

"I thought this place couldn't get worse before we left, but look at it now." Oleg muttered.

"Look at everybody," lamented Dmitry, "some of them look like skeletons."

As Valia scanned the camp, it was immediately obvious that one of the outside pens was now devoid of any military prisoners, but instead contained locals who for some reason must have upset their new Nazi masters. As Valia and his comrades became reacquainted with the surroundings, it became painfully obvious that many of the prisoners were ill, seriously ill. There were men who were struggling to breathe, many were constantly coughing, others were vomiting blood. Men were just lying there, on the frozen ground, surrounded by filthy, slushy, snow, and it looked like many of them had already died.

Valia asked one of the prisoners nearby, "What's going on here?"

"Can't you see for yourself. They're starving us all to death aren't they. We're hardly getting any food, and what scraps they do give us, are undigestible, rancid, and disgustingly putrid. Not only that, there's a lot of disease going around now. The doctors are saying it's typhoid, but they don't seem to be attempting to treat anybody."

"Is there anything we can do to help?" asked Oleg.

"I can't see anything anyone can do while these monsters are running the place. Each morning they take loads of dead bodies from each pen, and that Major Orland is a real bastard. He seems to have fun picking out some unlucky prisoner almost every day. They drag the poor soul out, and they either beat him to a pulp, or they hang him. It's almost like they think we're some sort of vermin. They look like they just want to have a bit of sadistic pleasure destroying us all."

As the dreary days slowly stretched into wearisome weeks, and the cold became more and more intense Valia, started to feel very tired, and began coughing a lot. He was all too aware of the symptoms. He'd seen so many of the other prisoners become sick, and eventually die from typhoid, he knew what he'd contracted. Dmitry and Oleg both had it too. As they became weaker and weaker, they were transferred to see the Russian doctors inside a small consulting room inside one of the buildings.

After a quick examination, the doctor that examined Valia, confirmed the news he was expecting to hear, however, the doctor also had an intriguing offer for him.

"Okay, Valia, you probably don't need me to tell you this, but you've got typhoid, and as things stand, I can't do anything about it. My best estimate is that you've probably got little more than a week left, but it could be a lot less, staying outside in this cold."

Valia's thoughts turned to his family, especially his loving mother back home in Yakhrobol. She'd never know how bravely he'd fought to save the Motherland. He knew that she'd be devastated with the news of his death. As well as feeling awful physically, he now felt awful mentally too.

The doctor could see the desolation in Valia's eyes. "There's a potential solution if you want to take it. I've been instructed by the Nazis, that we can treat prisoners who volunteer to work for them."

Valia gave the thought about half a second before breathlessly replying "How can I possibly do that, I'd become a traitor, it's impossible. I won't do it."

The doctor could see that Valia was angered simply by the proposition, but retained his composure, and patiently continued. "Look Valia, if I don't do anything to treat you, you will be dead within a week. Do you really want your mother and family to mourn for you, when there's a possibility they don't need to? Let me put it this way. If you volunteer, you'll get a bed inside one of the buildings and some proper food and treatment until you are back to reasonable health again."

Valia gave this proposition a couple of extra seconds before reiterating his position. "I appreciate what you're saying doctor, but there's no way I will be a traitor to my country. My decision really is final."

Not wishing to give up on Valia so easily, the doctor gave one final argument which he hoped might sway him. "I totally understand what you're saying Valia, but look at it this way. If you're dead, you can no longer do anything to protect our beloved Motherland. At least if you are alive, you still have the possibility to do something to actively fight the invaders. Don't forget, you will be in better health, and more importantly, you'll be out of this death camp. Who knows, you might even get an opportunity to escape, and then you would be in a position to fight the invaders again. Why not at least give it a little bit of thought?"

Doubts started to penetrate Valia's head. He wasn't quite so sure what he should do now. What an agonising decision to make; on one hand to face certain death within days, or to aid and abet the enemy, and hope to escape. Valia mulled things over for a little while before replying, "Can I think about it a little more, doctor?"

"Of course, Valia, but don't take too long, or you'll be beyond the point where I can help you."

Despite his desperate illness, Valia was returned to his pen outside in the harsh freezing conditions. He looked around, and didn't see Dmitry or Oleg anywhere. As time passed, he began to suspect that they'd been offered a similar proposition, and maybe they'd accepted it. All sorts of thoughts ran through his mind as he started to drift into a delirious sleep. Did he really want to die here on this godforsaken piece of ground? Nobody would care, nobody would bat an eyelid if he was dragged out of the pen and dumped into that dreadful pit outside the camp. He dreaded the thought of helping the Nazis in any way, but the doctor had put a tiny seed in his mind that somehow, an opening would present itself where he'd be able to escape and return to the fight.

When Valia opened his eyes and he looked around the pen again, neither Dmitry or Oleg were anywhere to be seen. His mind was made up. He couldn't tell anybody in the pen what he was planning to do, as they would surely kill him there and then. He managed to grab the attention of one of the guards and asked to see the doctor again.

On extremely unsteady legs, Valia was accompanied to visit the doctor one more time. This time, there was a Nazi doctor in the consulting room too.

The Russian doctor looked Valia straight in the eyes. "So Valia, what is your decision?"

Valia still felt uncomfortable, but it was the only rational decision he could come to in his near delirious state. "Yes, doctor, I will help the Nazis."

The Nazi doctor spoke briefly to a guard outside the consulting room, before administering Valia with an experimental antibiotic injection. Valia was then helped into one of the prisoner blocks, where he was thoroughly showered, before being issued with a new, clean, set of rags that masqueraded as a uniform, and an old pair of laced boots. He was also given some bread, clean water, and a bunk to recover on.

He was there for 15 minutes before he spotted both Dmitry and Oleg in nearby bunks. Valia felt a little less guilty now, he wasn't the only one who would be helping the Nazis. He closed his eyes and slept.

A surprising commotion at the window woke Valia from his fraught slumber. He got up and shuffled the short distance to the window to see what was going on.

He couldn't believe his eyes. A large hole had been dug just outside the prisoner pens, and in full view of everyone in the buildings. There, along with another 11 Russian doctors, was the doctor he'd seen just a few hours earlier.

Major Orland was there, wrapped up warm in a huge winter coat, along with a long, red, woollen scarf. He was joking and laughing with his follow officers as usual. A small group of prisoners brought what appeared to be the effluent from the toilet block, and poured the pungent mix into the hole. Water was then added, just to make sure the hole was filled with disgusting slurry. The doctors were then ordered to strip to their underwear in the terrible freezing weather. They were then forced into the hole at gun point, where they were compelled to fully immerse and bathe themselves in the disgusting, raw, sewage.

Major Orland found this hilarious, and several minutes passed while he laughed and joked with his men before his face abruptly turned into a vindictive stare. He turned to the guards and raised his right arm. On the click of his fingers, a volley of shots rang out and each of the doctors slumped into the disgusting morass, dead. Major Orland quickly returned to his quarters while the poor prisoners had the unenviable job of retrieving the bodies from the hole, and dragging them to the huge pit outside the camp, where they were unceremoniously dumped.

All the prisoners were visibly shocked. The last thing they expected was for their doctors to be executed. Valia was still somewhat delirious, so he quickly returned to his bunk bed, before slipping into another fitful sleep.

As promised, and mainly for their own protection, the group of volunteers were kept well away from all the other prisoners and they were also provided with improved rations. Not much improved, but at least they were unlikely to starve to death now.

Over the next few weeks their health and strength slowly improved, a few of them even undertook simple jobs, such as driving trucks around the city for the Nazis. In fact, more and more of the prisoners started to turn, and join the Nazi volunteers as the worst of the winter weather slowly ravaged those left out in the open.

On one particularly chilly morning, one which Valia would never forget, all the volunteers in the camp were, somewhat unexpectedly, marched out onto the parade ground and lined up to attention. Of course, as soon as the prisoners, still ensconced in their barbed-wire walled enclosures, spotted them, vitriolic heckling and jeering filled the air.

"Shit, what's going on now?" Dmitry muttered to himself. He

wasn't happy. He felt distinctly uncomfortable being paraded in front of the badly emaciated and very angry prisoners.

After ten minutes in the bitterly cold wind, a group of four Nazi officers they hadn't seen before, strutted out of Major Orland's office in fine order. The most senior looking of them soon addressed the assembled men.

"I would like to thank each of you for kindly volunteering to assist the Reich. We will be taking most of you back to Germany with us, where you'll provide useful labour in one of our glorious factories. We'll be leaving very shortly by truck, and will head north to Kiev, and from there we'll travel by train to Munich. You'll be issued with some proper clothes to replace those awful, stinking rags you're wearing, when we arrive in Kiev."

Near the camp gates, six large trucks were sat waiting for them, along with a few escort motorcycles, and several heavily armed guards.

"Oh yes, and before I forget, if there are any attempts to escape during any part of the journey, don't expect any mercy."

With that, the officers headed towards the trucks, closely followed by the volunteers, ushered as they were by several guards, and five or six glowering guard dogs.

"What do you think Valia?" The tone of Dmitri's question, reflected his anxiousness.

"I really don't know. Maybe we're on our way to Germany as they say, but we could just as easily be being taken to an execution site. You know what the Nazis are like."

"Let's hope it's a trip to Germany then," quipped Oleg, "I always wanted to visit the place one day."

The volunteers jumped into the trucks one after another, until they were full. The few that didn't get on were herded back to their barrack buildings. Valia was disappointed to find he'd ended up in one truck, whilst Dmitry and Oleg had been ushered by the guards onto a different one. This meant he wouldn't be seeing his friends again until they arrived in Kiev. Of course, this assumed that they were actually heading to Kiev.

Once the trucks were fully loaded, the convoy slowly rolled out of the camp. Valia was happy to finally be leaving that abhorrent place for good, but felt a distinct unease, and was very apprehensive about what the future would bring. He also felt a deep sense of sorrow for the remaining prisoners, the majority of whom were almost certain to die in that despicable camp.

With the deep growling engine, sporadically interrupted by extremely clunky gear changes, it wasn't long before they were into the countryside and heading north, in the general direction of Kiev.

Chapter 8
The Angel

The adrenaline that'd been pumping hard through his veins as he'd escaped from the convoy of trucks taking him to Kiev had long since dissipated as Valia was slowly, but surely, picking his way through the dark, dense forest with a certain degree of caution and foreboding.

Happy memories of his family, especially those of his mother, were a constant source of motivation and drive to keep him going. How he longed to be reunited with his whole family, in their lovely, cosy, wooden home in the small village of Yakhrobol. The stove was always lit during the winter months, keeping the whole house warm and welcoming, day or night, rain, wind or snow, and it was always a source of amazement to Valia how his mother was always able to produce all those wonderful meals from such plain and meagre ingredients. She really was a great cook.

How he could do with just a tiny portion of her delicious food right now. He felt himself slowly starting to starve again. Even though he'd recovered from his bout of typhoid, he was still a little weaker than he would've liked, so he really needed a good meal to sustain his strength.

Valia had a lot of things on his mind. His two most pressing concerns were the abject cold, and the dearth of available food.

You'd think that after a few months sleeping outside in freezing conditions he would be used to the cold by now, but even though the worst of the winter weather had now blown over, it was still uncomfortably cold. He needed to get some sort of warm winter clothing sooner rather than later, especially as the extra body heat from the other prisoners whilst trying to sleep in the Prison Camp was no longer available to him.

The other, rather obvious, major concern was how to keep out of the clutches of the Nazis. He knew if he was to be re-captured, his life expectancy would plummet to just a few minutes at most. Deciding who he could actually trust was going to be a major issue. From what he'd seen whilst he was a prisoner, a sizeable minority of the local population seemed surprisingly sympathetic to the Nazis, and if so, they'd probably be very keen to hand him in. Even for the majority who weren't, the incentives to hand in a runaway prisoner might well be too tempting. He knew that if he was discovered with anybody, those helping him were almost certainly going to be arrested, and very likely killed, so the chances of him finding anybody willing to overtly help him wasn't great. One thing was certain though, he'd certainly need to keep his wits about him.

Valia was keen to return to the fight as soon as he possibly could, but first he needed to have some idea where the Soviet Front Line actually was. Having nothing better to base his estimate on, he decided to head east, simply because it was more likely to be there than any other direction.

The one positive thing in his favour was the fact that he was already on the eastern side of the Dnieper River, so he didn't have the problem of trying to cross it undetected.

Each morning for the first few days, Valia would watch where the sun rose, and he would start walking in that general direction. During the day, he'd collect anything edible, and also check which side of the trees any moss was growing, and use this to try and get his bearings to ensure he remained on a roughly eastern route.

After being alone in the forest for some time, Valia's senses had become very sensitive and attuned to anything out of the ordinary, and if he did hear or spot anything suspicious, he'd immediately dart into the nearest available hiding spot until he was sure it was safe to carry on.

After a few days of navigating his way through the deep forest, Valia heard one of the things he really didn't want to hear. There were dogs barking. Immediately his thoughts turned to the ferocious Nazi guard dogs. Were they already on his trail? He increased his pace to try and distance himself from them, but after a short while, he realised the barks were getting louder, and that they weren't behind, but actually in front of him. Then Valia spotted some smoke drifting on the cold spring wind. He slowed right down and very cautiously made his way towards the sound.

Crouching down, he eventually came to what looked to be an opening in the forest with a small track leading to a large wooden house. He could now smell the smoke quite clearly, and more importantly he could smell the aroma of fresh cooking. He felt unbelievably hungry.

There were no motor vehicles anywhere to be seen, but he could make out recent tyre tracks in the snow. Were they from Nazi vehicles, or the house owner's vehicle? Valia had no idea, but for some strange reason, he had a very strong impulsive urge to go and knock on the door and ask for help. He really wanted to go inside and just spend some time warming himself next to the stove. He wanted to taste some of that wonderfully aromatic food. He wanted to feel safe, he wanted to feel secure. Luckily, before he could act on his strange impulse urge, Valia came quickly back to his senses. He knew, almost instinctively, that it would be a decidedly dangerous thing to do.

It felt a lot safer to stay where he was for a little while longer and just reconnoitre the place. He could see a small shed to the left of the building, which might be worth looking into. There also appeared to be a few chickens in the vicinity, as he could hear some clucking from somewhere too. The dogs were still sporadically barking, but as far as he could make out, they appeared to be safely locked away, inside the house. Valia decided to wait the few short hours until nightfall before approaching the house.

With the temperature falling and the sun drifting over the western horizon, Valia decided it was time to make his move. He needed to be as quiet as mouse, but he also needed to cover his tracks in the light snow as best he could. He found some fir branches scattered nearby, and he used those to brush the snow behind him as he moved around.

Moving very slowly and very carefully, Valia inched his way towards the shed. He was able to take a look inside through its small, dirty, cracked glass window and he spotted some items that would be really useful to him. The dogs started barking loudly again as a loud creak rang out as he tried to open the unlocked, rickety door. Valia had to move fast, he quickly grabbed the long, thick coat that was hanging on a peg inside the door, and stuffed a couple of potatoes into his pockets, and he also managed to grab an egg, before retreating back towards the trees as fast as he possibly could, taking care to cover his tracks as he went.

A young lady, who looked to be in her early 20's opened the door holding two large Alsatian dogs on their leads, and peered into the darkness outside. "Hello, who's there. Is there anybody there?" There was a slight tremble of fear in her voice.

Hidden behind a few trees, Valia was frozen to the spot. He didn't move a muscle. Then from his right, he heard a vehicle approaching. As it got closer, he could make it out to be a Nazi military car. Valia started to sweat. He was now in quite a precarious position. As the car came to a halt just outside the house, a tall, handsome looking officer got out of the car. "Olga, what on earth are you doing outside, it's so cold?"

"The dogs were spooked by something, and I was just checking. I guess they must've heard your car coming down the track."

"Of course, it can't be anything else can it, who's going to be wandering around these woods at this time of the night? Mmm, is that my favourite apple cake I can smell?"

"It is my darling, come inside and let's have some fun."

For a good five minutes after they'd gone into the house, Valia stayed rooted to the spot. The dogs had gone quiet again, so Valia risked taking a peek through one of the windows of the house. From the safety of the trees he could just about make out the couple kissing, and soon after, they started removing each other's clothes.

He'd seen enough. Valia needed to get away from this place as fast as possible, as this clearly wasn't going to be a safe place to rest up. Wrapped in his newly acquired thick winter coat, Valia immediately felt more comfortable, and as soon as he'd moved a safe distance from the house, he devoured the egg and the potatoes, raw. He couldn't remember anything tasting quite so delicious.

Apart from the ongoing issue of finding more food, getting rid of his tattered army uniform was now a major priority for Valia. Although it was hidden under the long, thick overcoat, it would surely be discovered if he was stopped for any reason, and that would surely be a death sentence for him. What he really needed now was some inconspicuous civilian clothes, if only he could find some somewhere.

A couple of days later, and several kilometres further on his long trek back to safety, Valia picked up some noticeable signs that he was approaching a small town or village. The trees were starting to thin out a little, and he could see plenty of smoke drifting gently into the sky not too far away. He cautiously moved forward before furtively emerging onto a small track that he could see led directly into a village.

As there were no visible signs of a Nazi presence anywhere, Valia slowly, and very watchfully, made his way towards the closest group of houses. He was very aware that he would now be visible from the houses, but his hunger was such that he really needed to start taking some calculated risks.

The village was suspiciously quiet, with no noticeable activity anywhere. As he got closer to the first house, Valia's gaze quickly fixed on an old man who had stealthy opened his front door. The man was vigorously beckoning Valia to come into his house as a matter of urgency. Something about the old man's demeanour gave Valia enough confidence to run up the nearby path and into his home. The old man swiftly followed him and shut the door quietly behind them. He then put his index finger to his lips, and went "Shhh." The old man then quickly went to one of the windows, and stared intently outside for several minutes, before visibly seeming to relax.

Turning to Valia he talked in a soft, hushed tone. "I'm sorry about that. Let me get you a cup of tea."

Valia was still unsure what to make of the old man, but he seemed friendly enough, certainly for now.

The old man slowly ambled over to the stove, and poured two cups of piping hot tea, before quickly handing Valia one of them "Hello, my name is Andrey, and before you ask, I'm 67 years old and I've lived here alone ever since my much loved and beautiful wife, Olga, passed away five years ago. May I ask, what brings you here?"

There was a pause for several seconds while Valia looked Andrey straight in the eyes. Could he really be trusted?

"Okay, if I tell you that I think you're a runaway soldier, and that I'm not going to report you to the Nazis, does that help at all?"

After a few seconds, Valia felt comfortable enough to introduce himself, and then proceeded to give Andrey a brief overview of his activities over the previous few months, which Andrey seemed to find really fascinating.

"Good, it's really nice to meet you Valia, and I'm so pleased I got to spot you first. I think it's only fair to tell you that you really need to be careful who you speak to, and where you go from now on. As well as regular Nazi patrols, there are a lot of informants around. I know for a fact that there's a couple in this village, in that house just over the road, and they'd have no qualms about handing you over to the Nazis. That's who I was checking on when you first came in."

Whilst Valia had been chronicling his tales, Andrey had been busy preparing some eggs and bread, and he now served them up to Valia along with another hot, steaming cup of tea.

"Don't eat it all too quickly," warned Andrey. "Your stomach will need to get used to proper food again, it might take a little while, but you'll be fine in a little while." Valia was just so grateful to have some proper sustenance after so long. It really was so delectable.

"If you don't mind me asking Valia, where did you get that coat? I only ask, because a Nazi patrol was here yesterday going door to door, telling us to report anybody wearing a coat just like the one you're wearing right now."

Valia recounted how he appropriated it, and Andrey just shook his head.

"It's a shame, it looks like such a lovely coat, but we'll have to burn it right now. If anybody sees you wearing it, the Nazis will definitely pick you up."

As Valia took it off, Andrey noticed the rags that once passed as a Red Army uniform underneath.

"We'll need to get rid of those too, and quickly." Andrey disappeared into another rooms, and Valia could hear him rummaging around for a few of minutes before re-appearing with a big smile across his face. In his well-worn, almost leathery hands were a selection of clothes. "I don't think I will need these anymore, so if anything fits you, you are welcome to have them."

"Are you sure?" asked Valia before trying them all on. Valia was able to pick a pretty nondescript combination, so as not to be too conspicuous when he was outside again. The coat and filthy rags that he'd worn with pride for so long were soon burning to ashes in the stove.

Valia was keen to find out the latest information, as he hadn't had any reliable news since he'd been captured way back in September. "What's the latest news Andrey?"

"Well, you'd better sit down, and I'll tell you what I know."

Andrey poured, and handed Valia another hot cup of tea. "The Nazis have been reporting that they captured well over 600,000 prisoners when they captured Kiev and the surrounding areas. Apparently General Kirponos and many of the Southwestern Front leaders were killed as they tried to force an escape from the encirclement."

"Yes, I'd heard that from a few of the prisoners in the camp who arrived a few weeks after we did, although I think most of those prisoners ended up in Kiev?"

"I think so, we've seen a couple of other lost soldiers over the winter months, and I've tried to get to them before the Nazi collaborators. I couldn't believe some of the horror stories they told me, but having heard your story about the executions near Kremenchug, I'm inclined to believe them now."

Valia wanted to hear more. "Have there been more executions you've heard about?"

Very solemnly, Andrey continued. "I had a soldier here a couple of months ago. He'd managed to escape from a prison in Kiev. He was a lovely young man, originally from Minsk. Most of his comrades who'd tried to escape with him had been mown down, or re-captured by the Nazis."

"You know, he was fine all the time he was here, until he recounted a tale about a place he'd been forced to work at in Kiev. When he mentioned the place called Babi Yar, he'd simply broken down in tears. Apparently, he'd been forced to go there to do some menial work while the Nazi soldiers, and even our own police forces were executing thousands of people, most of them Jews, but also some prisoners of war, and some others they wanted to get rid of."

Looking very sombre, Valia nodded. "I know just how he must have felt. I witnessed the executions of close to 3,000 Jews in Kremenchug, and that was a true obscenity, I can't imagine anything worse than that?"

Andrey looked empathetically at Valia before continuing. "The soldier I spoke to could hardly talk about his experience there, he was so traumatised. I don't know if you know it, but Babi Yar is a small ravine in Kiev. Apparently, the Nazis had arranged for all the Jews in Kiev to congregate near it on the morning of the 28th of September, under the pretence of being relocated. They were told to bring everything valuable they had, including all their money and documents as they'd likely need it after they'd been transported elsewhere. The soldier told me that over 30,000 Jews arrived, most of them in a positive spirit. They were so convinced that they were going to be taken to a better place to live."

"The Nazis were very organised, and so clever that the victims didn't realise they were heading to their deaths until the very last minute. The Nazis had local Ukrainians to put them at ease, then led them past a number of different places where they had to hand over their luggage, then their valuables, and finally their coats, shoes and eventually the remainder of their clothes."

Andrey continued. "Once undressed, the poor wretched men, women and children were taken into the ravine that was about 150 metres long and 30 metres wide and a good 15 metres deep. When they reached the bottom of the ravine they were seized by the Nazis and made to lie down on top of victims who had already been shot. The victims were then shot in the neck or back of the head by members of the Einsatzgruppen. As the day progressed, the bodies piled higher and higher, and the ravine filled with layer upon layer of dead or critically wounded corpses."

"Over two days the killings continued, before the Nazis had had enough. They covered the bodies, both dead and those still alive with a wall of earth from the side of the ravine."

Valia had tears in his eyes, he could vividly remember the small children being killed at Peshchanaya Hill, and having to cover the victims there, and it took several minutes before he managed to regain his composure.

Andrey, seeing the distress Valia was in thought it best to change the subject. "Where are you planning to go?"

Valia composed himself a little before replying. "To be honest, I'm just looking to get back to the front line and re-join the army, so I'm heading east. I'm not sure how far away the front line is though, do you have any idea?"

"Hmm, I'm not sure that's such a good idea Valia. You do realise that Stalin has more or less deemed that anybody who has surrendered, regardless of the circumstances should be considered a deserter, and as such you'll more than likely end up being shot as soon as you get there. In any case, the Nazis are not too far from Moscow, it would be almost impossible to get to the Front line without being caught. The soldier that was here a couple of months ago was going to head north towards his home in Belarus. He felt that the opposition to the Nazis would be really strong in that area, and there might even be some partisan groups forming in that area that he could join. It's really up to you to decide where to go, but maybe heading north might be the better option for you now. Whatever you do, try and stay away from big towns or cities, as you'll inevitably be stopped and asked for your papers."

Valia sat motionless for what seemed an age as he started to fully comprehend his position. His options looked pretty limited, and just maybe heading north might be the best option to take. He really needed to trust his gut instinct, and that was crying out "Go North Young Man."

"You can stay here tonight Valia, but you really will need to go before dawn tomorrow. The Nazis come and search the houses periodically, and if you're found here, I'll be shot, as well as you. I don't have much food as the Nazis take most of it, but I can spare you a couple of potatoes to take with you when you go."

It hadn't really occurred to Valia the full extent of the retribution that Andrey might suffer by sheltering him, but he now understood the risk such brave people were prepared to take. He really was a guardian angel. "Why are you doing so much to help me Andrey?"

"Well, I was in the Red Army during the Civil War, and any comrade in need, is a comrade I will gladly help, until my dying day." A tear welled up in Andrey's eyes as he continued. "Both my son's Sasha and Viktor are away in the Red Army, and they were sent west when the Nazis invaded. I've heard nothing from them since then. My heart tells me they will arrive home at any time, but my head is starting to tell me that it's less and less likely now. I always keep a watchful eye outside just in case they do come walking down the road, and that's why I spotted you so quickly, nervously approaching the village."

"I'd also like to think that if either of my son's found themselves in your position, somebody would be kind enough to help them as well."

Valia had tears welling up in his eyes. He was thinking about his wonderful family back home, and what their thoughts would be right now. Maybe they would think he was already dead.

After showing Valia a relatively safe place under the floor boards that he could sleep for the night, they shared a vodka or two together, whilst Andrey recalled the great victories he was part of in the great Civil War between 1917 and 1919.

Eventually, they both got to sleep. It was the first night that Valia could remember for ages where he'd felt like he was safe and secure. He longed to be safe and secure. He longed to be back with his family, he longed to be back in Yakhrobol.

Just before dawn the following morning, Andrey woke Valia with a hot tea. They shared an omelette together, before Andrey gave Valia two large potatoes, just as he had promised. "Oh yes, and here's something I think that you'll find very useful too." Andrey handed Valia a small sharp knife.

"That's brilliant Andrey, I can't thank you enough."

"Don't say another word, you really must be going now." Andrey opened the door quietly and checked that the way was clear. The two embraced each other with a big hug before Valia started out on his journey once more, this time heading north. It was certainly going to be a long walk to Belarus, but as things stood, he had all the time in the world.

Chapter 9
The Walk

I t seemed like a good idea, and it was probably the best thing to do under the current circumstances. Valia slowly evolved a strategy over several days of walking which he hoped would help him stay out of the clutches of the Nazis and their collaborators.

Walking through the dense forest was definitely the safest way to avoid being caught, however, the forest didn't cover the whole route he was taking, so he settled on a policy of staying in the forest where it was available, otherwise he'd walk along small tracks where he'd be less likely to encounter vehicles or people. He also made a point of making sure there were places he could quickly hide nearby before proceeding too far along any particular track. Whenever he encountered a major road, he would totally avoid it unless there was no other option available.

He also soon got to learn that deserted houses, or even dachas, of which there were many dotted around the countryside, were some of the best places to rest up and get some good sleep. He needed to be careful though, as some were permanently occupied, whilst others remained vacant for much of the year. If he noticed any signs of habitation, he would give it a wide berth, and move on to the next one. If it was vacant, Valia would sneak into a shed or even the main building if he could. Often there would be some basic food stored there, even if it was just a few vegetables in an underground store to stop them freezing during the winter months.

Very occasionally he would encounter local people on his long walk, and he'd have to quickly make a judgement if they were trustworthy or not. If he felt they were safe, he'd ask for some proper shelter for the night, and whatever food they might be able to spare. If he was unsure, he'd quickly make his excuses, and leave the area as fast as he could for the safety of the nearest forest. He couldn't risk being turned over to the Nazis by a rogue collaborator.

Within a few weeks he'd bypassed Kiev, and found himself alongside the Dnieper River again, although his time, it resembled a huge lake, off to his left. The waterway seemed to be full of boats, some were busy fishing, whilst others were transporting goods between Kiev and Chernobyl, a small town he could just about make out, far off in the distance, on the opposite bank of the river.

The occasional Nazi motorboat would speed up and down between the other boats at regular intervals, checking the paperwork of those on board, and whenever Valia heard their distinctive engines, he'd lie low, keeping a beady eye on their progress. If they spotted him by the side of the river, he'd have virtually nowhere to go.

Although the river was well stocked with fish, catching them was proving to be more of an issue. He didn't have a hook, a line, or even a net available, although he did have his sharp knife. He'd occasionally have some success scooping them out of the river with his bare hands, but certainly nowhere enough for a feast.

One afternoon as he continued his progress along the riverbank, Valia spotted a Nazi motor boat pulling into the bank little more than 100 metres up ahead. It seemed best to stay where he was, lying flat against the ground, and just keeping an eye on them until they left again.

However, within 15 minutes, there was some smoke rising from a makeshift fire, and he could hear a couple of men enjoying themselves. It looked like they were going to be there for quite a while.

As Valia reassessed his situation, he realised that he couldn't really avoid them, as there wasn't an obvious way to get past them without giving away his position. He decided he'd just have to wait until they were gone. He remained on his stomach as he observed what they were up to.

There was just the two of them, and they were in a small sandy cove with their boat tethered to a sturdy looking tree that overhung the river bank. It looked like they must've acquired a few of fish from one of the fishing boats and they were going to have a nice barbecue. Valia also spotted the men clutching a couple of beer bottles too.

Valia loved barbecued fish. Every summer, back home, he'd go out fishing for a nice carp or perch, in one of the nearby lakes, or even in the Volga River itself. He and his friends would often spend the whole afternoon and evening preparing, cooking, and devouring the nicely smoked fish, along with the obligatory bread, salad and most importantly, vodka. How Valia longed for those wonderful, carefree days to return.

After watching the men meticulously preparing, and then starting to cook their meal for ten minutes, he could start to smell that beautiful aroma wafting in his direction. It smelt fabulous.

However, Valia had also noticed something else. The men had left all their guns in the boat, and they looked to be a lot further away than he was from them. A plan quickly formulated in his mind. Could he possibly sneak up to the boat undetected, and take a gun, or better still, could he shoot the two soldiers grab their fish and make off in their boat?

The options he had seemed endless, until he realised the likely consequences of such actions. Okay, he might get a bit further up the river, but he was sure to be hunted down in double quick time. As things stood, they didn't know he was there, and as a consequence he was relatively safe.

Valia maintained his position, out of sight, but still able to observe the soldiers. Then from almost directly behind him, Valia heard talking, and the cracking noise of twigs snapping and breaking. A group of men were approaching him from behind, heading straight for the cove.

Valia looked around desperately as the voices got louder. There was nowhere obvious for him to hide. If he stayed where he was, they couldn't possibly miss him. Valia had to move, and move quickly. But where? He frantically looked around before his eyes fixed on the river bank. Valia figured that his only option would be to be immerse himself into the freezing water of the river as shallow waves lapped up on the shoreline, a short distance to his left. Just maybe he might get away with it.

"Hey, Klaus, got enough fish for us too?" A small squad of six Nazi soldiers approaching.

"Ah, there you are Uwe, don't worry, we've managed to get ten large Carp, and even better than that, we've managed to get a few bottles of the local beer too. Hurry on over."

"Great, we'll be there now."

"Have you found any renegades yet?"

"No, it's as quiet as a mouse out there, there's some great scenery, and some beautiful wildlife, but we haven't seen any runaways yet."

As the soldiers approached, Valia waited until the last possible minute before sliding himself into the freezing cold water. He almost convulsed as he immersed himself into the water as it was so cold, but he just about managed to control himself. Keeping just his head above water, hidden behind some reeds, Valia could just about still keep an eye on proceedings.

Luckily the squad seemed to be far more interested in their lunch than anything else, as they strode quickly past Valia, literally a couple of metres away, and out into the cove.

These soldiers kept their weapons within easy reach, so it was now going to impossible to execute any of the plans that he'd been thinking of a few minutes earlier, even if he'd wanted to.

Valia now had a huge problem on his hands. He knew he couldn't stay in the water for too long or he'd get hypothermia, but he couldn't really risk getting out of the water where he was either, as he'd more than likely be spotted. So, with a monumental amount of effort, he managed to start pushing himself along the river bank away from the soldiers, all the time, doing his best not to disturb the water too much. Only once he felt he was far enough away did Valia drag himself back onto dry land. He was absolutely freezing and shivering, and the bitterly cold wind blowing across the river only exacerbated his intense feeling of agony.

In the distance, the sounds from the cove had risen. The Nazis were having a wonderful time, laughing and joking, and drinking beer. The wonderful smell of cooked fish permeated the air, and was making Valia so hungry. Valia really needed to keep moving, if only to get the blood flowing through his body again, so he crawled as far as he could away from the soldiers, finally ending up in a small copse of fir trees. He didn't remember much else after that as he lost consciousness.

He had no recollection of anything at all until he started to come to his senses again. Strangely, he could feel warmth. As he focused his eyes, Valia could only register the vision of a beautiful young woman with long shimmering blonde hair smiling at him. She immediately whispered, "Shhh, there were some Nazis just over there getting drunk not so long ago, only a few hundred metres away. You must be quiet."

Valia looked up in amazement. Where had this vision of beauty miraculously appeared from? He then sensed that his wet shirt and trousers had been removed, and he'd been wrapped in a very coarse, dry coat. Before he could say anything, a young man approached them, walking very slowly and crouched over as much as possible, so as to avoid being seen.

"Good, I see he's still alive then," the young man softly whispered as he offered his hand to Valia. "Hi, I'm Lev, you can call me Leo and this is my sister Yana. I wasn't sure you'd make it, but Yana insisted we give it a try."

Looking somewhat stunned, Valia shook Leo by the hand. "You can call me Valia. I'm on a long walk heading to the North. I spotted the Nazis and had to hide from them, and the only place was in the river."

"I think it's okay now, I just went over to take a look and they seem to have gone, but we really do need to stay as quiet as we can for now, just to be on the safe side." Leo scanned the horizon once again, just to be sure. "What are you doing here?"

After almost certainly saving his life, Valia felt certain he could trust them. He slowly recounted his tales as both Yana and Leo continued to vigorously rub him all over to try and get some more heat into his emaciated body.

"Okay, it's a good job we found you when we did. I think you'd have probably frozen to death by now if we hadn't. You're probably wondering what we're doing out here. Am I right?"

"Well, the thought did cross my mind. I've been in this area for over three days now, and I've hardly seen anyone."

"Do you think you are strong enough to walk, we need to get you back to our Dacha, it's only a short distance away, but it's well hidden. I don't think you saw it when you walked past by earlier this morning. You seemed to be preoccupied with trying to catch some fish. Our mother spotted you, and then a little later the Nazis came and searched our place. Once we realised they were heading in your direction, we thought we'd better check you were okay, so voila, here we are."

Valia was totally stumped, how could he have totally missed a dacha. He felt a little stupid, but very grateful all the same.

With a little help, Valia dragged himself up, and they made their way to the dacha, where Lyudmila was waiting with some hot tea. "The Nazis come and search around here every two or three days, but they've already been today, so you should be okay for now. You can stay the night while we dry your clothes, and you can warm up properly. We've got a few extra fish hidden away that the Nazis can never find, so we'll have a few of them tonight."

As the evening wore on, the conversation was extremely convivial. It turned out that Lyudmila's husband had been killed at Uman, and she was doing the best she could to bring up her two children. Valia volunteered to do anything he could to help around the house, but it seemed that Leo, was very good and dependable son, and he'd kept the house in good order over the harsh, freezing winter months.

After a good night's sleep, Valia soon felt fully energised again, and gathered together his very few possessions as he prepared to leave. Lyudmila had some final words of advice. "You know, the Nazis are scouring the river banks for runaways. I've even heard from people that the Nazis often joke about how many they've found and killed. Perhaps you'd be better advised to head a little way in from the river. I'd suggest heading towards Chernihiv, and then north from there." They all embraced Valia as he left. "Thank you so much, I just wish there was something I can do to repay all of your kindness."

"You can join the partisans in Belarus, and continue to take the fight to our enemy. May God bless you, and give you safe travel Valia." With that she crossed herself several times, as Valia swiftly disappeared into the distance.

Taking Lyudmila's advice, Valia headed north-east towards Chernihiv. A few days later he approached the outskirts of the historic town. The further north he travelled, the friendlier the local people seemed to be towards him, and as he continued on his long walk, he encountered even more people who'd happily offer him shelter for a night.

Spring was a little late arriving, but by now, along with the multitudes of beautiful flowers adorning the gardens and fields, the weather was finally starting to get warmer, and the sources of food in the countryside were becoming more plentiful by the day.

For the next month, Valia walked and walked, and walked some more. He'd managed to evade any further close encounters with the Nazis, but if he wanted to cross into Belarus, he needed to find a way to cross the Dnieper River. There weren't too many bridges in the vicinity, and those bridges that were usable were heavily guarded and patrolled by the Nazis. He needed another way across.

Although the river here was a lot narrower than further downstream, it would still be a big challenge to negotiate. Valia considered swimming, but he wasn't sure he was strong enough, and there was also the potential for treacherous currents, so he decided another option would be needed. Spending a couple of days cautiously investigating the river bank, he eventually spotted a lone rowing boat in a secluded cove. It looked like it was frequently used for fishing, as there were some nets stacked neatly nearby. He couldn't just steal the boat, because there was a dacha overlooking it, and it was obvious somebody was living there. Ideally, he'd like to meet up with the occupants and see if they could take him over, but as had now become second nature to him, Valia scouted the dacha for a little while first, before he decided it looked safe enough to approach.

Without warning, the door flung open and a huge figure of a man stood there. With a deep, gruff voice he asked. "Hey, who are you, and what are you doing on my land?"

In the most pleasant and friendly sounding voice that he could muster, Valia replied. "Hello, my name is Valia and I'm looking to get a ride across the river. Is that something you can help me with?"

The man looked a little perplexed. "How did you get here, there's no tracks leading here?" The man was obviously suspicious of Valia, and his intentions.

"I'm just looking to get across the river safely, nothing more."

The man stepped out of the dacha holding a hunting rifle and pointed it directly towards Valia. "Why would I want to take you across the river, where's your paperwork?"

Valia was starting to get a bit concerned now. Most people he'd met recently had been very amiable, had he become too complacent. He was beginning to wonder if he'd made a catastrophic mistake. "I'm sorry, I don't have my paperwork with me."

With that, the man lowered his weapon and started to chuckle.

"Aha, I was right, you must be one of the runaway soldiers I've heard so much about."

Valia nodded sheepishly.

"I knew it, you're the first one I've seen along here, but a lot of my neighbours have come across them. I've heard that there's a lot of Partisan groups forming up around Minsk, are you heading up to join them? Come inside, I'll get you some tea."

He bellowed into the house, "Irina, we have a guest, get the tea on and open that old box of chocolates."

As Valia entered the house, it was immaculate. There were beautifully arranged flowers in vases, and the windows were flung wide open to fill the house with some fresh air. It felt so familiar, so much like his home.

Irina came over and shook Valia by the hand. She must have been in her early fifties, but could easily pass for being a lot younger. "Lovely to meet you, young man. How are you?"

As they settled on chairs with tatty red cushions around a large, wooden, rectangular table, they were both extremely keen to hear Valia's story. He'd recounted it so many times now, it was becoming second nature to him.

They treated Valia a little like a lost son, and Valia soon found out why. Artem and Irina had lost their only son at the Battle of Bryansk, as he'd been helping to defend the route to Moscow from the Nazis. They just seemed to be pleased to have a nice young man around the house once again.

With his gruff voice, and imposing frame, Artem sounded and looked every inch a giant, and Valia couldn't imagine anybody in their right mind wanting to pick a fight with him. In contrast, Irina seemed tiny, yet she exuded the sense of a very strong woman who obviously held sway over her giant of a husband.

"I'm not sure if you've heard Valia, but the Nazis have put a price on the head of runaway soldiers, so you will need to keep your wits about you. We also heard some news that Comrade Stalin has denounced all soldiers that desert, or surrender to the Nazis, no matter what the circumstances. I think your best course of action right now is to try and find a Partisan group and join it, if you can find one."

"Yes, I was planning to do that anyway. My current plan, once I cross the river is to travel up to, and explore the area around Minsk, and see what I can find there."

Irina interrupted the men's conversation, with a question all mothers liked to ask. "Would you like some food before you go Valia?"

"Oh, that would be great, thanks."

As the men continued to discuss the latest news that Artem was aware of, they enjoyed some deliciously cooked carp, and freshly made salad.

After a pleasant chat, Artem finally announced. "Okay, I think we'll head over at dusk. There's less chance of any Nazi patrol boats being around then, and you should be able to get a few kilometres inland before daybreak, so there's less chance of you being detected there either."

Artem was aware that Valia probably needed to get some rest before crossing. "I suggest you grab a nap now, and I'll wake you when it's time to go."

Valia was sound asleep within seconds of lying down on the soft and very comfortable couch. He felt so relaxed, it really was almost as if he were back home in Yakhrobol.

It didn't last though. His slumber was soon rudely awoken by Irina vigorously shaking him. "The Nazis are here. Quick, you need to hide."

Artem was already outside chatting with the translator for a group of Nazi soldiers, doing his best to buy as much time as possible.

Irina hurried Valia through a couple of doors into a room where straw was piled high and vegetables were stored in sacks.

"Hide under the straw, and just be as quiet as a mouse, they're probably only here to steal more food from us again."

Valia could hear the Nazi soldiers going through each room in turn. They were obviously searching the place. His heart was in his mouth. There wasn't anywhere to run. He pulled out the small sharp knife he was carrying in his boots, and waited.

The door burst open, and he could hear the Nazis talking as they looked around the room. Almost immediately, he could hear thrusts, as bayonets tore into the straw. Thrust after thrust, with one only just missing Valia by centimetres. After a few minutes they stopped, and then he heard the vegetable sacks being dragged out of the room. The soldiers returned a couple of times until all but one of the sacks had been taken.

Soon after that, Valia heard the sound of engines, as their patrol boat sped off again.

Irina came back into the room in a state of high distress. "It's okay Valia, they've gone now."

Valia rose from the straw slowly, and a little shakily and dusted himself off. That really was a close call.

"They don't normally do that. It looks like the Nazis are getting short of food again, and they're basically taking anything they can get their hands on. At least I can get some fish every day so we won't starve, but it really is a big blow to lose most of our vegetables just like that."

Irina was close to tears, the shock of just how close they were to discovering Valia had sunk in. She knew what would happen if they'd found him. Their beautiful house would have been burnt to the ground, and they'd have been hanged or shot. She was shaking uncontrollably.

Artem was hugging her as best he could to give her some reassurance that everything would be fine, but he turned to Valia. "I think we'd better get ready to go now Valia, don't you?"

"I understand, thanks for everything you've done for me." He came over and gave Irina a big hug too.

"Let's go." Artem led Valia down to the foreshore, and they were soon in the boat crossing the river. Their progress was swift as Artem's huge frame powered the boat quickly across the river. Constantly checking up and down the river for other boats, both men were on a high state of alert.

Just as they approached the far river bank, Artem spotted the patrol boat heading back up the river. "Go Valia. Go."

Valia jumped into the river and waded the last few metres ashore, staying as low to the water as possible so as not to be seen.

"I wish you good luck Valia." said Artem as he started heading back into the river, and started lowering his nets into the water, as if he was out fishing.

Valia, managed to get a few meters inland and found some shelter behind a large clump of rocks. He watched as the patrol boat drew up. The soldiers questioned Artem for at least five minutes before they seemed to be happy, and then sped off again up the river. Valia gave Artem a wave as he turned, and headed north west towards Minsk.

As his long walk continued through the rich and beautiful Belarusian countryside, the days seemed to merge into one another. Valia had the routine down to a fine art. At dawn, he'd wake, and reconnoitre the surrounding area. If there was a source of food nearby he'd have a delicious breakfast, if not, he'd check his bearings and head in the general direction of Minsk. Valia accepted any opportunities for food and drink that arose, be that from the surrounding countryside, somebody's garden, or inside somebody's house. As each day eked out its last glorious slither of sunlight, he would scout around for a safe looking place to rest up for the night. That could be under the wide-open skies, in a shed, or possibly in a comfortable bed provided by a kindly stranger.

The gentle warmth of the summer air really made a huge difference to Valia's outlook on life. For the first time since he'd been forced to surrender on that awful, bleak, September day, it really felt good to be alive. Spending most of the time wondering through the thick and bountiful Belarus forests, he also felt reasonably safe from being discovered.

Occasionally, Valia would come across remote houses or

hamlets, but as a general rule, he shied away from the populated areas. It was safer that way.

As the months slowly ticked by, Valia racked up hundreds of kilometres. He'd almost lost track of where he was and where he was heading, but he reckoned he wasn't too far to the east of Minsk by now. He'd heard there were partisan groups active in this part of the country, and he was hoping he'd bump into them one day.

Chapter 10
The Watershed

Since advancing hard past Kremenchug the previous September, Peter and his tank crew had been exceptionally busy. They'd remained part of General von Kleist's 1st Panzer Group for just a short while before re-joining the 16th Panzer Division as they participated in the fierce Nazi advance towards the Sea of Azov, just north of the Black Sea. As usual with the Panzers, they devoured the land at an incredible pace, crossing huge swathes of land in almost no time at all. However, the practical logistics of keeping the advancing forces supplied with all they needed with mainly horse drawn transport was starting to become a huge problem for the Nazi Army, and just a couple of short months after driving through Kremenchug in such a blasé fashion, their advance ground to a sudden halt. In November, the length of the supply lines had become simply untenable, and they were more or less sitting ducks.

As the Soviet forces ranged against them started to counter attack, the Division was only able to retreat courtesy of an emergency resupply from the Luftwaffe. Eventually they settled in the region around the city of Stalino where they spent the bitterly cold and treacherous winter of 1941/42 fighting desperately to hold their defensive positions.

During the few periodic lulls in the fighting, elements of the Division would also take part in anti-partisan operations in the area. Peter and his crew where happy to stay out of the worst of the winter conditions, as inside the tank, they were quite well protected from the biting wind and any rain or snowfall. To help them keep warm in their nicely cocooned environment, they'd even managed to get themselves some Soviet valenki from captured Soviet prisoners.

They did however need to light a fire under the tank each night when it was freezing to stop the oil and fuel in the engine totally freezing up, and also to prevent the tracks freezing solid into the ground. Peter and Werner were usually assigned the task, which they really hated. It involved them having to dig a small trench, then lighting a fire in it, then driving the tank over the trench.

Gloves were one of the most important pieces of clothing during the worst of the winter weather though. With temperatures sometimes well below -30°C, merely touching some freezing metal could result in loss of an unprotected finger or two, as they'd end up stuck solidly to the metal.

After the worst of the winter weather was behind them, it was finally time to move again. As April rolled into May, Hans finally received some good news. "Okay men, I don't know about you but I've had enough of all this retreating and holding a defensive line. I think it's time to take the offensive again, after all, that's what we do best."

The optimism inside the tank was palpable.

"What's the plan Skip?" Wolfgang was keen to know where they were going.

Hans jokingly tested them. "Okay, do you remember a city called Kharkov?"

They all remembered it well, and Werner wasn't overly impressed. "That's the place we took back in late September isn't it. What the hell are we heading back there again for?"

"Good question, well, it seems that the Soviets have launched an offensive and are trying to re-take it, so our boys there need a little extra muscle to help fight them off. Let's get ready, Peter, we'll be rolling in the next ten minutes, any problem with that?"

Peter was in a really positive mood. It was good to be going on the attack again. "Fine by me Skip."

As they approached Kharkov, Wolfgang and Werner were once again in their happy place. There were plenty of tanks and other targets to kill. What wasn't to like?

In the meantime, far away, Valia was busy on his long walk through the beautiful forests of Belarus trying to locate a partisan group he could join. Any partisan group would do. The paths that Valia and Peter were now treading could not be further apart, yet it was only a few short months since Peter had almost crushed Valia to death under the tracks of his trusty tank.

Here in Kharkov, it seemed like Groundhog Day. The Nazis were advancing in great number, and the Soviets were being encircled once again. By mid-June, well over 250,000 additional Red Army soldiers had either been killed or taken prisoner in the regions around the City.

"I've always said it my friends, let's face it, we're simply invincible. We're a special crew, and nobody's going to kill us, ever." Peter was obviously happy with the latest developments. "I know we missed out last year because of the appalling winter, but you've got to say the way things are looking right now, this will be the year we finally kick down Stalin's filthy front door."

The whole crew had been buoyed by the swift victory, and it brought back so many happy memories from the previous year's campaign.

"I'm hoping to have a Schnapps in Red Square for Christmas, what about you Skip?" joked Franz.

"I'll just be happy to get home safely and see my family again." Without realising it, Hans had brought a touch of realism back into the conversation. They'd been away from home an awfully long time now, and the mood dipped a little as they all pondered how their families might be faring back in Germany.

It had come as a bit of a shock to them when the Führer had declared war against the mighty Americans, and they were somewhat concerned how that might affect the folks back home. The British were already making a real nuisance of themselves, having had the temerity to start bombing the Fatherland. Peter had received a letter from his Mother and Father during the winter months and it had mentioned their shock and dismay after hearing that the Royal Air Force had actually dropped bombs on nearby Nürnberg during October.

With Kharkov now safely secured once more, Peter and his crew soon joined in with the new, major summer offensive deep into the southern heartlands of the Soviet Union. *Operation Case Blue* was effectively a follow-up to *Operation Barbarossa,* which had stalled during the winter of the previous year.

The main plan all along had been the seizure of the vitally important oilfields in the Caucasus, and to protect the flanks of this major thrust, a secondary, parallel drive to reach the Volga, near the City of Stalingrad had also been planned.

With the last of the summer sun baking all the tank crews to the verge of heat exhaustion, Peter along with the rest of the 16th Panzer Division finally reached their primary goal of the Volga River, just north of Stalingrad on the 23rd of August.

It wasn't too bad for Hans, at least he was able to get some fresh air when the commanders hatch was open at the top of the tank, but inside the cramped and furnace hot bowels of the tank, despite a few small fans to keep the air circulating, the rest of the crew were simply dripping sweat.

"Any chance of a nice dip in the river then Skip?" was a half joking, half serious request from Werner.

With his usual voice of calm and reason, Hans tried not to

disappoint Werner too much. "If only, unfortunately there's still some hostile forces in the vicinity, so unfortunately we're going to be cooped up in here for a little while yet."

"Peter, let's pull up behind those houses to the left over there please, and then we'll find out where we need to go next."

"No Problem Skip," and Peter deftly placed the tanks in a nicely sheltered location.

The crew took the opportunity to grab a quick drink, and a snack. It was also time to grab another pervitin pill. In the meantime, Hans was liaising with the other tank commanders to formulate their next move.

"So how long do you think it'll take us to clear out this city?" Werner asked.

"Well, based on past experience, I'd say no more than a couple of weeks at the most. At least the weather should be pretty good through into October, so hopefully it won't drag out too long." Peter was certainly being bullish about operations for the weeks to come.

"What's this place actually called? Stalingrad is it?" Werner had no idea.

"I think so, who knows, maybe Stalin will come and defend the place himself." Franz joked, and they all had a giggle.

It was just nice to have a little downtime after the non-stop action they'd experienced getting to the banks of the Volga River.

Hans came off the radio after quite a long chat. "Gentlemen, we'll hold up here for now, it sounds like our fly boys are going to bomb the crap out of the city. Once they've finished softening them up, we'll start our advance. That's likely to be in a day of two by current estimates. In the meantime, let's get some well-deserved rest."

"Could be some great fireworks later on then, I bet that'll make some great viewing". Peter was in high spirits in more ways than one. The crew spent a bit of time relaxing as best they could in a battle zone. They didn't have to wait long though before the action kicked off. Within the hour, the sky was filled with Luftwaffe bombers, and just a few minutes after that, that high explosive and incendiary bombs started to rain down upon the city.

Even where they were, just outside the City itself, the whole tank crew could feel the full percussive effect and shock waves of the bombs as they tore through the heart of the City, killing thousands in the process.

The destruction continued uninterrupted late into the night and throughout the next day. It was colossal, and totally complete. Very few buildings, if any, were left untouched as the City was turned into a writhing sea of fire. The flames devoured everything around them, and the horrible, dark, acrid smoke belched high into the sky. Huge flames roared from the smashed oil storage depots, and even the Volga River was set aflame.

Over the next couple of days, as the beautiful rays of light from sunrise and sunset weaved their way through the harsh, dense smoke, the colours that danced around the sky were simply unbelievable.

"What a great light-show, hopefully it'll be just as good tomorrow?" Franz had been awe inspired by the massive show of Nazi strength, and despite being thrown around the tank a few times, he'd really enjoyed the experience.

Hans, as always was on hand to provide a voice of experience. "Get some rest men, I'm not sure yet if we'll be moving in, or if the Luftwaffe are going to do another repeat show for us tomorrow."

The general consensus from the crew was that they'd be happy to let the Luftwaffe enjoy their little moment of glory, just that little bit longer. They'd certainly seen nothing like it before, and they were all more or less convinced that nothing could possibly survive after such a devastating ordeal. How could anything survive that onslaught?

For the next few days the intensive air raids continued, and the few remaining blocks that had somehow miraculously survived were mercilessly targeted for total destruction.

Once the Luftwaffe had completed their near obliteration of the city, Hans got the command he'd been waiting for. "Okay, let's get ready to roll. We've let those fly boys have their fun, it's now our turn to go and finish the job properly."

As the striking and beautiful hues of the sunrise reflected over the Volga River, the tanks started to roll into Stalingrad. They soon came up against the usual haphazardly determined defence as poorly armed and barely trained defenders would throw themselves against the advance. Peter was enjoying adding to the number of victims he had crushed to death under the heavy metal tracks of his tank. He was in his element. Initially their progress was good, but then something unexpected.

They came under sustained heavy shell fire from what appeared to be Anti-Aircraft guns. As an intense firefight ensued, the pace of the offensive slowed almost to a crawl.

"There's a flash 12 degrees to the right, 120 metres." Hans was calling out possible targets while Wolfgang and Werner were busy loading and firing as fast as they could.

The last time they'd faced such intensive fire was just after advancing past Kremenchug the previous year when they had encountered Valia and his comrades.

Explosions rocked them, and tanks to the left and right were soon engulfed in flames as they took direct hits.

"Don't worry my friends, don't forget we're invincible, they can't kill us." Peter shouted to encourage the rest of the crew.

"Thanks Peter, but it also helps a lot if we can kill them before they kill us." Wolfgang was trying to concentrate on aiming and firing, he didn't want any interruptions, no matter how well intended.

As the day wore on, the advance had almost ground to a complete halt, as the tanks tried to clear out all the anti-aircraft positions. Peter was finding it more and more difficult to manoeuvre as there were mountains of rubble everywhere.

"I thought they were supposed to clear the city for us, all they've done is create an area where it's almost impossible to drive a tank." Peter muttered under his breath as he cursed the aircrews that'd made his current task almost impossible.

By nightfall, the tanks had suffered terribly, with many badly damaged, and some totally destroyed, but at least it looked like the shelling they'd been under had finally been stopped.

As the fighting continued the following day, Hans received a radio call that seemed to shock even him. "You know those big guns we were fighting with yesterday, well our infantry units went to finally clear them out, and have reported that they were all totally manned by girls, no men at all, just young women, and it looks like not one of them left their posts."

"What, you mean we're now fighting the women, are the men too scared?" Werner joked, but he wasn't best happy. They were already more than familiar with facing women fighters, but usually just in very small numbers. This felt very different. For the first time this felt they were no longer fighting an army, they were now fighting an entire population.

For the next week the fighting was heavy, with rogue T-34 tanks springing out at them from the strangest of places. They faced even a few of them that hadn't even been painted. They'd obviously been driven directly out of the factory in the city and straight into the thick of the action.

The tank crews were just happy to have massive air superiority they could count on, if and when needed with the Luftwaffe having more or less total control of the skies, they were able to strike anywhere in the city as, and when they pleased.

As the days slowly ticked by, the fighting started to become more and more intense, and more and more attritional. The almost fanatical zeal with which the Soviet defenders fought for every single centimetre of the City came as a surprise for many on the Nazi side. Soviet soldiers and the civilian population fought side by side as they defended every single building, every floor, every room, they defended any piece of ground they possibly could.

Despite this, the Nazis very gradually continued to advance, and by the end of September they'd reached the 3 giant factories in the City: The *Red October Steel Factory*, the *Barrikady Arms Factory* and the *Stalingrad Tractor Factory*. By now, the joys and speedy advances of the summer months were already a distant memory, and the realities of the coming winter were starting to hit home. The constant, intense, close quarter combat now being fought was totally different to what they were used to, and it was unbelievably stressful. It had become savage, it had become primal, it had become personal.

A huge Nazi offensive against the factories was launched on the 14th of October, and for a time it looked like they were at long last going to finally capture the entire City, as the forward assault groups drove through and finally reached the Volga River, splitting the Soviet forces in two. However, a combination of last-ditch reinforcements bravely crossing the Volga River and extremely tenacious fighting meant that the ground, in and around the factories, were still being heroically defended by literally anybody that could fire a gun.

As the vicious fighting continued into November, the temperatures started to plummet fast, and ice floes stated to fill the Volga River. The Nazis now held 90% of the city. Surely it was only a matter of days now before the defenders were finally crushed.

"I can't stand this for much longer." Werner was at his wits end. The whole crew were.

Hans had been busy on the radio as usual. "At last. I've finally got some news I think you'll like."

"Well, they can't have surrendered, they're still shooting at us. What other good news could there be?" Wolfgang was struggling to control his emotions. The stresses they were all under was intense.

"They're going to replace us with a fresh Division shortly, and we're going to be relocated. They're not exactly sure where yet, but the rumour is that we'll be deployed to France, but we won't know for sure for a few more days. We'll have a couple of months back in Germany where we can go and catch up with families and recuperate whilst they re-equip the entire Division."

There was a silence inside the tank as the message began to sink in. It really did look like they were going to get out of this hellhole alive. They were heading home. Peter was right. They really were indestructible.

Only Peter didn't seem to be happy. "Bastards, somebody else is going to take all the glory off the back of all our hard work, sweat and toil." He wanted to stay there just a little longer, he wanted to savour in the inevitable, hard won, sweet victory. He wanted to kill some more people.

The next morning, as the brutal and barbarous fighting continued for control of the City, Hans ordered Peter to pull back a little from the front line, in preparation for their planned departure in a just a few short days. Some of the Division had already departed, but for now, the tanks had been requested to stay, just a little longer, to act as a temporary reserve.

Although the sun was doing its best to break through, the late autumnal fog was very thick. It felt like snow was in the air too. The tank crew were looking forward to getting home in time for Christmas. It would be cold, but nothing like the full, icy blast of another Russian winter.

As the crew settled down to relax for more or less the first time in almost three months, the radio traffic inexplicably started to pick up.

"Skip, I hope you are getting this?" Franz looked a little perturbed as he handed over the radio the Hans.

"Thanks Franz, yes, I was getting some chatter from the other commanders. I wouldn't worry about it too much for now." With that, Hans was busy for quite a while as he digested the latest updates. After half an hour he gave the crew a very downbeat update. "I'm not sure how accurate the reports we're receiving are, but it sounds like the Soviets are attacking our flanks to the West in huge numbers with what appear to be fresh troops, and large mechanised forces."

"How can that be, haven't we almost crushed them? They can't have any more forces, surely?" Werner asked quizzically.

"That's a very good question Werner. That was my understanding too. I think everybody thought the Soviets were a beaten force. Anyway, Peter, stand by to move, we'll wait for further orders."

Operation Uranus, the new Soviet offensive, had obviously taken the Nazi High Command by complete surprise, as they'd done nothing to defend against it. Their Romanian allies, defending the Nazi flanks to the west of Stalingrad came under savage attacks, first from the North on the 19th of November, and then from separate Soviet armies to the South the following day.

The Romanians, put up some initial resistance, but their inferior equipment and poor morale, as well as the lack of any meaningful mechanised Divisions meant they were quickly overrun, and were soon in headlong retreat in the face of the buoyant, rampaging Soviet forces.

By late on the 22nd of November, and before the Nazi Commanders in Stalingrad had fully realised the full seriousness of their situation and turned their mechanised Divisions to halt the Soviet advances, they found themselves totally encircled, as the Soviet forces linked up at the town of Kalach.

The following day, Hans had some crushing news for the crew. "My friends, I'll give it to you straight. The news isn't great I'm afraid, as you're already aware the Soviets have managed to encircle us in force. General Paulus has requested that we be able to fight our way out, but apparently that buffoon Goering has promised to airlift us the required support we need to keep fighting, so the Führer has forbidden any retreat. I guess it is what it is, and there's not a lot we can do about it, but I'm really sorry, the Christmas that I'd promised you at home isn't likely to happen this year after all."

It was already like a refrigerator in the tank, and the worst of the winter was still to come. Hans could see in the eyes of crew, the very first signs of fear.

Werner couldn't believe it. His mind had already turned to home, and the prospect of staying in Stalingrad any longer was not on his agenda. "Encircled. That's a bit ironic isn't it. We've been doing that to the Soviets since we first attacked them, and now look, we're going to reap the harvest we've sown."

The whole crew knew what happened to the Soviet armies that they'd encircled in the past, and it never ended well for them.

"Do you really think the Luftwaffe can provide all the support we need to keep going?" Peter asked.

There was stony silence. It wasn't looking great.

Over the following weeks the winter threw increasingly hostile weather at them. Temperatures plunged to unbearable lows, blizzards caused almost total whiteouts. It was horrendous. The Luftwaffe did their best with the limited resources at their disposal, but as usual, Goering's hollow promises were proven to be totally unreliable and unrealistic. There was nowhere near the amount of equipment and support material needed to sustain the now totally trapped 6th Army.

As the food stocks ran out in the tank, the mood became more and more morose. The tanks had been frozen solid for a few days, and the crew started to draw lots to determine who should head out to try and find something to eat. As the Soviets slowly and methodically closed the noose around them, all the crew could do was to fire what limited shells and ammunition they had left. Then finally, with all their fuel finally expended, the tank was effectively just a heap of useless junk.

Hans made the only decision he possibly could. "Okay Franz, destroy all the code books and the cipher machine, Wolfgang, make sure anything the enemy might find useful is destroyed. Werner, set up a charge to destroy the tank. We'll need a two-minute fuse. Grab anything warm you can lay your hands on, and any weapons and ammunition that you can carry."

The men followed their orders to the letter, just as they had always done.

With tears in his eyes, Hans made a final address to the crew. "Gentlemen, it's been my absolute pleasure to serve with each and every one of you over the last few years. I am only sorry that I couldn't get you home safely to your families again. The very best of luck for the future. Look after yourselves, and do whatever you can to survive." Almost as an afterthought, although it meant little now, he added "Heil Hitler."

The whole crew had tears in their eyes, as they embraced each other as a crew for one final time. One after another they exited the tank, and ran for whatever shelter and cover they could find. Franz left first, and zig-zagged his way into the ruinous doorway of what was probably once a very impressive looking building. He entered the building slowly and disappeared inside.

Next out was Werner. He made a bee-line for the same building, sprinting as fast as his legs could take him. However, just as he was nearing the doorway he halted dead in his tracks, and his head was thrown backwards. An explosion of blood turning to ice almost immediately filled the air. The crack of a sniper's rifle soon followed.

Wolfgang and Peter, as long-time boyhood friends, decided to make a run for it together. They sprinted hard and fast in the opposite direction to the others. With their hearts racing, and the adrenalin pumping harder than ever, they approached what looked like a badly smashed up building. It was difficult even to breath as the air was so cold, and the wind was roaring around them like howling wolves. They heard the crack of the sniper's rifle, and were relieved not to feel the deathly embrace of the bullet that had flown directly between them.

Hans knew the game was up. As far as he was concerned there was nothing more he could do, there would be no future. He would never see his pretty young wife and three-year-old son ever again. He was disconsolate. He said a short prayer for them, then he lit the fuse. He waited to be sure the fuse was working, then drew his revolver for the final time. He placed it inside his mouth, closed his tearful eyes and after pausing for a few seconds while happy images of his family flashed through his mind, he pulled the trigger.

Just a minute later the hulk of his trusty tank was ripped to shreds as the explosion deep inside its belly tore it to pieces.

Peter was looking hard. "Did you see which direction Hans ran?"

Wolfgang shook his head solemnly. "I didn't see him leave the tank at all. I did hear a muffled shot though."

Tears formed in their ears as they registered what had just happened. They needed to have their wits about them now. They were no longer tank crew, they were infantrymen. They needed to be extremely cautious and careful. Peter and Wolfgang were really unhappy to find that it was even colder outside the tank than it had been inside it, and the tears started to freeze on their faces.

"Where the hell do we go from here?" Wolfgang whispered.

"I'm not sure, but if we go outside, you can guarantee that a sniper is going to hit us at some point. Let's check the rest of the building, maybe some of our infantry are in here somewhere. I'll take that door, you look over there."

Wolfgang headed off to see what he could find in the room next door. As he opened a door, an explosion sent snow, dust and rubble throughout the room and blew Peter off his feet, flying backwards onto the floor. The door had been booby trapped. It took Peter a little while before he managed to lift himself up, and look around. All he could see were parts of Wolfgang spread all around the room.

For the next three or four days, Peter moved as carefully as he possibly could between the remains of once proud buildings, that had now been largely pulverised into rubble. If he did venture out, he was always very careful with his movements, to be sure he didn't attract the attention of any snipers in the area. Despite moving around to keep as warm as he possibly could, he didn't come across a single living Nazi, he did, however pass several that were already dead.

Every night was indescribably cold, and he just couldn't get any sleep at all. It was simply too painful, and all he could hear were Russian voices chattering nearby. When daylight finally came, he could barely feel some parts of his body at all, especially his toes. They'd just gone totally numb.

Peter now felt totally insignificant, and was starting to see the world for what it was. It started to finally hit home to him that all the lies he'd been fed throughout his life were absolute rubbish. He was not invincible after all. There was no Master race, how could there be if the Soviets were able to function like normal, whilst his countryman were struggling so badly.

At last, Peter started to understand. There was only life and death, and life is something very fragile, something that needed to be nurtured and treasured, not destroyed on a whim, and certainly not based on a pack of lies.

It was all too late now of course. He'd wasted his life believing the mendacity that people he respected and even adored had fed him. He had totally bought into their deceit, believing every exaggerated falsehood they made. The real tragedy was that a whole nation had, as so often does, been very cleverly duped by immoral and unscrupulous leaders.

What was he to do? It was Christmas Eve. He really should've been at home, back in Germany with his family. He didn't feel very festive at all. He was hungry, he was thirsty, he was exhausted, he was freezing cold, in fact he was struggling to do anything at all. He could hear the advancing Russians systematically working their way through the nearby buildings. They'd certainly find him tomorrow. He had nowhere to run. He needed to be ready and alert before dawn. As darkness fell, Peter slowly, and for the first time in many days, finally shivered himself to sleep.

He never woke. The next morning, as the Soviet soldiers were clearing their way through the building, they kicked Peter, to check if he was still alive or not. He was frozen solid.

Chapter 11
The Partisans

As the Nazi war machine scythed its way through much of eastern Europe in the summer of 1941, and then again in 1942, some things had remained a constant and impenetrable obstacle to the Wehrmacht. With their many dangerous bogs and treacherous areas of quicksand spread almost anywhere within their vast domains, the extensive, and very beautiful forests of Belarus were somewhere that the Nazis soon learnt to fear entering.

It was these very fears that prompted many Partisan groups to base themselves deep within the hearts of these wild and remote fortresses. No matter how hard they tried, the Nazis could not tame the wilderness.

After a relatively comfortable summer and autumn walking around Belarus, with the warm weather and an abundance of food in the countryside, Valia, once more, started to feel the cold winds in the air. The occasional snow flurry resulted in a beautiful white blanket covering to the trees, giving them a picture postcard appearance.

Another long, hard winter was looming, and it was looming very soon. He knew that he needed to be prepared for it as best he could, however, after all he'd endured and witnessed over the

193

previous year his primary aim was still to join up with a partisan group somewhere. He was desperate to take the fight back to the Nazis.

The previous week he'd met some travellers, and one of them had furtively handed Valia a special, secret leaflet, and it had given him hope. It'd been published by a partisan group calling themselves *The Red Banner*, and it was calling for any able-bodied person with military experience to come and join them in their fight against the Nazis in the forests to the south-east of the town of Cervien. It was the information that Valia had long been searching for.

Valia was already east of Minsk and in the Cervien region, when he heard the sound of horses rapidly approaching him along the narrow track. His eyes darted back and forth along the track, and also towards the nearby trees. Were they Partisans or were they Nazis? Almost instantly Valia dived into the trees. He didn't want to take any risks, especially now. Had they spotted him? He really wasn't sure.

As the four riders galloped closer, Valia squinted against the suns dazzling rays. They certainly weren't Nazis, but were they Partisans? There was only one way to find out. It was now or never. As they approached his position, he rose holding up a hand and slowly and very determinedly stepped out onto the track.

The riders pulled up in front of him, and a couple of them immediately swung the rifles that were slung over their backs to point directly at Valia. As the riders looked him up and down curiously, one of them asked Valia in a strong commanding voice. "What are you doing here?"

Valia felt the hairs on the back of his neck standing on end, and his heart was racing. "Hello, my name's Valia." He hesitated for a second while he briefly contemplated whether he was doing the right thing. He simply had to risk it. "I was wandering if you've heard of *The Red Banner* group?".

The leader started laughing, looking Valia up and down some

more. "And what may I ask is your business with *The Red Banner* group?"

Valia felt very exposed, and exceedingly vulnerable. The rifles were still pointing directly at him, and he still didn't know if they were friendly or not.

"I saw a pamphlet asking for people with military experience to come and join them somewhere in these woods."

With that, the leader clicked his fingers and one of the riders raised his rifle, and slung it back around his back again before dismounting his horse and striding over towards Valia.

The leader leant forward on his horse. "And what military experience may I ask, is that?"

"I was in the 56th Air Defence Battalion and we were involved in the defence of the City of Kremenchug back in 1941. Well, I was, until our Battalion was wiped out by Nazi tanks."

Valia seemed to have caught the leader's attention. "Search him Ilia."

Spreading his arms wide, Ilia frisked Valia quite roughly before pulling out the small knife from Valia's boot. "He's clean."

The leader smiled, however his next question hit Valia like a punch in the stomach. "We lost Kremenchug well over a year ago now. What dare I ask have you been doing since then, putting your feet up why your comrades have been fighting and dying?"

Valia was pretty angry at the insinuation, and it showed in his face. How dare he imply that he, Valia, wasn't a fighter. After all he'd been through, how could they possibly imply that. He wasn't having any of it, and with that Valia detailed his traumatic year for the horsemen to hear.

When Valia finished, the leader nodded sagely. Before responding, he contemplated things for a little while. "Okay, you know what, I think I believe you Valia. Ilia, he can ride with you, put a blindfold on him and let's head back to base. They can do a thorough debrief there."

Ilia placed a smelly rag over Valia's eyes so that he couldn't see, before he remounted his horse. He then trotted over and offered his hand, before pulling Valia up right behind him. "Hold Tight, we won't be stopping if you fall off." Ilia seemed a little irritated at having to share his horse.

The horsemen kicked on, and they were soon galloping on their way again. It must have been just a 15-minute ride before the horsemen carefully negotiated the cleverly concealed entrance into a large opening in the trees. They were particularly careful to cover their tracks as they entered.

Ilia seemed pleased to get Valia off his horse, and jumped down after him, removing the blindfold. Valia looked around him in amazement. There must have been at least 100 men and women busying themselves on various tasks. With its tell-tale dug-out appearance, and a flat roof made with branches, and covered with sods of earth for insulation, it looked like a new Zemlyanka was being constructed over to his right, and he could make out several more of them dotted around the clearing. Valia also spotted several well concealed defensive posts with heavy machine guns trained on all approaching paths and tracks. This was clearly a sizeable base, but was it *The Red Banner* group?

"Follow me Valia." The leader of the riders headed down the entrance into the bowels of one of the very well concealed buildings. Valia followed close behind. It was very smoky and quite dark inside the Zemlyanka.

A strongly built man who looked to be in his fifties was studying a large map on a huge table. He looked up and saw the men standing near the doorway. "Ah, you're back Ivan. What have you got to report?"

Ivan saluted, "Sir, today's patrol was clear, no new signs of Nazi activity that I think we need to be worried about. However, we did pick up another individual who seems to be interested in joining the group. Let me introduce you to Valia Ermolaev. We picked him up on one of the approach tracks. We didn't spot anybody else, and as he claims to be a former Red Army soldier, I decided to bring him in to see what you think."

Within seconds of Ivan's voice trailing off, a loud voice boomed out from the back of the Zemlyanka. "Valia, is that you? Is that really you Valia? I can't believe it. I thought they'd killed you along with the other prisoners in that convoy".

Valia knew that voice instantly. It was unmistakable. It was Dmitry. Dmitry swiftly barged his way over to Valia, and with tears running down both of their faces, they embraced each other just like long lost brothers.

"So, tell me Dmitry, is this somebody you can vouch for?"

"It is Sir. I can confirm that this is indeed Valia Ermolaev. I had the pleasure of fighting shoulder to shoulder with this hero in Kremenchug. Valia, let me introduce you to General Alexey Kanidevich Flegontov, the leader of *The Red Banner* group."

General Flegontov looked Valia up and down before shaking him by the hand. "Welcome to our Group Valia. Over the last few months, Dmitry has proven to be a great asset to our Group, and if you're anything like him, I'm sure you'll fit in here really well."

Valia was too emotional for words. He was still trying to come to terms with the fact that his great friend Dmitry was still alive.

The General was keen to get back to the map. "Dmitry, can you show Valia around the camp. I assume you'll be able to find him a place to sleep in your Zemlyanka? Also, I'll leave it up to you to get him up to speed with our current operations and procedures, especially the security procedures. Oh, and make sure you get him some fresh clothes, and for god's sake, get him cleaned up a bit. Off you go, we'll talk again tomorrow. I think the two of you have some catching up to do."

As Valia and Dmitri left the smoke-filled building, they could hear Flegontov. "Thank you, Ivan, come over here and check the map with me. We'll be initiating a new operation tomorrow and I want you to lead it."

Dmitry took his time showing Valia around the camp, and introduced him to everyone he knew. However, they spent most of the time recalling their adventures since they'd last seen each other. Dmitry was really impressed how Valia had managed to overcome each hurdle on his journey north.

For his part, Dmitry explained how he'd managed to hide in the forest after escaping the Nazi convoy too. He'd been convinced that Valia must have been executed with the other prisoners, that's why he was so surprised, and so delighted to see him again. He'd also spent a few months heading north on foot, but he'd been very lucky in that he hadn't had any meaningful encounters with the Nazis anywhere on his journey. Very luckily, he'd bumped into a couple of members of *The Red Banner* group about three months earlier, so he'd been in camp for a little while, and had actually been out on a couple of active operations already.

That evening, safely ensconced within their Zemlyanka, they shared some vodka, and had a good chat about everything.

"So, Dmitry, what do you know about this General Flegontov, is he a good leader?"

"Well, from what I know, he seems to be a bit of a legend around here. He's no spring chicken any more is he, but apparently in the time of the Civil War he fought in the far East against the Japanese and also against the White Army, who were strong in that region. He set up and commanded many partisan forces in that area at that time, so he's got plenty of hard-earned experience as well as a pretty good track record when it comes to Partisan groups and irregular warfare. He created some partisan groups near Moscow earlier in the year, and not so long ago he unified a few local groups around here to set up a partisan Division called *For the Motherland.*"

Valia pondered that for a few seconds. "So, we're working with other partisan groups?"

"Yes, I guess so. General Flegontov also commands the *Boevoy*, and the *Flame* partisan groups, so where necessary, we have the ability to conduct some coordinated operations using men from each group. Having said that, we're still distinct groups, so we can still do our own operations when we want to."

Valia was keen to sign up as soon as possible. "Who do I need to see about signing up?"

A rueful looking Dmitry slowly shook his head. "Valia, my good friend, because we've both been prisoners of war, we can't officially join the group at the moment. If anything, we're quite lucky they haven't taken Stalin's preposterous Order 270 literally."

Valia looked a little puzzled. "What the hell is Order 270?"

"Haven't you heard of it? It's the one that classifies any soldier that surrenders to the Nazis as a traitor, and they, along with their entire families, will suffer accordingly. You know, if Stalin was here, he'd probably be more than happy to shoot both of us on the spot. And it wouldn't just be us, there are quite a few ex-prisoners of war amongst this fabulous group of fighters."

"Luckily, General Flegontov is a pragmatist, and appreciates that we're much more useful to him alive than we would be if we were buried in some hole. Don't worry, I'll log your details with the General's administrative staff tomorrow, at least we'll both be unofficial members of the group."

Both men downed another vodka each, and continued in deep discussion early into the next morning before tiredness finally overcame them both.

Although Valia was still keen to see some action as soon as possible, he first needed to get familiar with his new comrades, and help out around the camp. He spent the next week helping construct a new Zemlyanka, cutting and shaping the wood, and then helping turf the roof once the framework was in place. He was also soon busy helping to manufacture several improvised explosive devices.

With the cold wind biting and swirling around menacingly, and the soft, white snow coating the ground all around, much of the time was spent in their self-constructed shelters, talking, and singing and planning, but periodically, patrols would head out to cause as much mayhem to the Nazis as possible.

Finally, over a week after arriving, Valia was summoned to General Flegontov's Zemlyanka. "Ah, good morning Valia, good to see you. I hope you've managed to settle in well. I've heard some very complimentary things about your work with us so far, so today is the day we'll find out just how well you're going to cope on active operations. You're going to ride out with Dmitry, Ivan and Ilia to destroy the Minsk to Smolensk railway line. Ivan will lead the operation. Dmitry and Ilia will lay the charges, whilst you provide cover. Ivan, I'll leave the rest of the details for you to fill in. The very best of luck gentlemen."

As they slowly strode out of the leaders Zemlyanka, Ivan called "Ten minutes at the horses. Get kitted up. See you there."

With snow now falling heavily, and the bitingly cold eastern wind showing no signs of abating, the men made sure they were wrapped up warm before picking up several belts of ammunition, a couple of bags of explosives, and a mix of rifles and sub-machine guns.

As they gathered near the horses Ivan ran a final checklist. "Okay, Ilia, you've got the mines, yes?"

"Yes, I've got them sir."

"Dmitry, you've got the fuses, yes?"

"I have them, sir."

"Okay, Valia, welcome along, make sure you keep up, and keep a watchful eye for anything suspicious at all times. Let's go."

The four horses started to canter out, with clouds of warm water vapour billowing from their nostrils in the freezing conditions. The group were soon galloping along at a good pace, with Ivan taking point, and Ilia the rear.

Valia was excited and nervous at the same time. He was praying for a successful outcome, and was expecting nothing less. As the horses ate up the ground beneath them, the men did their best to keep as warm as they possibly could against the biting wind.

After about 30 minutes riding hard, Ivan slowed down, and indicated for them to pull over. Valia was just happy that Ivan was leading, as he'd have needed to check the map several times en route to find where they were.

As they slowly rounded a corner, there it was. The target was large, and it was clear. A railway embankment stood above them, directly ahead.

"Okay, Valia, tie up the horses, and cover us as best you can. You two ready, let's go."

With that, the three men headed off as fast as they could go in the deep, thick snow. There were no signs of the Nazis anywhere, but Valia was on a high state of awareness, and had his sub-machine gun ready for action, just in case.

As the men slowly made their way up the steep embankment, Valia wished he was with them, he felt somewhat insignificant, but he knew his role was important, and he needed to make sure the horses were ready for the getaway. He'd surely be in the thick of action soon enough.

Valia watched intently as the men first primed the explosives, and then attached them onto a sleeper, directly under the line on both sides of the track. The whole operation took less than ten minutes, and the men were soon making their way back. Dmitry stumbled and ended up rolling head over heel a long way down the embankment. The others soon followed and before long, they were back with Valia. Dmitry smiled widely. "That was fun, but coming down that embankment was bloody painful."

Ivan checked his watch. "Okay, there should be a train here in five minutes time, let's mount up, but we'll stay here a few minutes longer, just to make sure we get it."

The unmistakable sound of a stream locomotive grew louder as it approached exactly at the expected time. The men looked on with bated breath. It was almost there. Just a few short seconds more. Then there was a massive explosion. The pressure fuses felt the full weight of the train and the locomotive was violently thrown off the tracks by the full force of the explosives. The tracks were utterly destroyed, whilst the locomotive ripped itself apart as it crashed and cavorted its way down the embankment, closely followed by all the wagons that dutifully followed the locomotive.

Valia was filled with excitement. It was the first time he'd witnessed such a successful act against the Nazis. It really felt fantastic, and the whole group were euphoric. As the broken loco-motive hissed steam and fire into the air as it settled at the base of the embankment, Valia could hear the screams of the crew, and the Nazi guards on the train. There must have been at least 20 wagons of valuable weapons and equipment that wouldn't be going to the front any time soon.

Ivan, waited until all the wagons were off the track and destroyed, then turned to the men. "Good job comrades, let's go home." With that, they kicked off and headed away from the scene of the carnage. Galloping through the snowfall as if they were ghosts on the wind, the horses brought their riders safely home again.

As they dismounted, Ivan came over to Valia, and shook him by the hand. "Very well done today Valia, a good piece of work for your first mission. I'm proud to call you a comrade."

The four men made their way into Ivan's Zemlyanka, and entered to a round of boisterous applause. The hot smoky air inside hit them immediately, and they quickly pulled off their thick hats, coats and gloves.

"Get me a bottle of vodka and four glasses please." Ivan was happy, and he wanted to celebrate the successful operation with his comrades. As they thawed themselves out near the piping hot stove, they warmed their insides with a few vodkas. It was a great evening. Patriotic and partisan songs abounded throughout the evening, it was a night for celebrations.

Over the next few weeks, the worst of the winter soon started to freeze everything in its all-encompassing grasp. Life in the camp revolved around making explosives, printing propaganda leaflets, eating, drinking and singing, and most importantly, staying warm.

There were frequent patrols, usually in pairs or foursomes, but occasionally lone riders would also head out, including Dmitry. The group continually needed to know the movement of the Nazi forces, and what they were doing.

A week or two earlier, Valia had been horrified on one reconnaissance mission into the small local town of Cervien to see 20 innocent young men hanging on makeshift gallows in the market square. Around one of the poor soul's neck was a large, very rough, wooden placard with the very badly scribbled message "These men have paid the price for the cowardly actions of the so-called partisans. If these heinous actions continue, more will pay the ultimate price for those cowardly vermin." They had obviously been hanging in the square for several days and nobody was allowed to take them down. It was awful. They had frozen solid in the freezing wind.

At regular intervals, small groups of raiders would head out from the camp to destroy railways, and bridges. Valia gradually notched up more and more operations, and as time went by, he started taking a more prominent role in those operations.

Instead of the typical revelry you'd expect from a Russian New Year, the celebrations ushering in 1943 were not surprisingly somewhat muted in the camp. The fighters did share a few glasses of vodka, but certainly nothing extravagant.

General Flegontov was starting to get a little worried and called the senior members of the group, which now included Valia, to his Zemlyanka. Standing behind his huge desk he issued them with a slightly concerning update.

"The reports I am getting from our patrols, and also from the other partisan groups in the area indicate that the Nazi forces have been reinforced and there's every indication that they'll be undertaking some kind of operation in the area very soon. We'll need to be on our guard. Ivan, can you step up the number of daily patrols we are sending out. We certainly don't want to be caught with our pants down."

"Sir, who have we heard from so far?" asked Ivan.

"General Korolev of The First Osipovichi Partisan Brigade has noticed additional police units in his area. General Volkov of the For Soviet Belarus group is reporting additional Nazi troops in his area, and all the other group leaders are reporting a similar situation."

"Okay, that sounds like a large-scale operation happening sometime soon to me." Ivan noted. "Our own patrols have also indicated some heightened activity from the Nazis too. We'll keep any eye out for anything likely to be a problem for us, but as well as increased patrols, I'll order increased perimeter checks around the camp for now."

General Flegontov quickly concluded the meeting, and sent the men on their way. "Thank you, Ivan. It's good to see you are on the ball as always. Thank you, men, continue with your normal activities for now, but be prepared for action at any time."

Just a few days later, on a bitterly cold morning, on the 6th of January, with snow falling all around, the radio traffic in General Flegontov's Zemlyanka went into overdrive. Reports started to flood in form all the partisan groups in the area. A massive cordon of Nazi Army and local police had surrounded the forests where many of the partisan's groups were located.

The partisan groups near the towns of Osipovichi and Babruysk to the south-east had been caught cold, and were under significant attack, and the infamous SS Dirlewanger Brigade, largely made up of convicted criminals, were heavily involved. With a notorious reputation for its extreme brutality, the SS Dirlewanger Brigade specialised in anti-partisan operations, but also revelled in the mass murder of civilians throughout Nazi-occupied Eastern Europe.

General Flegontov immediately ordered his fighters into combat formations, and for most of them to leave the camp and fight their way out of the encirclement if at all possible. As usual, Valia and Dmitry were side by side as they rode out of the camp with several of the detachments dispersing into different directions.

It didn't take long for some very heavy firefights to erupt throughout the region, as the different partisan groups fought for their lives. Valia and Dmitry were heavily involved, with both racking up numerous kills each as the partisan's groups tried to break out of the encirclement.

The fierce fighting continued for several days until the Nazi forces felt they'd finally drawn the sting from the partisans and withdrew from the area. It was certainly a costly few days for the fighters, and even more so for some in the local population.

The fighters started hearing harrowing stories about what'd happened in the region during the Nazi offensive, but it wasn't until General Flegontov called a meeting after a couple of days that the full extent of the carnage was laid bare.

"Comrades, thank you for returning for duty again so swiftly. As you probably know by now, it would appear that our Nazi enemies have finally withdrawn. I've been talking with the commanders of the other groups in the area, and we've tabulated as best we can the costs of the last few days."

"Nine partisan camps had been totally destroyed, and a huge amount of equipment captured, however the worst news from our perspective is that over 1,000 of our fighters were killed in the engagements."

"What I find most difficult to stomach though are the costs to our civilian comrades. Many villages were totally burnt to the ground, including Novaya Piva, Kobzevichi, Novye Lyady and Starye Lyady. Apparently the Dirlewanger Brigade carried out executions in many of the settlements in the Osipovich district, and the village of Tadulichi was totally destroyed. A newly built village called Makovye was also totally burnt to the ground, but here, over 250 of its residents were locked into a barn, and then burnt alive. For the life of me, I still can't believe anybody would commit such a heinous act as that."

"As well as these acts of barbarity, the villages of Veselovo, Britsalovichi and Bolshaya Gorozha were also turned to ashes, with as far as we know, over 900 civilians shot by the Dirlewanger Brigade in those settlements."

"As of today, we know of at least 20 settlements that were totally wiped off the map, with around 1,000 civilians killed, and a further 1,000 taken away as forced labour."

"Let these animals burn in hell I say. The sooner we can drive them from our homeland, the better. Ivan, from tomorrow, we resume operations as much as normal. Is that okay?"

"Yes, Sir, I'll make sure we'll plan a suitable response for any Nazis or collaborators we find."

With that, the meeting finished, and everyone headed back to their Zemlyanka's through the thick, clingy snow.

Valia turned to Dmitry. "Is there no end to this Nazi nightmare. After what we endured in Kremenchug, I thought it couldn't get any worse, but it seems there is no end to their depravity."

Dmitry was speechless. He couldn't believe the news. If he hadn't seen a couple of the destroyed villages with his own eyes, he'd never have believed it.

As the winter wore on, the news from elsewhere finally started to sound a lot more positive than it had done for an awfully long time. The big one of course came on the 3rd of February, with the news of a monumental victory over the Nazis at Stalingrad.

Having capitulated in the city the previous day, it was finally the proof they'd been waiting for that the Nazis could and would be beaten. There were raucous celebrations around the camp that day, and some very sore heads the following morning.

One February afternoon, the senior members of the group, were all called to General Flegontov's Zemlyanka. The General was there, smiling broadly, and he warmly welcomed everybody that could fit into the building. Standing next to him, making small talk to some of the staff was Ivan.

Once everybody was in, the General raised his arm to signal silence. "Gentlemen, I think you all know my number two, Major Ivan Zakharovich Kuznetsov well enough by now. Well, today is a very proud day for me. I have watched over the last year how Ivan has grown and matured as a commander, a soldier, and as a man, and I'm now more than convinced that he's ready for a new role. Today, I am delighted to announce the Ivan is being officially promoted into the role of commander of *The Red Banner* group."

A chorus of cheers and applause erupted all around the building.

"Oh, and before anybody asks, I will be remaining as commander of the *For the Motherland* Division. Where are the vodkas, let's celebrate?"

It didn't take too long before the fighters were soon singing patriotic songs. There were some fabulous tenor, baritone and bass voices on display and with the natural, rich harmonies that resounded throughout the building, the atmosphere and mood had become almost electric.

Valia loved to sing, and had such a distinctive voice, that everyone knew when he sang. Dmitry on the other hand was pretty tone deaf, so he only joined in the singing after having sunk several vodkas.

Each partisan group had their own favourite songs they enjoyed singing, but one of the most popular was written by *Alexei Alexandrovich Surkov* in 1941 and simply called *"In the dugout"*:

Fire is beating in a small stove,
On the logs there is tar, like a tear.
And the accordion sings to me in the dugout
About your smile and your eyes.
About your smile and your eyes.

Bushes whispered to me about you
In the snow-white fields near Moscow.
I want you to hear
How my living voice yearns.
How my living voice yearns.

You are now far, far away,
Between us there is snow and snow.
It's not easy for me to reach you, and to death, four
    steps.

And to death, four steps.

Sing, harmonica, in spite of the blizzard,
Call the lost happiness.
I feel warm in the cold dugout
From my unquenchable love.
From my unquenchable love.

Fire is beating in a small stove,
On the logs there is tar, like a tear.
And the accordion sings to me in the dugout
About your smile and your eyes.
About your smile and your eyes.

Whenever that song was sung, everyone joined in without fail, even Dmitry, and after one stirring rendition of the song, there was a slight lull in proceedings whilst most of the fighters downed another vodka. In the meantime, Ivan came over and sat with them.

"Gentlemen, have you heard the good news?"

Valia and Dmitry looked at each other quizzically. "What good news would that be, Sir?" asked Dmitry.

"Okay, as you both know by now, just because you were former prisoners of war, under Order 270, you were both technically classified as traitors, and therefore we couldn't officially let you join our group. Well, there's been some great news on that front. The High Command have just announced an amnesty for all prisoners of war, regardless of what they have done in the past, as long as they join up and serve the Soviet cause."

Valia and Dmitry looked at each other again quizzically. "Does that mean we can officially join the group now, Sir?" asked Dmitry.

"Well, in my considered opinion, being an active member of *The Red Banner* group would certainly be serving the Soviet cause. So yes, it does. Congratulations men, may I be the first to officially welcome you both to the group."

They were both so relieved, they grabbed each other in a huge bear hug, it was the news that they'd long been hoping for. With big smiles all around, they downed a vodka that tasted sweeter than any before. As Valia looked around the room, General Flegontov caught his eye. He had a huge smile across his face, and he raised his glass, and nodded in Valia's direction, before downing his drink.

The songs continued, and predictably, the last song was *The Partisan Song*. Everybody joined in at the top of their voices:

> We went into action in the darkest of nights,
> To crush the insidious enemy from our sights,
> We were seething with unquenchable anger,
> We did not value our lives, what did they matter.
> We sneaked up on the enemy's camp,
> The command was given "Forward!",
> Our friend the machine gun started singing a cheerful
> song.
> In the deadly battle, the enemy fled as far as he
> could see.
> The last salvo came in pursuit, we flew into the
> village.
> The winds whistled and the bullets were angry.
> The bloody battle was all around,
> My comrade suddenly fell, Shot by a fatal bullet.
> Farewell comrade, brave warrior, let this evil storm
> pass.
> High honour, our brave red partisan.

As the weeks ticked by, winter slowly loosened its vice-like grip over the countryside, and the raids by Valia and his comrades gradually increased, as did their intensity and range. Larger groups started being deployed, and they ventured further afield.

On the 11th of March, General Flegontov himself led a contingent of over 100 fighters from several partisan groups to the

Osipovichy region where they planned to attack and destroy an important road bridge across the Svislach River. Having travelled overnight, the partisans hoped to surprise a team of Nazi engineers that were there, busy strengthening the bridge ready to accommodate tanks.

As always, General Flegontov led the attack from the front. At the appointed hour, the Partisans started to swarm down a hill towards the bridge where the Nazi engineers were hard at work. They returned fire as best they could, but it was hopeless, they were totally outnumbered by the partisans.

As they closed in on the bridge for the final kill, partisans to the left of the group inexplicably started to fall in large numbers. It took the General a few seconds to fully grasp the situation. Approaching fast from behind some houses to the left were Nazi soldiers. There were lots of them. Then, they were coming from the right too. It was a trap.

General Flegontov was stunned. "Where the hell did they come from?" He called over to Ivan. "Lead the retreat and get the men home, I'll do my best to hold them off for as long as I can."

General Flegontov, along with around 20 of his most loyal fighters formed an ad hoc defensive line, and managed to hold off the withering Nazi gunfire and advances long enough for the bulk of the partisan force to disappear back into the forests. Despite their heroic defence, the General and his men were eventually cut down.

It was without doubt a body blow to the *For the Motherland* partisan Division. The cool, experienced, calculating head and logistical genius of the Division had just been severed. It was a disaster.

The inquisitions and soul searching went on for several days after the exhausted and demoralised remnants of the raid finally arrived back at their base camp. How could there have possibly been that many Nazi soldiers, just sitting there, waiting for them? It had been a deadly trap. How was it possible?

As far as the men in *The Red Banner group* were concerned there must have been an informant in one of the other groups. It was impossible to say who, but investigations would continue apace. In the meantime, Ivan called all the senior partisans together for a meeting.

"Comrades, as we mourn our great leader, General Flegontov, we must continue the fight in his honour. We need to re-double our efforts, and hit the Nazis as hard as we can."

The assembled fighters were still shaken, but the rallying call had the desired effect. It snapped everyone's concentration back to their reason for being. They had to fight the invading Nazis, and hit them where it hurt most.

"Dmitry, you lead the patrols today, Valia, you can lead them tomorrow. I want to get on top of what the Nazis are up to, and we also need to know when the next train shipments are scheduled."

Over the next few weeks, the raids increased in their ferocity and intensity, as more and more fighters joined the partisan ranks. Valia and Dmitry would often ride out together, and between them, they'd been involved in the destruction of several trains, as well as in the ambush of several Nazi troop concentrations.

As the summer months ushered in much more clement weather, Ivan called his senior fighters to his Zemlyanka to discuss a new operation.

"As you all know, the Nazis are coming under a lot of pressure from our brave comrades in the Red Army. The basic upshot of all this is that the Nazis are trying to increase the men and materials that they are sending to the front line, with the majority of it travelling by rail. Recent reports from the North indicate that they're now running another armoured train to support the normal trains. We've been asked to take it out."

Valia looked around the room, there was a look of trepidation on some of the faces. They all knew that these lumbering beasts were hard to kill. With armoured wagons and large guns, they packed quite a punch, and that was without the large number of soldiers that would normally travel on them.

Ivan pointed to a place on the large map covering the table in the centre of the room. "This is where we're going to hit them. Ilia will lead the raid, and he'll select around 30-40 of you to join him. Ilia, I'll let you go through all the logistics, but you need to meet the local resistance fighters here at 15:00, and they'll guide you to your attacking positions, ready to strike before 16:00 on Wednesday. I wish you the very best of luck for a successful outcome my comrades."

Valia had taken a mental note of the target area. It was a small town called Zhodzina, with the Plisa River running through its centre, and it sat about 60 kilometres north of their camp. It would likely take them a good couple of days to get there by foot, especially with the need to remain hidden from any Nazi patrols.

Ilia called Dmitry and Valia over to his Zemlyanka to discuss this major raid in more detail.

"Ah, there you are, thanks for coming comrades. I guess you'll have figured out by now that we'll be heading off to Zhodzina at dawn tomorrow. However, the main reason I've asked you here is because I want you to lead two separate groups in the attack. Dmitry, I want you to lead the main attack on the armoured train with around 20 fighters on the main line, whilst Valia, I'd like you to lead a backup group of around 15 fighters. Your main job will be to wait under cover near the bridge where the branch line crosses the Plisa River, and deal with any Nazi counter-attack that may come from that area. You also have leeway to join in the main attack if there's no immediate counter attack from the Nazis. Are you okay with that?"

Both Dmitry and Valia nodded to affirm their agreement.

"Great, get your kit together, and get a good night's sleep. We have important work to do tomorrow."

With that Dmitry headed off to make sure he had enough explosives and fuses for the mission, while Valia made sure his men had plenty of ammunition for their rifles, and sub-machine guns.

It was a beautifully warm and bright Tuesday morning with hardly a cloud in the sky, as the golden hues of the sun ushered in a new day. With the dawn chorus of birds chirping away happily in the trees, the large contingent of fighters started their trek north.

With the majority of the fighters on foot, Zhodzina was a two-day trek, and the first of those passed without any incident of note. As night-time approached, they found a secluded area of woodland and bivouacked safely for the night.

The following day the fighters made good time and were soon homing in on their rendezvous point with the Zhodzina resistance fighters, just to the South west of the town. With the main body of fighters safely hidden in nearby woodland, Ilia, Valia and Dmitry approached a couple of nondescript looking men who were chatting next to a sign that still proclaimed the town in its Russian name of Жóдино.

Ilia broke the ice. "Excuse me, I believe that you might be expecting a package from Ivan, is that correct?"

One of the men very carefully scrutinised Ilia, then Valia and then Dmitry in turn. "Good afternoon, indeed we are, we were expecting a slightly larger package though. I trust the rest of the package is nearby?"

"Yes, they're in the woodland over there." Ilia smiled and pointed in the direction where the rest of the fighters were waiting.

"Good, let me introduce myself. My name is Sergei, and this is my good friend Georgy."

The men exchanged warm handshakes before Sergei continued. "The latest news we have from the station master is that the target is still on schedule, it'll be leaving Minsk shortly and will arrive in just under an hour from now. I'll guide the main attack party to the best location for you to set up your explosives. Georgy will take the backup team down near the railway bridge over the Plisa River. The locations are about 400 metres apart, but we'll need to take you in slightly different routes, so we can keep you from being spotted by the Nazis."

Ilia seemed happy enough that Sergei and Georgy seemed to be genuine, and the five men headed back to the woodland together, before the fighters divided in two separate groups. Ilia, Dmitry and their men following Sergei, whilst a short time later, Valia and his fighters following Georgy. Moving swiftly but as unobtrusively as possible the fighters soon made their way to their respective attack positions.

At the main attack site, just on the edge of the town, Sergei kept a watchful eye on surroundings as Dmitry and a couple of other men crawled slowly up a small embankment to the main line from Minsk towards Moscow, and set about the delicate task of laying their explosive devices. After ten long minutes, they were done, and they crawled back to the main body of men who were doing their best to stay hidden in an area of lush, overgrown bushes at the base of the embankment. All they could do now was wait.

Valia and his fighters had found their own overgrown bushes near the railway bridge, and they were also waiting silently, weapons at the ready. Valia always found waiting to be the hardest part of any operation, there was always that frightening prospect of being discovered, or even betrayed. The fact that this operation was taking place inside a town, and in broad daylight, had put the hairs on the back of his neck on end. The chance of being discovered was that much greater.

Ilia looked at his watch. The train should be arriving any time now. He signalled for his men to spread out and get ready for the action to come.

Sergei who was now loitering close to the small railway station, a little way from the fighters, was first to spot a small detachment of Nazi soldiers come out of the station building and start to check the lines. There were only four of them, but two were heading directly towards the location where the explosives had been planted. If they discovered them, the whole operation could quickly unravel.

Ilia soon spotted the soldiers too, and had signalled to Dmitry and another fighter to get ready with their knives, just in case they got too close.

Sergei had to do something or the soldiers would almost certainly spot the explosives. Several scenarios instantly ran through his mind, and none of them ended well.

Ilia held his breath as Sergei started jogging down the track towards the two soldiers. He was powerless to stop him. As he rapidly closed in on the soldiers, Sergei pulled out a knife. The startled soldiers turned together as Sergei closed swiftly onto them. Ilia signalled to Dmitry to go, and go fast. The soldiers started swinging the rifles from their backs ready to fire, but before they could get a shot off, Sergei was diving forwards onto one of the soldiers and Dmitry, who was already sprinting as hard as he could up the embankment dived onto the other. With the guns knocked from their grasp, the soldiers met a swift and silent end as the brutally sharp knives tore into their defenceless throats.

Other fighters were quickly on the scene to drag the dead bodies out of sight. Ilia just hoped the other two soldiers were far enough down the track in the other direction that they hadn't heard or noticed the kerfuffle.

Just then the unmistakable sound of a large locomotive could finally be heard. It wasn't long before Ilia could make out the smoke flying high into in the sky. Their target was approaching. The other two Nazi soldiers wouldn't be able to stop it now anyway.

As the deep, growling sound of the engine grew louder, so did the anticipation and nervousness within the fighters. A short distance away under the bridge, Valia and his fighters could also hear the train. Despite their anxiousness, they were ready and eager to get started. The strain of waiting was getting unbearable, but at last they could now ready themselves for the fight to come.

Ilia could soon see the armoured train, with its engine straining hard to haul its huge bulk along the line towards them. The armoured train looked as impressive as it was intimidating. All the wagons were covered in thick armour, and there were large guns dotted along its entire length. It also had armoured wagons that housed heavily armed soldiers. To add to its potency, it also carried some tanks on flat carriages.

Dmitry was praying that the pressure fuses worked properly this time. He'd been on a few operations in the recent past where they'd failed dismally, if these failed too, it would be an utter disaster.

The train got closer, and closer, and closer, and then the front wheels made contact. There was an almighty explosion that could be heard for miles around. The engine broke apart and erupted into a fireball as it drove itself into the stony embankment. The wagons, one by one, started to leave the shattered track and flop over onto their side before coming to a singularly, inglorious and abrupt halt. A few of the wagons exploded from within as the shells they were carrying detonated.

The main body of fighters didn't need a second invitation, they quickly rushed towards the stricken monster to administer the coup de gras. Amidst the taut, tangled wreckage, any surviving Nazi soldiers were dispatched in double quick time.

The massive blast had echoed around the town, and almost immediately the detachment of Nazi soldiers based there were sprinting en masse to cross the railway bridge and provide support for their fellow countrymen, and take the fight to the partisans.

Near the base of the bridge and still not visible to the charging Wehrmacht soldiers, Valia and his group of fighters were lying in wait. As they got to less than 50 metres away, Valia let out a roar. "For the Red Banner and mother Russia. Let's go." Rushing up the bank directly towards the advancing soldiers as quickly as he could, Valia was firing from the hip with his sub-machine gun. The Nazi soldiers were stunned, they'd been taken by complete surprise. They were soon falling right, left and centre as Valia's shots hit home. With the rest of his fighters following closely behind, the air was full of bullets, with the Nazis halted dead in their tracks. Some of them started to return fire, and figures left and right of Valia were hit. The deadly firefight continued for at least ten minutes before the guns fell silent, the partisans had done their job.

With any immediate threat from the south of the river elimi-nated, Valia led his remaining group of fighters north over the bridge, and they joined up with the main group of fighters, who were already picking over the carcass of the armoured train.

The fighters were ecstatic, the operation had gone like clock-work, and all their objectives had been met. Sergei and Georgy were simply relieved, but at the same time quite sad. They knew they could no longer stay in Zhodzina, as it would simply too dangerous for them.

Within the hour, under a fabulously, beautiful blue sky, Ilia was leading his triumphant fighters on their cheery two-day trek back to their camp to the South. Sergei and Georgy tagged along. They were certainly worthy of becoming members of *The Red Banner* group.

The daily routine of the partisan fighter varied little from week to week. The main activities fell into a few different categories. Collecting food was a high priority, as was the defence of the camp, but the main focus, and the activities that Valia and Dmitry spent most of their time on was patrolling, obtaining intelligence and carrying out both clandestine and overt operations to disrupt as much as possible the Nazi war machine.

One late summer's day, while they were getting some well-deserved rest, both Valia and Dmitry were summoned to Ivan's Zemlyanka. No reason was given.

As the two friends crossed the camp in the bright and delight-fully warm afternoon, they pondered what this latest summons would mean for them.

"What do you think Valia, where will Ivan be sending us this time?"

"You're asking me my friend? Your guess is as good as mine. It could be anywhere couldn't it."

As usual at this time of year, it took a few seconds for the men's eyes to acclimatise from the bright sunshine outside to the inherent darkness within the Zemlyanka. As their pupils grew to attune themselves to the lighting, they noticed most of the senior fighters were present.

Valia whispered to Dmitry. "Looks like it's going to be a big operation this time." Dmitry didn't say a word.

"Ah, there you are comrades, welcome." Ivan welcomed them in his normal, warm manner. "You're probably wondering why I've called you both over, aren't you?"

After a few seconds Valia responded. "Well, we just assumed we have another major operation lined up, isn't that so Dmitry?"

Dmitry was of a similar mind. "Why else would you call us over Sir, if it wasn't to go through the plans for a new operation?"

Ivan laughed out loudly, and picked up one of several large vodka bottles from his sizeable table. "Grab some glasses men, this is a time to celebrate."

Valia and Dmitry looked at each other a little puzzled. What was there to celebrate?

After filling all the glasses, Ivan asked. "To what should we celebrate?" After a few seconds silence, Ivan continued. "Valia and Dmitry, you have both become trusted and indispensable members of *The Red Banner* group. I, and all the men here are more than happy to call you both comrades and friends. For outstanding heroism and valour beyond that expected of a Partisan fighter in the attack on the armoured train at Zhodzina, it is with the greatest pleasure that I am now able to award you both the Partisan Medal, second class."

Valia and Dmitry looked at each other somewhat stunned. That was the last thing they were expecting.

Ivan continued. "Dmitry, please step forward."

Dmitry marched in good order over to Ivan and stood at attention directly in front of him. With that, an aide handed Ivan a brass Partisan Medal, with its light green silk ribbon, and a two-millimetre-wide blue stripe down the centre to indicate it was of the second class. Pinning the medal onto the left breast of Dmitry's jacket, Ivan embraced Dmitry kissing him warmly on both cheeks. "Congratulations Dmitry, very well done."

Dmitry saluted before returning to join Valia.

"Valia, please step forward."

A tad embarrassed by all the attention, Valia marched forward to receive his medal.

Ivan repeated the same procedure, pinning the medal on the left breast of Valia's jacket and embracing him tightly. "Congratulations Valia, you are a credit to your family, *The Red Banner* group, and the Soviet Union. Very well done."

Valia saluted before returning to join Dmitry.

As the very short medal presentation ceremony ended, Ivan toasted them, before inviting everyone to have a few drinks to celebrate.

After a few hours, the men headed back to their Zemlyanka's. Valia turned to Dmitry. "When we were suffering in that awful Prison Camp in Kremenchug, I'd never have envisaged this happening. It's such a proud day. I'm just so happy we've been able to share it after all we've been through together in the last year."

As the glorious summer turned to another frigid, icy winter, the intensity of the partisan raids noticeably dropped off. A few attacks on the railway lines continued, but other operations were generally curtailed unless they were deemed to be critical.

The ranks of the partisans continued to grow at a steady pace, as more and more local people and a few isolated Red Army soldiers came on board.

As the winter months brought more and more positive news from the main battle fronts, the general mood within the partisans themselves improved. They could sense their defiance was making a difference, and with the recent victory in the monumental tank battle at Kursk, it really did seem like the Nazis might finally be beaten as an attacking force.

In late January 1944, the news started to filter through that the dreadful siege of Leningrad, which had lasted over two years and four months had finally been lifted. Things were definitely starting to look like they were heading in the right direction.

As the days ticked by into weeks, they soon ticked over into months. Valia and Dmitry remained busy, racking up more kills, and destroying more trains.

As the beautiful summer weather finally returned in all its glorious splendour, the news they'd longed to hear for so long finally came through. Ivan called a meeting of all the fighters in camp to give them the good news.

"Men and women of our glorious *Red Banner* group, I've just received some truly wonderful news. The Red Army is about to launch massive attacks against the fascist Nazi enemy. Operation Bagration will begin in just a couple of days from now, with the main assault scheduled to commence on Friday, the 23rd of June. It's a pleasure to tell you that well over 1,500,000 of our brave comrades are right now lined up and waiting to attack the Nazi invaders."

A big cheer erupted around the camp with the news, one thing was for certain, the fighters would be celebrating with extra vigour tonight.

"I'm absolutely delighted to tell you that we've been given the honour of lighting the fuse that will see our fellow countrymen vent their full anger, fury and might against the enemy. We've been instructed to disrupt communication lines, destroy any Nazi head-quarters, disable as much enemy equipment as possible, and conduct reconnaissance to provide the Red Army useful intelligence they can use when they finally advance."

"As well as that, we'll be working with the other Partisan groups to capture and hold important roads and bridgeheads on rivers until the Red Army arrives."

Ivan slowly looked around the assembled fighters. There were now well over 1,000 men and women in *The Red Banner* group, originating from all corners of the Soviet Union, but by far the biggest group were those from the surrounding locality.

"I know that a great many of you are from communities local to this area, so for you, this final request will mean a lot. We need to organise the protection of all settlements in the vicinity, and wherever possible we should disrupt the export of any Soviet citizens to Germany."

Valia could feel the excitement emanating from the fighters. This was their time. They could make a huge difference, and they knew it.

Ivan continued. "We'll be reviewing potential targets with immediate effect, but I'm sure I don't need to remind you that these tasks are of the utmost importance, and I charge each and every one of you to undertake the operations that are assigned to you with the utmost patriotic zeal and drive home your attacks with every last ounce of energy that you possess."

Ilia stepped forward and briefly mentioned something into Ivan's ear. Ivan raised his hand, and addressed the massed fighters once more. "We'll begin our operations of disruption on Monday, so tomorrow we'll be sending out protective squads to all the nearby villages, and we'll be assigning every other fighter a list of targets for Monday or Tuesday. We need everybody ready for action from tomorrow. Go and get your weapons ready, and then get some good sleep, you're going to need it."

With that, Ivan and Ilia headed off to Ivan's Zemlyanka deep in conversation. The air was filled with excited and somewhat apprehensive conversations as the fighters visited the stores and workshops to make sure they were fully equipped for the actions to come.

The next morning, the camp was a hive of activity, with runner's zig zagging all over the place as they took messages to every Zemlyanka and workshop. Soon, large numbers of fighters were heading in different directions. Their role would be to try and defend the local villages and population as best they could.

It wasn't long before Valia and Dmitry were summoned to see Ivan. As they were making their way over to Ivan's Zemlyanka they bumped into Sergei and Georgy who were also heading in that direction.

"Are you going to see Ivan too?" enquired Georgy.

"We are, I'm sure we'll have a challenging operation, we normally do." Valia replied with a wry grin.

The four men continued chatting all the way to the Zemlyanka, but stopped as soon as they entered. Valia could see the huge map on the table with lines and notes in different colours written all over it.

Ivan was very animated as he finished discussing an operation with a couple of the women snipers. Valia caught the end of their conversation. It sounded like they were being instructed to head into Cervien itself, and target any Nazi officers they could near the Nazi headquarters and also the railway station in the town.

As the snipers departed, Ivan briefly looked up. "Ah, there you are men, come over here, I want to show you something on the map." With little hesitation, Ivan pointed to a railway line about 20 kilometres away from the camp. "Here are your targets for tomorrow. I want you to spread several mines along this line, and also on this connecting branch line. We need to destroy as much of that line as we possibly can. We can't have Nazi trains sending reinforcements to the front. Are you okay with that Gentlemen?"

Valia looked at Dmitry and nodded. "Yes, Sir" replied Dmitry.

"Oh yes, I'm also assigning Sergei and Georgy to join you on this raid. You'll need to work in pairs to cover as much of that line as you can. I'll leave it up to you exactly how you wish to divide the work, but I wish you the very best of luck men."

Ivan immediately bowed his head and stared intently at the map again, he was obviously deep in thought, contemplating whether there was anything else he could possibly do. He was so deep in his own world of concentration that he didn't even notice as Valia and his three comrades turned and left.

Over the previous year, Valia and Dmitry had planted quite a few explosives along this particular stretch of the railway line, so they pretty much knew all the best spots to hit.

As the four comrades made their way to the stores to pick up a few bags of mines and fuses, Dmitry made an eminently sensible proposition. "Sergei, as we're already familiar with it, how about Valia and I target the main line, while you and Georgy take the branch line?"

Sergei looked at Georgy quickly before replying. "I don't think that'll be a problem. If we head to the spot where the branch line splits off from the main line together, I should think we'll be able to deal with the branch line ourselves, no problem."

"Great, then can I suggest we leave at dawn tomorrow, it won't take too long to get there on horseback, and we really want to be there before the Nazis start sending out their own patrols."

Everybody seemed happy enough with the plan that Dmitry had formulated, and were soon back in their own Zemlyanka's, and readying themselves for some much-needed sleep.

With a deep orange glow just starting to form low in the sky far to the East, the camp was awash with fighters departing on their various operations. Valia and his three comrades rode out amongst them, bags of explosives aplenty, and with machine guns stowed safely around their backs.

Within the hour, they were busy laying their destructive mines. Somewhat surprisingly, the easy bit was laying them, the hard part was camouflaging them well enough so that they wouldn't be spotted easily by the Nazi soldiers often sent to sweep the lines for explosives.

After a couple of hours of intense work, Valia and Dmitry had safely planted eight sets of mines along a ten kilometre stretch of line. They made their way safely back to the appointed meeting place where they waited, safely hidden in some trees, for Sergei and Georgy to return. They waited, and waited, and waited some more.

"Where the hell are they, they should've been here a long time ago?" Dmitry was getting quite agitated.

"How about we give them another ten minutes, then I think we'll need to make a move back to camp alone." Valia hadn't totally given up on them, not just yet anyway.

Just then, they heard gunfire from not too far away coming from the direction of the branch line. It sounded like a heated firefight.

Fearing for their comrades, Valia and Dmitry immediately kicked their horses in the direction of the gunfire. Then there was silence. Whatever had happened was intense, but it was very swift.

Valia and Dmitry carefully and very cautiously continued in the direction of where the gunfire had come from, until, less than five minutes later, slowly emerging from between some tall trees, they spotted Sergei, somewhat slumped on his horse. There was no immediate sign of Georgy, but Valia and Dmitry sped towards Sergei, who looked like he was about to fall off his horse. As they got closer, they spotted the bloodied body of Georgy lying right behind Sergei.

"What the hell happened?" Dmitry demanded know.

"It was a trap. There were six of them. Six of them just waiting to ambush us. Luckily Georgy spotted them, and opened fire. I think he managed to get three of them before he got hit in the head. I managed to get to him quickly, but he was already dead by the time I got there. The remaining Nazis kept shooting, so I jumped behind a fallen tree. Somehow, they didn't manage to hit me, and after a couple of minutes I eventually found their range and took them out, one by one. I did get a slight graze on my left leg for my troubles, but otherwise I'm okay. I just couldn't leave my good friend behind, so I put him on the horse and started to head back to find you."

"Shit, when that patrol doesn't report in, this place will be swarming with Nazis. Let's get back to camp as fast as we can. Are you going to be okay, or do you need help Sergei?"

"I'll be fine, I'm just a little slower than I'd like to be."

With that they headed off in the direction of their camp, as fast, but also as cautiously as they could.

Later that afternoon, after getting his leg patched up by one of the camp doctors, Sergei, Valia and Dmitry dug a shallow grave, and tears flowed freely down Sergei's distraught face as they solemnly laid Georgy to rest in the makeshift burial ground at the edge of the camp. It was a sombre occasion indeed, especially for Sergei, who had known him since they were at school together.

Each day thereafter, Valia, Dmitry and Sergei headed out of the camp on a new, daring, and very likely deadly dangerous operation. Sometimes they would target trains, sometimes they would target Nazi vehicles travelling by road. Other days they would surreptitiously enter Cervien and cut communication lines, or ambush troop movements.

Soon however, the full, herculean forces of the Red Army descended upon the ill-prepared Nazi Army Group Centre like a fully coiled spring rebounding with unimaginable force and menace. The advances made in just a few short days were staggering, and by the 3rd of July, just ten days after the main assault of Operation Bagration had commenced, the 2nd Guards Tank Corps of the Red Army were already fighting in the outskirts of Minsk. The following day, after extremely fierce fighting, Minsk was finally totally recaptured by the Soviet forces.

During 1941 and 1942, the Red Army had lost hundreds of thousands of soldiers in various encircling actions by the Wehrmacht, this time the boot was on the other foot, and an encirclement of virtually the entire German Army Group Centre was achieved by the Red Army, trapping over 300,000 Nazi soldiers and equipment behind Soviet lines. It was a crushing defeat for the Nazis, who were never able to replace the experienced men and equipment that had been lost.

The Red Army proceeded to decimate the surrounded Nazi forces, with the help of the Soviet Air force, as well as the rampaging Partisans. In the Cervien region alone, there were around 9,000 partisan fighters by now, in their different groups and brigades.

In Cervien itself, the Red Army finally retook the town on the 2nd of July. The fighting, as always, had been fierce, but the sheer, overwhelming numbers of Soviet forces ranged against the Nazi defenders was just too great from them to resist.

There were wild celebrations across the whole area, and

retribution against Nazi collaborators was often swift, savage and often deadly.

Back in camp, amongst all the unbridled revelry that was going on around him, Ivan was still working hard. There were still Nazi forces on the loose in the region, and this time, rather than destroying the lines of communications, they needed to protect them.

As they were busy polishing off a special bottle of Samogon that they'd been keeping safe in their Zemlyanka for this exact moment in time, Valia, Dmitry and Sergei were surprised to be summoned to go and see Ivan again. Not wishing to waste a good bottle, Valia took it along with them.

As the men entered Ivan's Zemlyanka. Ivan looked up. He looked as serious and concerned as always. It was clear to the men that he wasn't celebrating like most of the fighters.

"Thank you for joining me men. I'm sorry to interrupt your celebrations, but unfortunately I still have a few critical operations that need to be carried out, and you three are best suited to one of them."

The men put their now empty glasses on the large table, and Ivan pointed to a new location on the map.

"I've been instructed that we need to hold this small, but strategically important road bridge until relieved by a Red Army unit. It's only 25 kilometres away, so you can be there in just over half an hour. The soldiers should be there to relieve you in just a few hours' time, but for some reason it's something that's been flagged up as critical."

Valia looked at Dmitry, then at Sergei. He was just glad they hadn't opened the other bottles of Samogon. They'd just have to wait a few hours more.

"Get plenty of ammunition, and head there as fast as possible. With luck you'll be back by nightfall. Then I promise, you can celebrate. In fact, I'll come and celebrate with you." Ivan smiled as he watched the men jog out of the Zemlyanka, and over to the stores.

Riding as fast as they could, the men arrived at the small stone bridge to find it still intact. After a quick search of the area, they found a safe and secluded place to tie up their horses, and also some good defensive positions that they could take up around the bridge. It certainly wasn't a big bridge by any means, being no more than 50 metres in length, and the river below, if you could call it that in the summer, looked to be quite shallow and narrow.

Valia thought it made good sense to double check the bridge. "Sergei, can you cover us while we check there aren't any explosive devices under the structure?"

"No problem, I can do that, I'll position myself behind those rocks over there, it'll have a good range of fire in all directions, if needed."

"Great, Dmitry, you check this side, I'll check the far side."

With Sergei acting as cover, Valia and Dmitry spent a good 10 to 15 minutes checking carefully underneath the bridge.

"All clear here," shouted Dmitry.

A few minutes later, Valia emerged on the far bank of the small river, and crossed over the bridge.

"Yes, all clear my side too."

They strolled over to Sergei, and sat down next him.

Dmitry was a little frustrated. "I hope those soldiers get here quickly, I really could do with some more Samogon." The men settled down quietly and waited. There was no activity at all, apart from the birds singing and flying around high in the trees. They could hear some animals nearby, but there was no human activity at all. It was dead quiet from their perspective.

After a couple of hours of getting more and more frustrated, Dmitry asked the question they were all subconsciously thinking. "Why the hell is this bridge, stuck in the middle of nowhere, so bloody important then?"

The men pondered the question for a little while before Valia pipped up. "I guess some officer, somewhere, with no real understanding of the countryside around here has looked at a map, saw a river crossing, and thought, that bridge must be critical. It's probably as simple as that. They won't have a clue if it really is important or not."

"Shhh, what's that?" Sergei could hear something.

"Yes, I hear it too." Dmitry could make out what sounded like approaching tanks in the distance.

"I'm sure the tanks won't need to use the bridge, but I guess any other vehicles probably would. I just hope they get here quickly, so we can get back to camp, we've got a couple of bottles of Samogon waiting for us there."

As Valia, Dmitry and Sergei looked on, a convoy of vehicles slowly trundled down the narrow forest track towards them. Valia felt huge pride surging through him as T-34 tanks led the column heading towards them, with their sizeable frames filling the entire width of the narrow track.

The men of the 56th Air Defence Battalion had been right all along back in Kharkov. Although he had doubted it many times over the last couple of years, Valia now, finally saw the proof. The Red Army was indeed the best army in the world, he knew it, he could see it and it was truly undeniable.

There were four tanks in total, and each was adorned with at least ten soldiers perched on top, each cradling a machine gun. Behind the tanks, there were quite a few trucks, and also several soldiers on horseback.

When the convoy was little more than 400 metres away from the bridge, Valia, Dmitry and Sergei slowly stood up and started waving. The men on the leading T-34 soon spotted them, and a couple of them started waving back.

Valia left his position and strolled down to the bridge, closely followed by Dmitry and Sergei. The soldiers on the tanks jumped down as the column came to a juddering halt just short of the bridge. They jogged over to greet the relieved men, and there was much hugging and back slapping all around.

"Good afternoon comrades, I'm Major Balakin from the 110th

Rifle Division of the 50th Army. Thanks for keeping an eye on the bridge for us. We've been trying to track down some rogue Nazi units that appear to have moved into this area after we liberated Cervien yesterday."

Dmitry was happy enough with that. "That's no problem, I'm Dmitry, and my comrades over there are Valia, and Sergei. We're members of *The Red Banner* Partisan Group, are you happy to look after the bridge from here, we have some important business back at our camp?"

"That's fine, we're going to make camp here tonight anyway, so I'm happy for you to go. Please send our greetings to your comrades, we've heard a lot of good things about the great work of *The Red Banner* Group."

Sergei had already jogged off and had collected the horses, and within minutes the three fighters were heading back in the direction of their camp, along one of the many small tracks that crisscrossed the forest like a vast spider's web. They were in a jovial, almost celebratory mood, and for some reason, far less cautious than they normally would be. They were chatting amongst themselves, paying no great heed to their surroundings, when, from out of nowhere, there was the unmistakable sound of a crack of gunfire. Almost instantaneously, Valia, Dmitry and Sergei found themselves under intense fire from up ahead.

Heavily camouflaged, and hiding in the at the side of the track just about 200 metres away, a group of 20 to 30 Nazi soldiers, were now firing for all they were worth. After a momentary pause to take in exactly what was going on, Valia screamed. "Get back down the track, FAST." The fighters pulled hard on the reins and spun the horses around as fast as they could before galloping back the way they'd just come.

With bullets whistling all around, the fighters kicked the horses on to get away as fast possible, then just ahead and to the left of him, Valia saw Sergei's horse collapse under him. Then, just a split second later, Valia felt a searing pain in his right arm. He'd been hit. The next thing he knew, he was smashing into the hard ground, and then coming to a juddering halt after rolling along it for several metres. The pain was utterly excruciating, but his adrenaline was now flowing freely throughout his body. Although heavily dazed, Valia knew he had to move. He quickly looked around, and could see Dmitry riding off, far in the distance, then he quickly became aware of gunfire from nearby.

Looking back, he could see Sergei on one knee, using his dead horse as cover, firing back at the Nazi soldiers with his machine-gun. Valia looked down, he was still in once piece, but he had an intense, piercing pain in his right upper right arm, and blood was oozing from a gaping wound. A bullet had sliced through his meaty biceps and triceps, but luckily it seemed to have missed any major blood vessels.

Still somewhat stunned by his heavy fall, Valia spotted his machine-gun about 15 metres away. He quickly crawled over to it, while bullets ricocheted off the ground all around him, and hurried over to join Sergei.

While Sergei was loading a fresh magazine into his gun, Valia checked how he was. "Are you okay Sergei?"

"I'm fine, apart from some bumps and bruises. My horse has copped it though."

With that, he resumed firing. Valia had more or less lost the use of his right arm, it was hanging limp by his side, so he struggled hard to load a fresh magazine into his machine gun for Sergei to use.

Although the Nazi soldiers were advancing towards them cautiously, Sergei had managed to hit at least five of them. With its magazine exhausted, Sergei passed Valia his machine-gun to be reloaded, and picked up Valia's gun and continued firing. Whilst struggling to replace the magazine with his one good arm, Valia heard a loud thwack next to him, and almost instantaneously he was showered with blood. A bullet had found Sergei, and he was smashed backwards onto the ground with immense force, with a big, bloody hole in his forehead, dead.

Valia's mind was racing, he tried to raise his machine gun to fire, but it was impossible with the state of his arm. With nobody returning fire any more, the Nazi soldiers started to run towards Valia's position.

Frantically looking around, Valia quickly targeted the thick woodland next to the track as his only realistic chance of escape. He'd done something similar in the past, just maybe it would work again.

Without a second thought, Valia started sprinting as fast as his injured body would allow. The pain was excruciating, but he knew if he didn't run, he'd be dead as soon as the soldiers got to him.

With salvos of shots following him all the way, Valia somehow managed to make it into the trees. Splinters flew all around as the bullets crashed into them, but at least the trees provided Valia, just a modicum of protection. He must continue, he knew it. Pain was etched across his face as he forced every sinew of his battered body onwards. He was sprinting like he'd never sprinted before. The only thought in his head was. "Run, run hard, and don't stop, no matter what."

After a few minutes, the shooting subsided, and Valia slowed almost to a stop. Gasping hard to get his as much air into his lungs as he possibly could, he leaned hard against a huge spruce tree to stop himself falling over. There were no more shots, and Valia couldn't hear the Nazis shouting any more either. Had he really managed to get away?

Slowly slumping to his knees, the relief of the realisation that he was still alive was short lived. The intense pain flowed through him in waves of unbridled agony. Valia knew he had to stem the blood that was still oozing from his arm or he would lose consciousness soon. Unbuckling his belt, he managed to formulate a makeshift tourniquet which seemed to stop the blood loss, for now at least.

It was only after he sat down for a few minutes, resting against the mighty spruce tree that Valia recalled hearing that the Nazi soldiers were often terrified of entering the forests and woodlands of Belarus on account of the large number of dangerous bogs and areas of quicksand that they hid.

Just to be sure there was no immediate threat, Valia waited a further ten to 15 minutes without hearing any human activity before he felt safe enough to start moving around again. He knew it was imperative to get help. He really needed to see a doctor to treat his injured arm as soon as he possibly could or he be in big trouble.

Valia figured returning to the track would be his only real hope of survival. He'd doubted he'd ever be found if he remained in the midst of this lush, thick woodland. The only problem was the Nazi soldiers. Would they still be there when he returned? Hopefully they'd have moved on by the time he made it back to the track. He agonised over what he should do for several minutes, before deciding that he really needed to take that risk.

With a multitude of birds singing and warbling brightly in the branches high above him, Valia decided he had to move. With his virtually useless right arm hanging limp beside him, he started to make his way back along the route that he'd come in. It was starting to get late, and the already dim and dingy lighting under the extensive canopy of the trees was starting to make visibility on the ground even more difficult.

With his eyes nicely attuned to the subdued lighting, Valia could just about make out the various natural obstacles the woodland had to throw in his path. Sometimes there were large pools of water, sometimes, nasty roots that could easily trip him up, and sometimes even the odd narrow streams to overcome. Although he could negotiate most of these hurdles quite easily, a few times he needed to take a running jump to clear them, especially some of the slightly larger pools and streams.

By now, the strain on Valia, and the loss of blood was starting to have an effect on him, making him quite weak, and his progress was slow to say the least.

As he was finally nearing the track, there was one final pool to clear, so Valia jumped over it cleanly, but on landing something didn't feel quite right. It wasn't a firm landing at all, his feet simply kept sinking into the ground. It didn't take Valia long to realise what the problem was. He'd landed right in the middle of some quicksand. How could he have been so stupid? He just couldn't believe it. By the time he was up to his knees, Valia knew he had a major problem on his hands, and for just a few seconds, started to panic. It would soon be dark, and he couldn't hear anybody on the track at all. The more he moved and struggled, the further he seemed to sink into the dirty, filthy morass. It was frightening. All his instincts were to try and force his way out, but it made no difference, he just kept sinking deeper. After a while he was sunk up to his waist deep.

Rather than continue to struggle to free himself, Valia concentrated his mind hard to try and relax himself, and he did the best he could. He needed to clear his tired, aching mind and think.

As his body relaxed, he noticed that he was no longer sinking, but, and it was a big but, he was still trapped up to his waist.

Valia looked around for anything that could possibly help him, and spotted a few thick branches hanging not too far away, just overhead. If he could possibly reach one of them, just maybe he could extricate himself from the dire situation he found himself in. He reached up with his good arm and could just feel a branch against his fingertips. It was tantalisingly close, but he needed just a tiny bit more effort to be able to grab it properly. Valia composed himself, and tried to grab the branch once more, but again to no avail.

Valia's energy was quickly fading. He started to think of his mother, waiting anxiously for his safe return at home in Yakhrobol. He was desperate to get home and embrace her tightly once more. One thing was for sure though, he certainly didn't want to die here, not in such a desolate place, not in a place where nobody would ever find him.

Valia summoned up every last ounce of his fading energy, as he reached up for the branch one more time. The relief that flowed through his whole body as he finally managed to properly grab hold of a branch was indescribable. He kept a tight, firm grip, and after composing himself for several seconds, slowly started to pull with all the might he could now muster.

He could feel himself rising slowly out of the dirty quagmire with each pull, and after each pull, Valia quickly repositioned his hand further along the branch, without ever really releasing his grip fully. After what seemed an eternity, he could just about make out in the darkness, some tree roots very close to hand. He kept working his way along the branch until he could grab the tree roots instead. Slowly but surely Valia pulled himself to safety. As he finally freed his legs, Valia was absolutely shattered. He managed to crawl to the edge of the tree-line, no more than 20 metres further on, before blacking out and losing consciousness altogether.

Valia felt nothing, his mind was totally blank, except for an image of his wonderful mother that seemed to keep appearing. Then, all of a sudden, in his mind, he could vaguely perceive his long departed, loving father, saying, "Don't go Valia, don't give up. Now is not your time to come and join me. Your mother needs you, and she needs you more than ever."

Then Valia started to imagine another voice. It was a voice he knew well. Was it real? He simply couldn't make out what it was saying, but it forced his conscious mind to start working again.

"I think he's still breathing, but only just. Look at the state of that arm, he must have lost a lot of blood." Dmitry was kneeling over the unconscious body of his close friend. "Come on Valia, fight. Stay alive, and come back to us. Please fight."

Dmitry was there with Ilia. Dmitry was working hard on the arm to staunch the blood loss, and Ilia was cradling Valia's head on his lap, so that he could give him some much-needed water.

Valia spluttered out the water, and started to move, just a little.

"Come on Valia, we know you can do it." Ilia implored Valia to wake up.

Valia moved a little more, and then his eyes flickered open. He couldn't focus properly at first, but a few seconds later he could make out the anxious looking faces of his two friends.

Managing to formulate a few simple words, Valia finally managed to speak. "What kept you so long?"

Dmitry and Ilia smiled, they knew their friend would make it. After all, he was a born fighter.

"Well, better late than never," quipped Dmitry, "but I have to say, it looks like your fighting days might be over."

After removing the tourniquet, and stemming any more blood loss with plenty of bandages, they gave Valia some more water, and a small bite of food.

With Valia in as good a shape as they felt they could make him where they were, Ilia said. "Okay Dmitry, let's get him back to the camp now. The doctors will need to take care of him from hereon in. If we tie Valia behind you on the horse, we should be able to ride back to camp in 20 minutes or so."

It took a lot of effort the get him up onto the horse behind Dmitry, but once there, Valia grabbed hold of Dmitry as if his life depended on it. As Ilia mounted up, they slowly trotted their way back to camp.

Valia had somehow survived again. In his mind, he was certain he'd resume the fight against the Nazi invaders once again, but was that even a realistic proposition, given the state of his shattered arm?

Chapter 12
The Finale

I t had been a good two weeks since Dmitry and Ilia had brought the badly injured Valia back into the camp, barely alive. The doctor had done a fabulous job though, he'd managed to save Valia's arm. He'd managed to clean and stitch up his wounds nicely, and also straighten his badly fractured humerus.

In a perverse sort of way, Valia had been exceptionally lucky, the bullet had travelled right through his arm, entering at the back, it had seared its way through the triceps, and continued to slice through the bicep muscles, and out through the front. He had both an entry and exit wound, which the doctor needed to fix. It seemed that the nasty fracture had been caused by the heavy impact of falling from his horse, rather than being damaged by the bullet.

It had been very much touch and go for the first few days though, with Valia suffering from a high fever and delirium. Valia would sometimes talk absolute nonsense while he was sleeping, and he'd sometimes cry like a baby, but the nurses in the Zemlyanka that acted as a small field hospital looked after him like he was their own brother.

Since his fever finally broke, Valia had been convalescing as well as could be expected for such a nasty injury. His arm was heavily

236

bandaged, and he was in sling, which meant his movement wasn't great.

Dmitry visited Valia as often as he could between his ongoing raids and Major Kuznetsov and Ilia visited a couple of times to see how Valia was too.

There were around 20 fighters laid up in the hospital with a range of injuries, from amputated limbs, through to simple gunshot wounds.

As he slowly recovered his strength over a period of time, Valia started to regain some very limited use of his right arm. It would obviously never be the same again, but at least he still had an arm.

The fighters in the beds either side of him had both had appendages amputated. One had lost both legs beneath the knee, whilst the other had lost his left arm just above the elbow. As they whiled away the days, Valia learnt that one of them, Evgeny, had originally come from Kremenchug, and was a member of the 102nd Infantry Division who'd been deployed to the town of Bykhof back in 1941 in the vain hope of holding back the initial Nazi thrust towards Moscow. Apparently, the Division had been utterly destroyed over a couple of days of fierce fighting in the region around Gomel.

Evgeny, along with a couple of his comrades had managed to elude the Nazis for several months by sheltering in the forest, and when *The Red Banner* group formed, they had become founding members of it.

On one operation, Evgeny and his comrades had been sent to plant some explosives under some Nazi vehicles in Cervien, but unfortunately an unstable mine had exploded prematurely, killing his comrades instantly. Luckily for Evgeny, Ilia had been nearby, and managed to bring him back to camp with his legs shattered and shredded.

The patients in the field hospital received daily updates from the nurses, so despite their debilitating injuries, they were filled with hope and enthusiasm for the future as news of the Red Army advances continued.

Eventually, Valia finally managed to get some time with Dmitry to discuss what had happened on their way back to the camp from the bridge.

"Tell me Dmitry, what happened to you after Sergei and I had been knocked off our horses. I saw you riding off into the distance?"

Dmitry looked a little guiltily at Valia before replying "To be honest with you Valia, it was a really gut-wrenching decision to keep on going. I very nearly headed back to help the two of you, but it was a split-second decision, it just seemed that the best thing to do was to try and get some help for you, so I galloped as hard as I could back to the bridge, which was a little closer than the camp."

Although this was hard to hear, Valia could empathise. He'd have probably done exactly the same thing if their roles were reversed.

"As soon as I informed Major Balakin that there was a Nazi formation travelling on foot just a few short kilometres away, he dispatched his cavalry immediately to intercept and destroy them. A couple of the tanks also started to follow us down the track, just in case they were needed, as we galloped ahead. When we finally arrived at the place where you'd been hit, we spotted your horse aimlessly wondering around, and we immediately found poor Sergei, lying in a huge pool of his own blood. There was no sign of the Nazis though, they'd obviously moved further westwards. We searched the area for you as best we could, and followed a trail of your blood into the forest a little way before we lost it in the fading light. We even shouted as loudly as we could but there was no reply. As it was getting dark, Major Balakin's men were pretty certain you'd also been killed, so they decided to return to the bridge to rest up for the night. I had a gut instinct that you'd still be alive though, as I know the type of a fighter and warrior you are."

Valia smiled a little. "Did you stay the night searching for me?"

Dmitry looked a little guilty again. "No, it made no sense. As much as I wanted to, the light wasn't good enough to properly search for you. I decided the best thing to do was to take Sergei's body back to the camp, and look for you again in the morning."

Valia nodded. He'd have probably done the same thing too.

"Before leaving for the night, I draped Sergei's body over the back of your horse, with his arms hanging down one side and his legs down the other side of the horse. Once I was sure the body was securely attached, I mounted mine, and very slowly led it back to camp. When I arrived, I reported what'd happened to Major Kuznetsov, and he agreed that I could do a final search for you first thing in the morning, and Ilia was insistent on joining me too."

Valia was just happy to hear that Dmitry hadn't just given up on him, as he was sure that many would have.

"Just after dawn, Ilia and I rode along the track where Sergei's horse still lay, with flies swarming around it, and we shouted again to see if you'd respond. We went up the track for a good couple of kilometres but still didn't see any sign of you, so figured that you must have died somewhere in the dense woodland. It was only when we were returning back down the track, that something caught my eye as we were about to head back to camp, just 200 metres away from the dead horse. I spotted you right by the tree-line, and a little way back from the track, so it was just a matter of pure luck really that we noticed you at all."

"I don't know what it was, whether it was just an instinct, but somehow I just knew you were there. To be brutally honest with you, when we finally got to you, we thought you must be dead, you looked in a terrible condition, caked in dry mud and blood. It's only when we realised that you were still actually breathing that we tried everything we could to revive you. It took quite a while for you to come around, but once you did, we managed to manoeuvre you onto my horse and Ilia tied you behind me, so that you wouldn't fall off. When we eventually managed to get back to the camp, the doctor, was quick to spot you, and came out to give you treatment straight away. They only brought you into this field hospital after a couple of hours."

Tears were running down Valia's face. He knew that without a trusted friend like Dmitry, he'd surely be dead by now. He'd never forget Dmitry's determination and courage to rescue him. He now knew what a real friendship was.

"Dmitry, what happened to Sergei's body?" Valia asked with a solemn look and a slight tremble in his voice.

Dmitry was lost in his mind again for a few seconds, as he remembered yet another lost comrade. "After we'd got you safely here, Ilia and I carried Sergei to the small burial ground, and laid him to rest right next to his old friend Georgy. I'm sure that's what he would've wanted."

Although *the Red Banner* group was still planning and carrying out their own operations in support of the Red Army, the Nazi forces in the area had by now, more or less been eliminated as the Red Army continually pursued and drove them back westwards.

One afternoon late in July, Ivan called another meeting for all the active partisan fighters, but unfortunately those in the hospital were unable to attend. As the meeting continued for over an hour, Valia and Evgeny started to hypothesise why the meeting was taking so long. Ivan was usually very succinct and to the point, meaning his meetings were usually finished quite quickly. Obviously, something was going on.

"I bet they're going to decommission the whole group and send everybody home." Evgeny postulated.

Valia thought for a few seconds. "Why would they do that? I wouldn't be surprised if they assimilate our fighters into the Red Army units around here to replace the soldiers that they've lost in the advances so far."

"Hmm, I guess so, you've got to admit, our fighters are probably much more experienced than most of the Red Army soldiers, so you're probably right. I take back my bet."

Eventually the meeting broke up and the doctor entered the hospital with some quite interesting news. He was accompanied by a couple of very imposing looking men in the neatly pressed uniform of the NKVD.

"Gentlemen, as I'm sure you know by now, the area around Cervien and further westwards, well past Minsk, is now safely under the control of our glorious comrades in the Red Army. It has been decided that there is no longer a requirement for active Partisan groups in this area. The plan is that by the end of July, *The Red Banner* group, along with many other Partisan groups in the area will officially be disbanded. All the active fighters have had a choice. They can either join one of the Red Army units in the area, or remain as an unofficial Red Army commanded detachment, still under the control of Major Kuznetsov."

Valia looked at Evgeny with a smile, almost as if to say, "I told you so."

The doctor continued his update. "Major Kuznetsov will mobilise what remains of his command in the next day or two, and they'll be moving westwards to continue the fight against the Nazi invaders. In the meantime, you patients will remain here for now. Engineers are busy repairing the hospital in Cervien, and once it's ready to accept patients, you'll be transferred there. I'll be staying with you until the hospital is ready, then I will re-join Major Kuznetsov's unit."

After the doctor had finished his update, one of the NKVD officers addressed the patients. "Thank you doctor. I am here to tell you that we will be checking the condition of each and every one of you. If anybody is capable of being returned to active duty, rest assured they will be. We will, of course, also be interviewing each and every one of you individually about your activities over the last three years. Anybody found to have taken part in any treasonous activity will of course be appropriately dealt with. Are there any questions?"

As none were forthcoming, the NKVD officers turned and left the building.

With no active operations now taking place locally, Dmitry was able to pop into the hospital to visit Valia each afternoon before the group deployed westwards. The visits always cheered Valia up, and Dmitry was far more ebullient than Valia had seen him before. On the last visit before his departure, Dmitry's demeanour, had changed again. He looked far tenser and sombre than the previous few days, with the weight of the world appearing to be on his shoulders. He was heading into action again, and knowing exactly what he was likely to face was obviously causing him to feel apprehensive.

"Well, we're more or less ready to go Valia, so, it's finally time for me to say goodbye my good friend. I just wanted to wish you the very best of luck for the future. It's been a real pleasure to have had you at my side over the last couple of years. Make sure you keep in touch, and promise me that you'll come and spend some time with me in Leningrad when this war is finally over. We can then properly celebrate our small part in all this madness."

Valia was struggling to contain his emotions. The two of them had been through so much together, he really wished he could continue the fight alongside his great friend, but it was simply impossible.

"I wish you the very best of luck my good friend. I will certainly make every effort to visit Leningrad once everything settles down again in the world. I'll miss you. Take great care."

With that, the men tearfully embraced, before Dmitry finally strolled out of the hospital and onto the next, and so far, unwritten chapter of his life.

Valia was unable to stop the tears running down his face as his best friend finally disappeared. Minutes later Major Kuznetsov paid a last-minute visit to the hospital, and wished his former charges his very best wishes for the future, and with that, he too was gone.

The camp, which had once been a hive of furious activity, now felt decidedly empty. It felt just like a mortuary. There were very, very few people left, just the field hospital patients, the medical team to look after them, a couple of cooks, and a handful of fighters to provide at least a semblance of a rudimentary defence.

Over the next two to three weeks, each new day was more or

less identical to the previous one. There was very little variety, and with so few people in the camp, there wasn't much news around that could be used as the basis for conversation. Despite the best efforts of the medical team, a couple of the patients finally succumbed to their wounds, and they were solemnly taken out, and were the last to be interred in the camp's burial ground of heroes.

By the middle of August, the NKVD had thoroughly checked and cross checked all the records for each of the patients left in the field hospital. As was to be expected, they had been thoroughly scrupulous and where there were any concerns that needed to be addressed, the patients were called for a personal interrogation.

One after another, patients were wheeled out to a separate Zemlyanka where they were intensively interrogated by a team of four NKVD personnel.

Usually the questioning would last an hour or two, before they were returned to the hospital. However, after being questioned for an inordinately long time, one of the patients was for some reason taken outside. A single shot soon reverberated around the empty camp.

Evgeny turned to Valia with a look of trepidation in his eyes and whispered. "What gives them the right to go around executing our brave fighters. They've no idea what we've been through. I thought there'd been an Amnesty for all fighters in March last year. Obviously, that wasn't worth the paper it was written on was it. It's criminal."

Valia simply nodded. He was now feeling somewhat concerned himself. He hadn't been expecting any of the patients to be sent to the horrific, forced-labour camps of the gulag, let alone executed on-the-spot.

Within the hour a couple of NKVD approached Valia. They simply said, "Come with us, we'd like to ask you a few simple questions." A couple of nurses helped Valia onto a very basic wheelchair, and wheeled Valia into the Zemlyanka that was acting as their interrogation centre.

A tall, dark haired NKVD officer with piercing blue eyes was staring straight a Valia. He proceeded to sit down behind a table upon which were several boxes of paperwork. Some of the records were strewn untidily around, and a lone cigarette was smoking away on the edge of a small red ash tray.

"Good afternoon, I hope you're feeling comfortable?" Valia nodded without saying anything.

"Good, as I'm sure you know, we're only here to find the facts, and nothing more. All we need from you are truthful and simple direct answers to our questions. Is that clear?" Of course, it was clear, it was crystal clear. The hairs on the back of Valia's neck started to rise on end. He was getting quite nervous now. Valia nodded again.

"Okay, let me start with a simple question. What is your name, and where were you born?"

Valia looked a bit puzzled. "My name is Valerey Alexandrovich Ermolaev, and I'm from Yakhrobol, which is a small village in the Nekrasovsky District of the Yaroslavl Oblast."

The officer spent a few minutes looking through the pile of records. "Hmm, that doesn't match a name listed on any of the records for *The Red Banner* group. There is somebody listed as Valentin Alexeevich Ermolaev from a place called Yahrorova in the Nekrasovsky District of the Yaroslavl Oblast. Could that person, possibly be you?"

Valia looked a little surprised. "Well, my Comrade Dmitry actually registered my details, so it's likely he made a couple of mistakes I guess. I've never heard of a place called Yahrorova before, and everybody knows me by the name Valia. As Valia is actually short for Valentin, maybe the person who wrote the records down assumed my name was Valentin because of that? I can only assume they made some spelling mistakes with Alexeevich and Yahrorova."

Looking at Valia somewhat suspiciously, the officer then proceeded to read the records for Valentin Alexeevich Ermolaev once again. When he finished, he slowly looked up, and in an almost menacing manner carried on. "Let's hypothesise that that is the case for now shall we." Then, in a slightly more amiable tone he carried on. "From what's written here, you seem to have been very well respected in *The Red Banner* group, and I see that you were even awarded the Partisan Medal, second class. That is the mark of somebody who is a good, courageous fighter, and a proud citizen of the Soviet Union. I don't see a problem with that."

Valia, felt a little less anxious now, but was still quite nervous, as it was common knowledge that the NKVD were a law unto themselves. He still had no idea how things were going to pan out.

"So, Valia, please tell me in your own words how you came from Yakhrobol to becoming a member of *The Red Banner* group?"

For the next couple of hours, Valia proceeded to detail exactly what he'd done, and where he'd been since he'd left home. He went through in detail about his initial training just outside Moscow. He covered the period he spent in Kharkov where he had joined the 56th Air Defence Battalion, through to their defence of the Railway bridge at Kremenchug, and the battle of Kryukov. He detailed how the 56th were completely destroyed in a battle with tanks, and he went into great detail about his time in that awful prisoner of war camp, and detailed all the atrocities that he'd had the misfortune to witness. He even mentioned that under extreme duress he'd agreed to work with the Nazis, but had escaped at the first opportunity. Finally, he detailed his various exploits on his long trek from the Ukraine through to where they were now.

On a table to the left side of the Zemlyanka, another NKVD officer was carefully writing down everything Valia was saying, and if he wasn't clear about anything Valia was saying, he'd ask additional questions to clarify the facts.

Once Valia had finished his story, the officer sitting in front of him smiled. "Thank you Valia, I think that will do for now. It sounds like you've had quite an eventful couple of years. We'll double check these details as far as we possibly can, but for now, I'm happy to release you back into the doctor's care. Thank you."

With that one of the two NKVD officers who'd been stood by the entrance of the Zemlyanka throughout the interrogation process moved forward, and carefully wheeled Valia back to the hospital.

Once Valia was ensconced in his bed once more, and the NKVD officer had left, Evgeny was keen to know what had happened. "How did it go Valia, you were in there quite a long time?"

"Well, I was as nervous as hell, because you have no idea what they are thinking. Having said that, I think they were generally happy with my story, and the answers I gave to their questions. You can never be sure what they'll do though, as they're going to double check everything I said."

"I hope it doesn't take long. You know what, whenever I'm interviewed about something, I always end up feeling guilty about it, even when I know I've done nothing wrong." Evgeny was a bag of nerves, and he was next up for the interrogation.

After the NKVD had finished their dreaded interrogations, life in the field hospital returned back to more or less normal. Valia was getting a lot stronger, and the exercises the nurses were giving him to strengthen his right arm were starting to pay dividends. He could now grip things lightly, and he could even pick up a few light objects with his right hand, but there was no way his arm would ever be the same as it was again, and he knew it.

The beautifully warm breezes that had flowed gently into the Zemlyanka over the last few weeks started to cool slightly as summer started to wane. Just before noon on the 24th of August, the doctor entered the Zemlyanka with a slight spring in his step and a wide smile on his face. "Comrades, I'm pleased to say that tomorrow we'll finally be travelling to the hospital in Cervien as the work on it has now advanced enough for you to be transferred there. This will be your last night in Camp, so make the most of it."

Valia didn't know whether to be sad or happy. The camp had been his safe haven for well over a year, and he'd always felt safe and secure within its boundaries. He'd be sad to leave it for sure, but a nice comfortable bed in a newly refurbished hospital did sound very appealing. It was also one step closer to him getting to see his mother in Yakhrobol again.

The following morning, just before the wagons arrived to transport the wounded into Cervien, all of the partisans that still remained in the camp either walked, or were pushed in a wheelchair, the relatively short distance to the secluded burial ground. Each of the partisans knew at least one, and sometimes many, of the 100 or so former comrades who were interred there. It was the last time that they'd be able to pay their last respects to these brave men and women, so Valia went directly to the graves of Sergei and Georgy. There he stood for several minutes, his mind in deep contemplation, recollecting the many times that they'd stood shoulder to shoulder on one operation or another. Each of the surviving partisans had their own treasured memories of their close comrades, and it was such a sad way to finally say goodbye to them.

Being transported on a horse drawn wagon which was very slowly meandering its way along the long, dark, forest tracks wasn't how Valia remembered travelling into Cervien before. He missed his comrades, he missed his horses, but most of all, he missed the exhilaration and excitement of riding swiftly through the forest on a dangerous mission.

As they travelled through Cervien itself, he could still see the scars of the bullets and explosions on almost all of the buildings. One thing that Valia was pleased not to see though was the temporary gallows that the Nazis had installed in the centre of the town. The sight of those 20 innocent men just hanging, frozen solid and lifeless was etched into his memory. It was a memory he wished he didn't have to endure.

When they finally arrived at the hospital, those that could walk unaided, were taken to a ward upstairs, whilst those that couldn't, were wheeled into wards on the ground floor. The young nurses fussed over the wounded fighters like they were celebrities. Valia was quite pleased, as he'd been given a lovely, and very comfortable bed, right next to a window overlooking the main road through the town, so at last he could view the world going about its daily routine outside.

Rehabilitation for the fighters depended on the injuries they'd suffered, and it didn't take long before Valia was told it was likely he'd need to stay in the hospital for a further three months.

Compared to life in the partisan camp, the hospital felt almost like a holiday camp. The food was good, nutritional, and varied, the medical care was fabulous, but the greatest boon though, was their regular access to newspapers. Valia soon became an avid reader, and it wasn't long before he became known around the hospital as the expert on the current state of the war.

He'd been somewhat surprised to find out that the Americans had joined the British in opening up a second front in the far west of the continent. The general consensus in the newspapers seemed to be, "Better late than never".

As August rolled into September, the doctors and nurses worked hard to get movement and feeling back into Valia's arm. It was often a painful and frustrating experience, but looking back to what he was capable of doing when he was in Camp, he could see real progress.

As for the world news, Valia devoured whatever was written in the popular newspapers, especially the comprehensive content provided in *Pravda*. He was happy to see that the Romanians had finally signed an armistice, and the Red Army had pushed deep into Poland, and was even now, nearing Warsaw. It was also great to read that the Bulgarian capital of Sofia had also been captured. With the Finns finally signing and armistice too, the support for the Nazi regime was quickly dwindling, which could only be a good thing.

The daily routine in hospital soon became somewhat tedious though, and Valia really appreciated his time reading the newspapers.

As October thrust itself upon the world, Valia received some unexpected, and devastating news. One of the doctors had come personally to let Valia know that his good friend Dmitry had been killed in action not too far outside Warsaw. Valia was shattered by it. He laid down on the bed and simply cried. Why wasn't he there to protect his friend? Valia felt absolutely crushed. For a couple of days, he completely went into a shell, and couldn't speak at all. His mind was devoid of anything except the feeling of guilt. Why had Dmitry been risking his life while he'd been safely ensconced in this very safe and secure hospital?

It took the nurses considerable effort and several days to break Valia's depression, and it took a few weeks before he was more or less back to normal. Reading the newspapers had helped tremendously to bring Valia out of his shell again.

This time, he was pleased to hear that the Red Army were attacking the Nazis in northern Finland and Norway. In fact, they were advancing everywhere, with Cluj in Romania, and Szeged in Hungary just examples of the cities liberated, and Hungary itself signing a peace accord with Moscow.

The world outside the hospital was really changing, and not just the weather. The snows had already begun by the time November ushered in some bitterly cold weather. The hospital, in its neatly, centrally heated bubble bore no resemblance to the freezing winter days that Valia had experienced over the last few years.

On Thursday, the 23rd of November, Valia was called into a small, cramped office to see the head doctor. As Valia entered the room, his heart sank as he saw the doctor flanked by two officers in the distinctive uniform of the NKVD.

Valia's mind raced into overtime. Surely, they weren't going to send him to a gulag, not now, just because he'd been a prisoner of war, were they? As the doctor began to speak, Valia focused hard again on what was being said.

"Good morning Valia, I believe we've done all we can to rehabilitate your arm, and unfortunately we can't get it into a good enough state for you to re-join the army, so sadly, I'm going to have to sign papers declaring you unfit for further active service. All the paperwork from the hospital will be completed tomorrow, and you can leave the hospital on Saturday."

Valia was still nervous about the presence of the NKVD officers, but he needed to reply to the doctor.

"I'd like to thank you and all your staff for the wonderful treatments and the dedicated work you have done on my behalf. I'm truly grateful. I'll make sure I say goodbye to all the staff before I leave."

The doctor picked up some paperwork from the desk in front of him. "Thank you Valia. Ah, yes, these officers would like to speak to you for a few minutes. I'd better leave you alone with them."

As the doctor closed the door behind him, one of the officers asked Valia to sit down.

"Hello, Valerey, I'm sure you remember a chat you had with some of my colleagues a few months ago. Anyway, we've been checking the account you provided them for your actions. We were able to corroborate some of the facts you provided, but weren't able to check absolutely everything. So, on the balance of probability, and the exemplary references on your behalf from Major Kuznetsov, we will be releasing you to return home."

Valia was somewhat relieved, and very excited at the same time. He would really be going home, and going home soon. He couldn't wait.

As one of the officers handed Valia his clearance documents, and a travel warrant to get home, he added ominously. "Oh, and by the way, don't forget, we will continue our investigations, and if we do find something untoward, we will be in touch again."

With that, the officers both shook Valia's hand and left. The relief that ran through Valia as the officers closed the door behind them was indescribable.

The next couple of days flew by in a blur of official documents and emotional farewells with the nursing staff and doctors.

Missing In Action

It was soon Saturday, the 25th of November, and Valia found himself almost alone, wrapped up warm against the cold winter winds and driving snow at Cervien station. As he looked down the track at the approaching train he was struggling to come to terms and comprehend just how much he'd been through over the last four years. It was simply unbelievable. When he'd left home, he was an innocent young man full of optimism and looking forward to the adventures ahead. Now, here he was, starting his journey home, having gone through more in a few short years than most people would experience in a whole lifetime.

With steam billowing high into the cold air from its locomotive, the train to Moscow pulled to a halt right in front of him. Valia climbed the steps, and took his seat in a carriage full of military uniforms and smoke. A few minutes later, the train pulled out of the station and started to wend its way towards Moscow.

Looking out of the window over the snow-covered forests, Valia thought back to another time, not so long ago, when he'd be blowing up the tracks they were now travelling along. It just felt really strange.

A few short hours later Valia was at the bustling main railway station in Moscow, and boarding another train, this one bound for the city of Yaroslavl, only about 300 kilometres to the north-east. He was getting closer to home, and couldn't wait to get there. Again, the carriage he was in was packed with military personnel heading for their next assignment. Valia had no more need to worry about such things. All he was thinking about now was his wonderful mother, and getting home.

After a pretty uneventful four-hour journey, the train was finally crossing the Volga River bridge and pulling up into the main Yaroslavl railway station. Valia immediately felt at home. It was Yaroslavl after all, a place he knew well. There was a familiarity to it that made him feel very comfortable.

He'd love to go and just walk around the city again. Of course, the river would be frozen solid by now, but the boat station would be there, he could walk along the embankment. He could stroll along the strelka where the Kotorosl River joins the mighty Volga River, then the short distance to the City Kremlin. Of course, he would love to, but more than that, he wanted to go home to Yakhrobol and to see his mother and his family again.

It was too cold to stand around outside for any length of time, so Valia sought some shelter in the large waiting room in the railway station. It was pretty hectic inside, with most people wearing a uniform of some sort, either of the military, or of the rail persuasion. After checking the timetables, and talking to a few of the staff, Valia found that the next service to Krasny Profintern would leave in less than 30 minutes, so there was little point finding a seat, and making himself comfortable.

Being made up of just four carriages, the train to Krasny Profintern was much shorter than all the other trains coming and going through the station. Despite this, as Valia walked along the platform, he noticed that there were plenty of empty seats, with each of the carriages almost deserted. Valia boarded the rearmost carriage, but only after a very officious guard had thoroughly interrogated him and triple checked his travel papers.

As it was a stopping service, the train was unduly slow compared to the rest of the journey. Nevertheless, the excitement and anticipation grew within Valia as each stop was ticked off, until the train pulled into the tiny, very nondescript stop of Svechkino. This was as far as Valia was going, so he grabbed his bag, and was soon descending the carriage steps into the deep, thick snow. He took a few steps back and away from the carriage, and put his bag down as he waited for the train to move on.

Just a few minutes later, as he watched the train depart on its short journey onwards to Krasny Profintern, Valia picked up his bag again with his good hand and started walking again, first over the railway tracks, and then in the direction of Yakhrobol. The snow was already many centimetres deep, and the sharp piercingly cold wind was blowing the new snow all over the place. With the sun having long since faded over the horizon, Valia had to navigate through the bright darkness with the moonlight doing its best to fight its way through the thick snow laden clouds.

Navigation here though wasn't a problem, as Valia knew the area like the back of his hand, and even in these atrocious conditions he would be home in less than an hour, after all, it was now just over three kilometres away.

Head down, and with great determination, Valia maintained a good, steady pace, and before too long, he was walking along the long, undulating track leading to the village. Occasionally he'd stumble over an obstacle such as a large stone hidden from view by the fluffy carpet of snow, or he'd slip and slide on a particularly icy section of the track, but eventually he reached the tiny, main street in the village of Yakhrobol.

Initially, the village appeared to be devoid of any life at all, as everything was so quiet and still. All Valia could register was the brutally cold wind, gusting and swirling around him causing the snow to dance and fly chaotically into the air. It didn't take too long though for dogs to start barking as he passed some of the houses, and then, through the windows of some of them, he could even make out the silhouettes of village people going about their daily business against their flickering candle or electric lights.

It didn't take long before he was finally standing outside the family home. It was just as he'd remembered it. It was the thoughts of coming home that'd kept him going through the worst of his ordeals, all those harrowingly, desperate low points, and now, here it was. He really was home.

Although he was feeling tired and weary after his long journey, he was overjoyed. He was simply ecstatic. Tears welled up in his eyes, as against all the odds, somehow, he'd made it home alive.

As he stood there, trying to compose himself, the very familiar and comforting aroma of his mother's cooking enveloped him. It was so divine. Then, as he started to approach the door, all of a sudden, his pent-up emotions, started to overwhelm him, and he couldn't stop himself from crying out loud. It was with tears of happiness and excitement running down his face, that he eventually knocked on the door and waited. There was no response. Valia did his best to wipe some of the tears from his face with his dark, thick gloves, before, after several seconds, he knocked again, this time a little louder. The sharp, gusting winds were howling all around him, but after a while, he could just about make out the sound of footsteps approaching, and a lady inside muttering "Who can that be at this time of night, especially in this awful weather?"

Then, Valia heard the distinctive noise of bolts slowly being slid open, one after the other. Then, with a low, dull, creaking noise, the door slowly opened a little. It was his mother, holding a candle lamp, with its flickering flame jumping around brightly. She squinted as she peered outside, trying to get her eyes acclimatised to the darkness. "Who's there?" she nervously enquired.

As Valia started to talk, she instantly recognised the trembling voice, shot through with a mix of happiness, affection, and joy, that greeted her. "Hello Mama, I'm home. I promised you that I'd come back."

Valia's mother dropped the lamp into the snow and fell to her knees, totally overcome with shock. Valia rushed forwards to help, and at the same time to embrace her. "Is it really you Valia, I just can't believe it. It's a miracle" Valia's mother was in floods of tears as she finally held her son close again after his years away from home.

"Who's there, Mama?" called out a voice from inside the house. Nobody replied, Valia and his mother were totally speechless as they were both so overcome with emotion.

Valia's sister Vera came to see what was going on. She couldn't understand what was happening until Valia removed the thick hat, that was partially obscuring his face, to finally reveal himself. "Valia, it can't be. Is that really you?" she cried out, and immediately burst into floods of tears and joined them, kneeling on the ground, in a tight family embrace.

It took several minutes for the shock to wear off, and for each of them to finally compose themselves properly.

"Come in out of the cold Valia, you must be freezing, let's get you warm. Vera, please get some hot tea ready for Valia, he'll need something warm inside him."

As they settled down around the table near the stove, Valia's mother rushed around getting food ready for her beloved son. "You know, at the end of 1941, we received an official letter to say you were missing in action. Everybody was telling me you must be dead, but I wouldn't believe them. You promised me you'd come home, and you never ever broke your promises, so I knew you'd be home one day, and thankfully, here you are. Tell us your story Valia, we want to know everything you've been up to since you left home."

Throughout the long evening, and deep into the night, Valia recounted his whole, often harrowing story. His mother and sister were mesmerised and horrified in equal measure.

Noticing that neither of his brothers were at home, he asked his mother if she knew where they were. "Have you heard anything about Anatoly and Victor, Mama?"

His mother went quiet for a little while before answering. "We haven't received any news from Anatoly for several months now, but the last we heard, he was driving a tank in the 125th Tank Battalion as part of the Volkhov Front, helping to bravely defend Leningrad. Apparently, he was even awarded a battle merit medal for his valour too. We've no real idea if he's still alive and well, but at least that's what we're hoping and praying for."

"And what's the news about Victor?"

His mother said nothing, but a look of pain crossed her face. After a few seconds Vera interjected. "Valia, did you know that Victor was a sailor in the Black Sea Fleet stationed at Sevastopol in the Crimea? Well, the Nazis captured it in July 1942, and Mama got a letter at the end of 1942 to say, just like you, that Victor was missing in action as well. We are just hoping for another miracle, and pray that he'll come home safely one day soon."

Valia felt awful. Not knowing what was happening to her sons must have been emotional torture for his mother, and now he was safe at home, he felt the same way about his brothers as his mother must have felt about him too.

E. W. Butcher

Over the next few months, the special bottle of Samogon on Valia's top shelf remained untouched. He refused to touch a drop of it, unless both his brothers where there to share it with him.

Finally, in the summer of 1945, Valia, now a married man, and with a baby on the way, reached up to that bottle. He took it down, and blew the dust off it. He headed into the kitchen where there were five glasses on the table. Sat around it were Valia's mother, his sister Vera, and his two brothers, Anatoly and Victor. They had all, against all the odds, eventually, come home safely.

Epilogue

Against all the odds, Valia had somehow managed to survive the horrors and deprivations that the war had thrust upon him. On so many occasions, as he valiantly battled and jousted with death, just the idea of being able to return home to be with his family once more, seemed nothing more than a pipe dream. Yet, home he came, and within months, Valia was married to Pavla, the love of his life. A son called Vladimir soon followed, and the prospect of finally getting to enjoy the relative peace and tranquillity of a normal family life, enticingly beckoned.

However, with the Nazi invaders now soundly defeated, large swathes of the countryside lay in total ruin. The Nazis had totally and utterly devastated much of the land that they'd occupied, and help was desperately required to begin the colossal reconstruction work that was now essential, and so vitally important to the psyche of the nation.

Former prisoners of war that hadn't already been executed or transported to the gulag by the NKVD, were the first to be called to action. As such, Valia and his family soon found themselves in the severely shattered and destitute city of Leningrad, where, for the next decade, they helped with the work to return the city to its former glory. Despite the hardships of endless toil and labour, during this time, Valia and Pavla were overjoyed to welcome their first daughter, Tatiana, into the world.

After ten years, in what is now Saint Petersburg, the family relocated once again. This time they settled in the very far north of the country, inside the Arctic Circle. Kovdor was a small, largely inaccessible, closed town, very close to the Finish border, and not too far away from the huge Soviet naval base at Murmansk.

If it wasn't for the large mineral resources and mining operations in the area, it's hard to believe that Kovdor would exist at all, in the harsh, inhospitable and desperately remote countryside it found itself in. Living inside the Arctic Circle wasn't the easiest of places to bring up a family, but Valia and Pavla seemed to thrive there, even welcoming a second daughter, Tamara, into their household.

Eventually though, the pull of their birthplace grew inexorably stronger, and towards the end of his working life, Valia, and his family moved again, one final time. This time, back to the city of Yaroslavl.

In 1985, during the celebration of the 40th anniversary of *The Great Patriotic War*, it was decided that all surviving veterans of the war would be awarded the *Order of the Patriotic War* medal, either first or second class. Valia received the first-class version.

Finally, after a long and truly remarkable life, Valia joined his long since departed colleagues of the 56th Air Defence Battalion on the 7th of April 1990, and was buried, a hugely respected and honoured Soviet war hero.

Yet, to this day, the Soviet military archives in Russia, list Valia as *Missing in Action*, on the 12th of September 1941, the day that the 56th Air Defence Battalion were utterly destroyed.

The city of Kremenchug was devastated by the Nazi forces. In just over two years of occupation, much of the city was destroyed, and a large number of its inhabitants either killed, or deported as slave labour. Soviet forces finally re-took the city on the 29th of September 1943.

The picture below was taken soon after the Nazis captured Kremenchug in 1941. You can see the damage to the railway bridge that Valia and his comrades had tried so hard to defend, as well as the pontoon bridge that the Nazi's built adjacent to it.

The city is now an important industrial centre, and in 1975, the city of Kryukov was finally merged with Kremenchug to form a single municipality.

The damaged Kryukov Railway bridge, 1941

Nikita Khrushchev was a political commissar during the war with the Nazis, where he acted as an intermediary between the local military commanders and the political rulers in Moscow. As the Nazis advanced, Khrushchev worked with the military to defend and try to save Kiev. As the Kiev area collapsed, he survived a breakout, but General Mikhail Petrovich Kirponos wasn't so lucky, and was killed by a landmine. Eventually, Khrushchev ended up in Stalingrad, where he remained for most of the battle, narrowly missing death on more than one occasion. After the war, he emerged as a political force, and ended up as leader of the Soviet Union. He was involved in a high-risk nuclear weapons face-off with the United States during the Cuban Missile Crisis. Overthrown in 1964, he eventually died in 1971.

During Nikita Khrushchev's second wave of destalinization in November 1961, the city of Stalino was changed to the now, very familiar name of Donetsk, in order to distance it from the former Soviet leader, Joseph Stalin.

If you were wondering what Valia actually looked like, here are a couple of photographs of him.

Valia with his mother, just before leaving home.

Valia, after the war.

Additionally, if you hadn't realised, the face of the soldier on the front cover of this book is also Valia, and the document extract shown on the back cover is also his.

Oh, and don't forget, if you enjoyed reading this story, please do leave a review.

Acknowledgments

Special thanks go to the following for their inspiring support and helping make this book a reality: Janice Wilkes, Gaynor Stockwell, Ryan Winchcombe, Susan Wall, Louise Kennedy, Louise Wilcox, Mark Keohane and Ivan Dolphin.

Also, a special mention must also be given to local historian, Slava Ivushkin, for his excellent historical information about the battles that took place around Kremenchug in 1941. You can find his excellent website here: http://gorod-kremenchug.pl.ua/Kremenchug_1941-1943/Stran_Istorii.html

Extra special thanks to Elize Watkins for producing such a fabulous cover design. If you are looking for a great, original design, you can contact her here: https://99designs.com/profiles/elizew

About the Author

After a long and successful career in world of IT, working for several large corporations across Europe, Eric Butcher came to writing quite late in life. In 2021 he published *Countdown to Zero*, the first in *The Visioner* series of short stories. *Missing in Action* is his first full novel.

As well as writing, Eric enjoys most sport, music and photography.

For more information about Eric, you can visit his website at:
www.ewbutcher.com

Printed in Great Britain
by Amazon

93e654e0-b18c-4c2f-b6bc-d70ebd5c6e76R01